A Place Nowhere

Birte Kont

Translated from the Danish by Nina Sokol

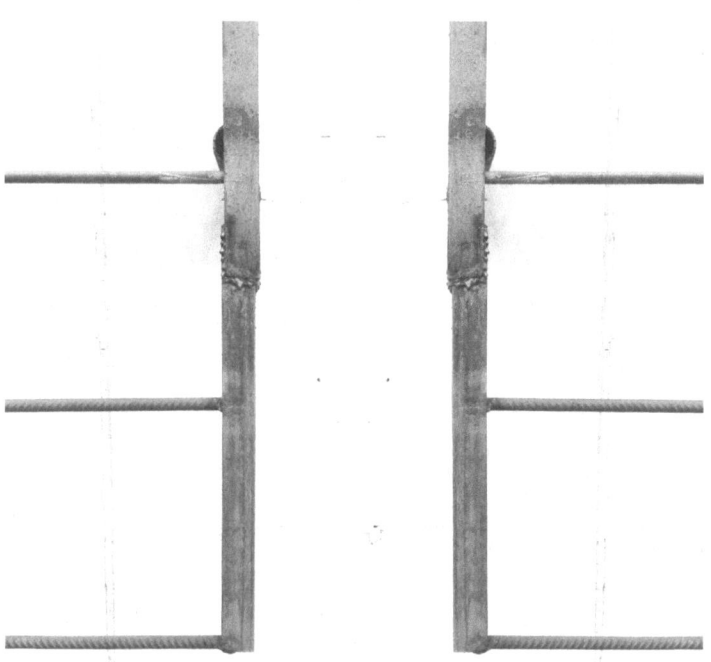

Spuyten Duyvil
New York City

Special thanks to The Danish Arts Foundation for financial support towards the translation and publication of this book.

Danish Arts Foundation

© Birte Kont & Gyldendal,Copenhagen 2011.
Published by agreement with Gyldendal Group Agency.
translation © 2021 Nina Sokol
ISBN 978-1-952419-75-1
cover image: ©Joel Fulgencio via unsplash.com

Library of Congress Cataloging-in-Publication Data

Names: Kont, Birte, author. | Sokol, Nina, translator.
Title: A place nowhere / Birte Kont ; translated from the Danish by Nina Sokol.
Other titles: En by i Rusland. English
Description: New York City : Spuyten Duyvil, [2021] |
Identifiers: LCCN 2021007165 | ISBN 9781952419751 (paperback)
Subjects: GSAFD: Bildungsromans.
Classification: LCC PT8177.21.O58 E513 2021 | DDC 839.813/8--dc23
LC record available at https://lccn.loc.gov/2021007165

A PLACE NOWHERE

I
WORDS ARE GOLD

"**G**od is punishing you!" Mom said as I turned round the corner of the house, crying, in my muddy clothes and blood trickling down my leg. I limped along the sidewalk toward the main door where she stood waiting for me. My dad and my big sister, Helle, were already sitting in the car, the Yellow Captain, parked at the curb right outside our building. Now she would have to take me back up and start all over again. And just when we were on our way to Pesach at my grandma and grandpa.

He always did. She had been saying that for as long as I could remember. But still it was like hearing it for the first time.

I was sitting in the back seat next to Helle. My head was spinning wildly. Had my fall really been God's punishment?

It burned when Mom dabbed iodine on the wound with a wad of cotton. Then she put a band-aid on my knee. But even though she scrubbed my clothes not only with a cloth but also a nail brush (which made her cheeks blotch), she could not make all the dirt disappear. I had to take off my stockings. White stockings had to be white otherwise you could just forget all about them.

And had it really been on account of God that I looked like a ragamuffin and, on top of that, the reason why we'd be late?

We turned at the corner of Grandma and Grandpa's street in the North West neighborhood and arrived at the same time as the rest of the family. We were so many that we took up practically the entire sidewalk in front of the entrance. Even though it was spring, a freezing wind penetrated my jacket.

A gust of wind grabbed ahold of Dad's hat when he, like all the uncles, raised it. He caught it in mid-air as had it been a matter of life and death and placed it firmly back on his head.

The aunts shrieked, leaving lipstick marks as they kissed everyone's cheeks. Mom's kiss didn't leave any marks and she was the only one who wore a fur coat with a spotted pattern on it. It was luminous next to the black Persian lamb coats that my aunts were wearing.

I rubbed my cheeks and took a deep breath. So we had managed not to arrive too late after all.

Everyone had brought flowers. Although Lord knows I hadn't deserved it, I was allowed to hold our bouquet. You could smell the flowers right through the wrapping paper. They were freesias. Grandma loved freesias.

"You have to hold them upside down, like this!" Helle said as she turned my hand.

The bouquet tipped. I tightened my grip and kicked at Helle's nylon stockings. But she managed to jump aside.

"Now now, girls!"

"Look, I'm holding it the right way!" I held the bouquet upside down and stretched out my arm so she could see.

"Yeah, *now* you are!" Helle said.

Cousin Siggi was standing in the doorway, holding the door open with the tall frame of his body. He was the technical hope of the family and he was now an apprentice in the TV business. He was holding a thin rod in his hand. It looked like a television antenna and it shone as he swung it, directing us all into the entrance stairway.

The well-known aroma of family celebrations filled my nose: a blend of flowers, perfume and chicken soup and something else which I wasn't quite sure what was.

Winnie, our cousin, took my hand. I sensed the warmth spread through my body. Who would you be without your family? Without all the people who had always known you? I forgot everything that had happened before, forgot myself and turned into a floating nobody, and yet I remained myself as we walked up the stairs. All the way up to the open door where Grandpa stood waiting to welcome us, saying, "*Gut jontef, gut jontef!*"

Grandma's stout, apron-clad body appeared and we gave her the flowers. Grandpa, an erect man with a side-parting in his gray hair that had been combed over to cover the bald spots, took our coats and furs and ran into the bedroom carrying the humongous pile of outer garments in his arms.

I squeezed past Mom and the aunts who were scampering back and forth between the kitchen and the living room carrying dishes in their hands as well as vases with flowers that had an array of colors, and went out into the kitchen. I went over and stood next to Grandma in front of the kitchen table. A cooked chicken, its rump facing us directly, lay on a platter, swimming in the leftover juices from the cooking and with carrot slices floating about like gold fish.

Grandma lifted the nubbly chicken skin, stuck her hand inside the chicken and removed something. It was a yellow lump from the egg which she now was offering, her hand stretched toward me. I shook my head no. Then she put it into her own mouth and took a sharp kitchen knife from one of the drawers. Her hands were shaking as she started cutting into the chicken with the knife while using her other hand to keep the chicken in place. I held my breath. But she managed to cut the chicken meat into numerous small pieces without cutting herself.

Grandpa clapped his hands and called us to the table. Just like Grandma, he could speak three languages: Yiddish, Russian and Danish. But it sounded like they were speaking all three languages at once. That's what you call broken Danish, Dad said. And we were the only ones who understood at the first get-go.

As always whenever there was a family gathering, all the tables of the house were assembled to form one long table. The pieces of white tablecloth overlapped one another in order to cover the fact that the tables had different heights. Between the vases with the flowers of all different colors were plates and bowls filled with food. There was gefilte fish and fish balls with carrot buttons, gehaktes leber, sour pickles and chren that would make your nose burn and could even make the big boys cry. On one plate there was a pile of Matza.

Uncle Sem, the oldest of my mother's brothers, took a piece of Matza and broke it in half. He sent the plate around and, laughing, he said, "Whoever created this must have been an anti-semite!"

"What is 'anti-semite'?" I whispered to my mother.

"Just something you say." She spoke in a very low voice, almost without moving her lips.

"It's the bread of misery!" Dad said across the table as he took a piece of Matza.

"As though there wasn't enough misery in this world, my dear brother-in-law," Uncle Kam said, sounding as though he had some unfinished business to settle with his tongue behind his large lips under his mustache.

"Now now, Kam, you're not here to talk business today!" Aunt Manja also took a piece of Matza before passing it around. "Anyway, with a little chren it doesn't taste so bad."

"Pesach comes only once a year," Aunt Katja said as she broke off a square for herself and stuck a tiny piece of Matza that had fallen off in between her carrot-colored lips.

"What's Pesach, Mom?" I whispered again.

"It's a Jewish Easter meal, now that's enough with the questions!" She placed a Matza and a fish ball on my plate. There was beet-colored chren.

The laughter rose and fell. They raised their glasses.

"*Na zdorovje!*"

"*L'chajim!*"

"Dat gefilte is fan-tastic !" said Aunt Pavla, who was Swedish and speaking her own form of broken, sing-song Danish.

"Then you should try the gehakte!"

"Yeah, and tomorrow it'll all be gekakte!" Uncle Jafet, the youngest of our uncles, snorted.

"What are they saying, Mom?" I whispered once more.

"It's nothing, now stop asking so many questions!"

"Oh oh oh!" Jokke, the oldest of our cousins gasped with gaping mouth as his eyes glazed over.

"Yes, well, chren is a *richtigeh* sinus opener. Here, have something to wash it down with!" Aunt Manja leaned forward and flipped a small bottle of lemon soda across the table.

Jokke caught it, poured a little in his glass and placed the half-filled soda bottle at the edge between two tables. It tipped over and yellow soda spilled across the table.

"You're all thumbs!" Aunt Manja said. She moved her head in tiny, energetic jerks and lifted her eyebrows so that her face almost always had a surprised look on it. Now she was giving Jokke a reproachful glance.

While laughing, Grandpa held out his napkin and said, "You shouldn't cry over spilled lemonnn!"

He jumped out of his chair and carried the empty bottles out to the balcony. He came back, placing new bottles with soda and beer on the table. Then he ran out to the kitchen and came back with a foggy-looking bottle of Akvavit in his hand. He lifted it in the air and said, "*Nuh, trink!* Lets kill this joyous day of Freedom!"

"Now dat is fan-tastic!" Aunt Pavla yelled with her Swedish accent.

Everyone around the table laughed too.

Mom told Grandma to stay put as she and the aunts carried the used platters and plates into the kitchen. They went back and forth with new sets of food-laden plates and platters which would soon be stripped of their contents and once again carried out to be refilled with food. But Grandma got up anyway in order to help with the soup.

Apart from Grandpa, the men in the family remained seated during the whole meal. With their ties slung over their shoulders they shoveled down the food as their noses turned red. But not our Dad. He was a total abstainer he always said, whereupon after a short pause he would add, "More or less, that is!"

After the chicken, dessert would be placed on the table, a large crystal bowl filled to the rim with stewed fruit. The juice had the same color as the spots on my mother's fur coat and tasted sweet.

"This is the reward for all the plagues we've had to endure," Uncle Sem said as he dried his flushed face with his napkin.

"Cheers to that, Brother!" Uncle Jafet said as he lifted his glass. "Also to the rest of you!"

"*L'chajim!*"

"Why does Uncle Sem always say that?" I whispered. I took a spoonful of fruit stew and chewed on a prune.

"It's just something you say. Hold your head over the plate, you're spilling!" Mom gave my back a gentle push and dried my chin with her napkin.

After the meal Grandpa grabbed ahold of the aunts, swinging them round one by one.

"*Gott in himel*, father-in law!" Aunt Katja pursed her lips as she pushed his hand away from her bottom.

The uncles tilted their heads back and guffawed.

Grandpa swept aside the few strands of his side-parting and went over to Grandma and put his arms around her just as she was carrying a pile of plates out to the kitchen.

"Elias!" she said as she wriggled herself free.

Then he put his hands behind his back and stuck his mouth out across the pile of plates.

"*Kush!*"

"*Kush majn toches!*" she said, almost without moving her lips.

My mother and the aunts, giggling, followed my Grandmother into the kitchen carrying dirty dishes in their hands. The sound of clinking porcelain and the aunts' frequent burst of laughter could be heard all the way into the dining room where my dad and uncles helped Grandpa move the tables back. They pushed the dining room table up against the wall, put their jackets on the back of the chairs and sat down at the card table.

"Pooh!" Uncle Kam looked at my dad as he loosened his tie.

I went over and opened the door to the bedroom where Helle and Winnie were sitting on the edge of the beds amidst all our coats. I encountered a harsh and sweet scent. It was Winnie, she was apprenticed at Magasin du Nord's perfume department and was holding a small, round mirror in her hand. She broadened her lips and applied some lipstick. Afterward her mouth looked like a red heart, but then, everything about Winnie was heart-shaped.

Helle noticed my presence and got to her feet.

"You can't be in here," she said. "Only those who have been confirmed can!" "

"Oh, let her," Winnie said as she smiled at me.

But Helle took me by the arm and pushed me toward the door. I resisted and tried, unsuccessfully, to pull her long ponytail but she was stronger than me.

The next moment I once again stood in the living room facing the closed door. My cheeks were flaming hot. I would have liked to have heard what they were talking about. It wasn't hard to see that Winnie had gotten a boyfriend. I wasn't so sure about Helle, she never wore lipstick. I heard laughter and looked around. The sound came from the balcony.

Jokke and Siggi were standing out there amidst the beer and soda crates where they took turns drinking from a beer bottle. When they were finished, Jokke placed the bottle in the crate. He wasn't all thumbs, he had a wide gold ring on his little finger that glistened in the sun.

"One more?" he asked as he let out a burp.

Siggi shook his head. He was once again holding the antenna in his hand and pulled it back every time Jokke reached out to grab it.

"And from now on, call me the Prophet! That goes for you,

too!" Siggi said as he spotted me. He ran his hand though his hair which was already starting to grow thin just like his father's, Uncle Sem.

"What is it again prophets do?" I asked.

"Predict the future!" Jokke said as his thick lips slowly parted into a skewed smile.

"I *know* that. But how do they do it?"

The Prophet pulled out the antenna so that it grew double its length.

"This works just as well as a prophet's staff. Whenever people in the building across the road are glued to the TV, that's when I predict the future," he said, attempting to keep a straight face, "Because that's precisely when I'll tell them, 'In just a few minutes you'll be jumping up from your easy-chairs!'"

Jokke started laughing. His round belly moved up and down beneath his white shirt.

"And do you know what they'll do then?" The Prophet didn't wait for an answer, "As if by command, they'll all jump up and start to turn the dials and knock on their TV sets."

Jokke sniffled and reached out for the antenna. The Prophet pulled it back.

"Keep your fingers from big Daddy's business!" he said.

"Oh boy, a static-maker!"

"And the next day the whole building will be calling for a new TV." He folded the antenna and put it in the inner pocket of his jacket. Then he made a sign that it was time to smoke. "Well, Cousin, are you coming along to look for Elias?" He took a long stride across the doorstep. Jokke followed him.

"Can I come down and look for Grandpa, too?" I asked.

They didn't answer. Their gaze fixed straight ahead of

them, the two cousins trotted through the living room and out to the hallway. If I told on them they wouldn't get their driver's licenses. I had a dizzying sense of power for a brief moment. But I wasn't a tattle tale. I missed my cousin Ralfi, he played the guitar and had taught me a couple of chords. But he was in the hospital. The hallway door closed shut.

I went over to the card table where Dad and the uncles were sitting with cards in their hands and cigars dangling from the corners of their mouths. As opposed to Dad, who had thick, curly hair, the uncles were thin-haired and had unbottoned the collars of their shirts. The knots of their neckties hung down at their chests where tufts of hair stuck out through their undershirts. Uncle Jafel's tie hung down his back. Their eyes were gleaming.

"Full house!" Uncle Sem shouted with his skewed cigar-mouth as he slammed his cards down on the table.

No one took their eyes off the game. But Uncle Jafet reached out and offered me a piece of chocolate. I put it in my mouth and went over to the buffet. There was a silver jug on a tray that was also made of silver. Mom used to stick her hand down into the drawer where the silverware was stored and count it all. There was nothing in there now, only green felt.

She and the aunts brought in the coffee. They poured it and carried the cups over to the card table. Then they settled down into the red plush furniture, rested their hands on their stomachs as they talked about the pills they took against all sorts of things. Also small hexagonal ones that weren't against anything in particular but that nevertheless still made you feel *azooy fil mer* better, Aunt Manja said as she looked over at the card table.

The men in the family never talked about pills.

"Where is Elias?" Grandma had entered. She sat with a straight back in the easy chair with a wrinkled brow.

"Dad will be here soon, Mom!" Mom said. She had gotten that same "Where is Elias?" look which also made her brow wrinkle. For a moment her gaze grew distant, as though she were trying to see where he was deep within in her skull. Dad always said she was able to see things just around the corner. She focused all her attention back on Grandma who was fidgeting in the armchair and smoothing out the folds in its decorative upholstery.

I heard voices and went out to the hall. Jokke and the Prophet were laughing as they entered. Grandpa stood in the open door to the hall and had just offered the neighboring couple, who were on their way up the stairs, a saline injection.

"You don't have any children and your wife is so beeyoutiful!" Grandpa kissed his fingers. "You're lucky, because I'm a trooly grrreat artist!" he asserted with a trace of laughter in his voice. "I come from Vitebsk, just like Chagall!" he added as though that explained everything. He flung out his big hands sticking out from the open shirt sleeves.

The beauty stuck her hand in her purse. Her lucky husband turned toward Grandpa.

"Did you really know Chagall, Mr. Elias?"

"Did I know?" bellowed Grandpa as he gestured with his finger for the neighbor to come closer, his head hovering close to his, he said, "Do you know anyone who doesn't know Chagall? But remember, I, too, am a trooly grrreat artist!"

"Thanks a million, Mr. Elias, but we won't be accepting your offer," The neighbor stroked the front of his wife's coat with his hand. He smiled at Grandpa and winked at me.

Then he took the key from his wife's hand and put it into the keyhole of their door.

Mom had joined us. She grabbed ahold of my arm and pulled me back into the hallway.

"Really, Dad!"

Grandpa stretched out his hands and looked at her with a pleading expression on his face.

The neighbor's door shut closed. From inside there was laughter.

We went back to the living room and Mom sat back down on the sofa.

"Why don't you crawl up here beside me?" Aunt Pavla moved to the side and lightly tapped on the seat beside her. Then she took a lock of her dark hair in her mouth and looked up toward the ceiling as innocently as a circus clown about to do something mischievous.

I curled up to her on the sofa, placed my feet on the smooth material of Aunt Pavla's dress and buried my nose in Mom's scent. She readjusted my position a little and pulled her herringbone patterned dress slightly down. I felt her hands in my hair and looked up. I followed her eyes, they seemed to touch the fabric of the aunts' dresses. I envisioned the grimaces on her face before me whenever she spoke about dear Manja. But not just about her, also dear Pavla, dear Katja, dear all of you with your jewelry and make-up, ruffles and dyed hair.

The aunts just continued talking. Aunt Manja praised Aunt Katja's new hair color. I myself had seen Pavla smear a foul-smelling, greenish mud substance into Katja's hair. It was henna, she said, and it made your hair turn the color of a carrot! Aunt Pavla had a hair dresser's salon in their bathroom where all her friends would come to get their hair done. They would sit in the living room joking around and squealing as they waited for it to be their turn. And the lucky woman who already sat under the hair dryer would shout for them to speak louder so she wouldn't miss out on anything. Then Aunt Pavla would tell them to shut up and not holler so much. But she was the one who hollered the loudest.

And when Uncle Jafet came home from the shop, he put his arms around Aunt Pavla. He said that he would cut off a bit of her breasts in order to better be able to reach all the way around her and he went out to get his tailor's shears. The long blades slid away from one another. She grabbed her breasts and shouted, "I'll kill you!"

"Aw, can't you take a little fun?" He winked at me and left the living room carrying the shears.

But when, with a stiff gait, he headed directly for the bedroom it meant that he had a headache. Then the doctor would come and give him an injection and we'd all have to keep quiet.

Loud voices drifted in from the card table. Once again Aunt Manja looked over in that direction and her red-painted mouth stiffened in a grimace, "Only a pogrom could stop them from..." and here she'd stop herself and say, "Men!"

"What's a pogrom, Mom?" I whispered.

"It's just something you say," she said, practically without opening her mouth.

She was still running her fingers through my hair but now she too was looking over at the card table where Grandpa went from one player to the next, giving them his advice.

I closed my eyes. The Jewish celebration meal weighed

like a stone in my stomach. What did it mean to be Jewish? I had heard Mom talk about us to other people. She would always lower her voice to almost a whisper and say that we were members of the Mosaic Religious Community. And in the same breath she would always add (as though to assure that it wasn't contagious), "But we're not Orthodox!"

Whenever I asked about it she would always say that we are just like everybody else; just ordinary Danes. Yet still I had always felt that we were different. But then I had always felt that I was different in another way than Helle was. From one moment to the next I could suddenly get scared. Of nothing. Then I'd feel an oppressive sense of heaviness in my stomach, as though something awful was about to happen to us all. If I were to say it aloud.

Somebody had left a scratch on the Yellow Captain. The light from the street lamp shone right on it, it was on the door just under the lock, a long, deep scratch.

"Were they trying to steal it?"

Helle looked at me. How could I ask such a stupid question? her eyes were asking.

Dad touched the scratch and made a face. The Captain would now have to go the auto repair shop so it wouldn't start to rust.

On the way home he talked about the card game, he had hit the jackpot, he said. But the uncles had gotten annoyed, which wasn't the first time when he'd won. Uncle Kam had said straight out that he refused to support our expensive habits. There came a small outburst from Dad. But what could you expect? They were vulgar and greedy, every single one of them.

Uncle Jafet had collapsed, he had also hit the jackpot. No, not the jackpot, he had been hitting it up, rather!

Mom sighed.

I looked over at Helle but her eyes were closed.

And Grandpa ... Mom sighed again and said that Lord only knew she didn't know what to ... she turned her head and looked at us.

I quickly shut my eyes but she didn't say anything more.

I was annoyed that I had fallen asleep while so much had been going on.

... And so was Aunt Pavla, she just shut her eyes, Mom said. Such a shame that Winnie ... she lowered her voice. And Aunt Manja had had dark circles under her eyes that she tried to cover up with eye shadow, the same color as her new dress. Uncle Kam had gotten a new assistant at the shop, she was only 23 years old.

"The apple doesn't fall far from the tree," Dad said.

The words fell more scattered now.

It sounded as though there was something wrong with all of them and that was strange since they were our family. The only ones there was nothing wrong with were us, and Grandma.

"You spare the rod and spoil the child," Mom said and sighed again. "Grandpa ..."

Then they both talked about the scratch on the car. Would the insurance cover it if you didn't know who the instigator of the incident was?

When we got home Nora was sitting on our doormat, leaning her head against the door.

Even though she wasn't Jewish, she was still more or less

a member of the family. On her head she was wearing a small white cap. It had slid down over her one eye along with a lock of her fair hair. She was breathing deeply and snoring.

When I placed my hand on her shoulder she shuttered. Then she half opened her other eye and smiled through the slit.

In the hall she took out a bottle from her purse and handed it to Dad. Mom got a box of chocolate.

"You didn't have to do that, dear Nora!"

I got the best gift of all: I was allowed to fall asleep close up against Nora's warm body on Helle's and my convertible couch.

*

My mother had been awarded the Danish Fire Brigade Medal of Honor because she had a *nose*. A nose and presence of mind. Because had she not detected the smell of gas and kicked opened the neighbor's door, flung open the windows and turned off the gas in the oven, we would all have been as good as dead!

I had *ears*. You didn't get a medal for that. I had always been drawn to the sound of voices: words were gold.

One night when I got up to pee the door into the living room was ajar, and when I approached the streak of light that fell across the dark hallway a sound came from within, "Shh, di kleine!"

It was my mother and it was me she meant!

Mom burst out, "Shh...!" It sounded like a shot in the night. And like a bullet it penetrated underneath my skin. The outburst was followed by a moment of silence, then the voices continued to talk in a different tone of a voice.

I ran back to the safety of my bed, pulled the eiderdown over my head yet didn't quite dare to fall asleep. My heart was pounding. What could it be? As always, whenever there was something I wasn't allowed to know I imagined the worst.

One day I went over and stood in front of the gas cooker that on straddling metal legs balanced on a terrazzo plate in the corner by the kitchen door and stared into the burner with the black holes.

It was strictly forbidden for children to turn on the gas. But I was split. One side of me refused to obey the rules and managed to convince the other side to push the kitchen stool over to the gas cooker. Then I got up on the stool, turned the knobs and sniffed as I whispered the words, "Gas, to gas, the gas, gasses."

I started to get dizzy and all at once I turned off the gas. I moved the stool back in its place in front of the radiator under the window. I sat on it and tried to collect myself a little.

Mom entered the kitchen and sniffed.

"It smells like gas in here," she said, checking to see whether she had forgotten to turn it off and rushed to the window. She leaned over me and pushed the window all the way open. Through the thin cotton material of her smock I could sense the warmth of her body. She turned around and looked at me, but she didn't say anything. She just walked out of the kitchen again.

I placed my elbow on my knee, resting my hand against my burning cheek. Why couldn't I just leave the gas alone? All I knew was that there had to be something in the word "gas" that I probably could not bear to be told about. Just thinking about what it might be made my stomach ache and I squatted down in front of the gas oven. I stared into the darkness of its interior. Or I paced back and forth in front of the gas oven until my mother yelled, "You're not turning on the gas!"

Once I stood in the bathroom observing Dad's straight razor, I asked myself whether it in reality might be a sharp pogrom. Carefully I pulled the handle from the metal holder that lay beside the bowl with shaving cream and the shaving brush made of marten hair that tickled when you dragged it across your chin, just like he always did.

Mom and Helle used the straight razor for their legs. As soon as the razor touched my skin I was cut and screamed at the sight of all the blood that started running down my shin. Mom came rushing in, "That's God punishing you! You know very well you're not supposed to take Dad's pogrom!"

She hadn't said that last word. Pogrom had to be something other than the straight razor.

Another time I was about to throw some food away that I couldn't finish and when I opened the cabinet below the sink where the garbage bin was, I froze. From the cabinet a coarse gurgling could be heard, "Pogrom!"

So that's where it was!

I stuck my head inside the cabinet. All the pipes criss-crossed one another. There was one that was thicker than the others..

"Po-grom," it gurgled once again. It seemed to be coming from the thickest pipe that sounded as though it was about to turn itself inside out. I examined the pipe more closely. It was wrapped in a sack cloth and brown liquid would drip from it whenever there was a new gurgling sound. It was sticky. I pulled my hand back and stuck my nose into it. The stench made the muscles in my stomach contract.

Right at that very moment I heard Mom's voice and backed out of the cabinet. I just managed to get on my feet and close the cabinet door when she entered the kitchen.

"Right this way, sir," she said to the plumber.

A man dressed in brown work clothes followed her right at her heels. He smelled almost exactly like the thick pipe. He placed his bag on the floor and opened the cabinet. He took the newspaper she offered him and spread it out on the floor in front of the cabinet. Then he placed his knees on the newspaper and started to haul tools out from the bag. There was a hole in one of his socks.

The plumber went out to the hall again. Was *he* a pogrom?

I shut the door as fast as I could. But now he knew where I lived! I took short gasping breaths. What if he came back? With his pogrom hand he could sweep me right up from the carpet. And no matter how loud I screamed no one would be able to save me as he carried me out to the dark woods.

The front door shut closed. There was no way of knowing what might happen from that day on. But one thing was for sure: you could die from it.

*

One late afternoon someone rang our doorbell. Mom yelled from the bathroom for me to open it.

There was a man in brown work clothes. My heart skipped a beat. It was him, the pogrom! I quickly slammed the door.

The door bell rang again. I wanted to scream but nothing came out when I opened my mouth. At that same instant Mom came out of the bathroom, scolding me as she went to open the door.

There he was again. I stared at him, unable to move, but he gave my mother a big smile and said, "Congratulations on your new TV!"

She said that there must have been some mistake, we had not bought a television. Then I saw that there was a big wooden box next to him.

The man scratched his neck, checked the nameplate on our door and the piece of paper he was holding in his hand. And then he checked the nameplate once more. He had no intention of returning with the box.

Then Mom wiped her hands in her apron and asked him to kindly wait for a moment while she made a quick phone call.

"Well, my little friend, you'd like to have a television set, wouldn't you?" he asked.

I nodded as I examined the box more closely, its four legs had wheels.

When Mom returned she opened the door wide this time as she said, "My husband is a real rascal. I'm really sorry about that! Please come this way!"

At that very same moment my playmate, Lasse, and his mother entered the hallway of the building and they just *had* to come in and see our TV. It was placed in the corner of the living room right across from the couch where there was an outlet. The man set up an antenna on the TV, then he went down on his knees and started turning some knobs. A picture with gray and black shaped squares became visible on the screen. And at that very same moment, the television set started making a howling sound so we had to cover our ears.

"And this is just the test screen, " the man said.

Lasses' mom grabbed her shopping bag and thanked us for letting them have a look, it was time for her and Lasse to go up to their apartment. I saw them out. Before I closed the door I heard Lasse ask why anyone would want a howling thing like that in their living room.

The main door opened and Helle entered. Her skirt swirled about her legs and she was carrying her brown leather school bag.

"Come hurry up and see the TV!" I said. "I've already seen it!"

"What are you babbling about?"

"Television is nothing less than the way of the future," Dad said when he got home from the shop. He looked at Mom, grinned from ear to ear and continued, "Can't you envision its future perspective?"

She still didn't look too pleased but Dad continued to smile and said that the six-day race would be transmitted from the indoor track at Forum. And, of course, that would be soon.

I had once been to the six-day race in Forum. That huge auditorium was a boiling inferno of lights, noise and people. People shouted, sang and whistled whenever a row of bicyclists, crouched over their handlebars, whizzed right past us. Nora was also with us. Her temperament was practically tailor-made for bike racing, Dad said. She sat next to Mom, laughing and stomping her feet. She stuck two fingers in her mouth and whistled.

I sat on Dad's knee and when another row of bikers whizzed past us again he pointed toward the cabins in the middle of the auditorium. It was in there that the bikers would sleep when they weren't sitting on their saddles. Helle shook her head so that her long ponytail swung from side to side and shouted that she couldn't fathom how anyone could sleep in all that noise.

But now we wouldn't have to go all the way out to Forum to watch the bicycle race, we could just sit at home and watch it from the sofa, Dad said. And he looked forward to the moment when everyone in the family, especially my mother's brothers, could see his name on television as it was displayed on one of the many advertising banners in the auditorium. But the best thing of all was that more people would come to buy clothes at his shop.

"And they'll bring new customers with them, see?"

She still didn't look entirely pleased. And that may have been precisely due to the future perspective she was envisioning: from now on the entire family would come over to our place to watch TV. But first they would have to have something to eat. And that's exactly what happened, our living room was transformed into a veritable movie theater.

In the evening Mom and Dad stood behind all our chairs that had been lined up in front of the TV. It didn't matter one bit that they had to stand, Dad said, he had been standing up in the shop all day anyway. And Mom would have to get up at any rate since she was always having to run back and forth between the living room and kitchen when we had guests over. Just when the TV program was about to begin he took her hand and said, "Look what I'm holding! It's *The Best!*"

Everyone in the living room turned around. Then he put forth his other hand which he had been hiding behind his back and in which he was holding a small magazine called *The Best (of Reader's Digest)* that he always took with him to bed at night after a hard day at the shop when he needed to replenish his spiritual depot. One of his favorite pastimes was to retell some of the stories from the magazine. He was an expert at telling stories and would always add his own spice to them.

Mom wrenched her hand free as she smiled and asked him to stop that nonsense, but everyone in the living room was laughing. Then they turned their heads back toward the TV screen.

A proud smile spread across Mom and Dad's faces as they peered right into the future across the heads of their family members.

When the program was finished and the test screen and the howling sound had returned, everyone in the living room clapped and cheered. The aunts shrieked and held their ears.

Dad squeezed in between the chairs and turned off the TV. He turned around, and with a grin that reached from ear to ear he said, "Now just listen to this: Hershkel meets his friend Mershkel on the street and says, 'You can't live without a TV!' 'Oy!' says Mershkel, 'And how can you be so sure?' And Hershkel says, 'That's obvious! In the old days they didn't have TV, and look what became of them...they're all dead!'"

Grandpa and the uncles tilted their heads back and guffawed.

"You're a true Victor Borge!" Uncle Jafet said once he was able to catch his breath again.

At that same moment Mom shouted from the kitchen. Nora, who lived with us when she wasn't at sea, turned and counted us on her fingers. Then she yelled back in her sing-song Jutlandic accent, "Foourtayn!"

Uncle Sem got up, big and broad-shouldered, and carried his chair to the dining table. His eyes would follow Nora and the aunts who bustled about the table distributing cups and plates as they talked about how marvelous it was that they could sit in our nice warm living room and watch TV.

"*Gott in himel*, it's being sent *directly* into this very living room!" Aunt Katja said and dropped whatever she had in her hands so she could pull down her skirt that had crept up above her knees.

"To think, from now on we won't have to sit outside in front of the TV shop in all kinds of weather," Aunt Manja said, "I mean, you were liable to get chronic bladder infections and things that are *azooy fil mer* worse!"

Aunt Pavla and Aunt Katja gave Aunt Manja a sympathetic look. And she nodded with such vigor that her long earrings danced about her broad cheeks. Mom always said Lord knew she herself would never wear earrings. Then she'd always put forth her hands and turn her rings, a golden wedding ring on her left hand and an eternity ring with real diamonds on her right.

"Hopefully there's no risk of getting contaminated with show-off infection as well!" Uncle Sem said as he nodded toward our Dad who was bending over the TV and fondling all of the dials.

Aunt Katja sent Uncle Sem a look that could have meant a number of things, but Aunt Pavla also looked over there with a look of admiration in her eyes. "He's adamant about preenciple," she said in her half-Swedish, "A mann with a backbone!" And of all the aunts, her judge of character was the best, Dad said.

Uncle Sem clicked his heels as he laughed.

Grandpa also placed his chair at the dining table. He did not make do with merely looking, but placed his hand on Nora's bottom, grabbed a hold with his fingers and praised the quality of her pleated skirt.

She turned around and gave a crooked smile.

Helle entered the living room with a basket full of home

made rolls in each hand and placed them on the table. Mom was carrying the coffee pot.

"This is the perfect time for your coffee, Sis!" Uncle Sem said, "and one can clearly taste that you always boil the water twice!"

"What are you driving at?" she said.

"*Emmes*!" Uncle Sem said as he put his hand on his heart.

Uncle Kam remained sitting restlessly in his chair as he fidgeted with his mustache,

"Uh hum," he began as he pointed to the TV, looking at it as though the mere sight of it hurt his eyes, "how much does a thing like that actually cost, Brother-in-law?"

I knew you could have your teeth straightened, but what about your tongue?

Dad turned and looked at Uncle Kam who was a guest and therefore had to be treated properly. So, he put on a calm face and said, "You know, when you're located on the main drag, people are always dropping by!" He lifted his hand and straightened the knot in his tie, "But I got a good deal on it."

"Uh hum," Uncle Kam kept quiet and exchanged long glances with Uncle Jafet.

We were lucky because the market forces were on our side, Dad said to Mom after the guests had left and Nora was taking her bath. And of all the men in the family he happened to be the one who had the most sense of reality, he said, at least he had more of it compared with her brothers. Not to mention her father. Mom didn't say anything.

And so that was how the evenings were spent, night after night. The future, Forum and the big wide world had entered our living room to stay. And little by little what Dad had predicted started to happen. The future became so financially accessible that other members in our big family could take part in it. But by that time we were already on our second TV with a wider screen.

*

Mr. and Mrs. Sand were not Jewish either. They were kind of friends of the family. Mrs. Sand was friends with Aunt Pavla, and Winnie and Mrs. Sand's daughter, Else, were practically the same age. Mr. Sand was a police officer. Mom used to say that they were so terribly cultured which made it sound like an invective,

Mrs. Sand said that Danish culture thrived on the inspiration it received from abroad and took me to the museum so that I could see for myself. Sometimes we went to Tivoli, or to a concert at the Radio House Concert Hall. It was perfectly fine that I fell asleep, Tchaikovsky's music was something you had to get to know, she would say. We also looked at paintings, Chagall. He was also Russian and turned everything upside down. His floating couple were either on their way out the window or hovering above the city's roofs, away from Vitebsk. What Chagall wanted was a new and better world, Mrs. Sand said.

"Look at the goat," she said, pointing at a painting, "there, under the clock, it symbolizes hope!"

Whenever our parents went out Mrs. Sand would come to our place or I would sleep over at their place. Also sometimes when mom needed a little vacation from me and that way, I too, would get a vacation from being a little sister.

"Well, that's settled then, Mrs. Sand!" my mother said in the telephone. "What would we do without you?"

As always, Mrs. Sand was the one who came to pick me up. We took the bus to their place, they didn't have a car. She had gotten a poodle hairdo at Aunt Pavla's that morning and was wearing a hairnet that covered her curly hair. It would help make the curls last longer, she said. She also said that there were flags on the busses that day because it was ten years since peace had been declared.

I couldn't remember hearing anything about a war.

Their house was situated behind a small park. Mrs. Sand opened the front door of the building and together we walked up the stairs to the first floor. In front of their door she took out a bunch of keys from the pocket of her light-colored cotton coat and winked at me.

I nodded, placed my finger on the doorbell and pushed hard.

The door opened and Mr. Sand appeared in the doorway dressed in full police uniform.

"Who's that rascal who keeps ringing the door-bell so that the whole house is shaking?" he said and slammed the door.

We looked at one another and chuckled. Still shaking with laughter, Mrs. Sand inserted the key into the lock and flung the door wide open. Then we walked into the hallway and shortly afterward Mr. Sand appeared from his hiding place behind the door. He was also laughing as he took my duffel coat and hung it on the coatrack on the wall. Then he took off his uniform jacket and placed it on a hanger.

I followed Mrs. Sand out to the kitchen.

"There's nothing like a good little ritual," she said as she reached for their kettle and turned toward me. "Isn't that right?"

"Yes, that's true" said Mr. Sand who had joined us in the kitchen, "It keeps us poor urban creatures from falling apart. Without all our little pranks we would be in bad shape," he said as he smiled and pointed toward the open window, "like a window pane without putty."

I looked at him. His police cap had left a circle on his head where his hair had been pressed flat.

"Come with me" he said as he placed his hand on my shoulder. We went into the living room.

He sat down in one of the armchairs and pointed at the footstool upon which he normally placed his big feet with the chequered slippers. I sat down. In the middle of the coffee table towered a glass vase with red and white carnations. In front of my plate there was a glass with juice and there were napkins with the Danish flag.

Mrs. Sand entered and poured coffee into their cups. Placed the blue coffee pot on the table and sat down in the other armchair. I leaned over my plate and took a bite of pastry. Drank some of the juice.

After a little while Mr. Sand looked at his wristwatch and turned up the radio, they didn't have a television.

"Daa-dee-daa-dum. Daa-dee-da-dum..."

It's Beethoven's 5th symphony," said Mrs. Sand as shouts and cheers could be heard from the crowd gathered in front of the City Hall.

Later Mr. and Mrs. Sand talked about the "five evil years" when the Germans occupied our country.

"You had to have black shades pulled down in front of the windows," Mrs. Sand said, a shiver running through her body. "And everywhere you looked you would see their horrible flag."

With a sense of graveness and fervor in his voice, Mr. Sand told about the Liberation. And about America that helped us after the War. The Marshall Plan. He said that America was God's own country. But American culture had gotten its foot in the door.

"Donald Duck, you know him, right? Ketchup. Chewing gum and crap like that. It all comes with the package," he said, feigning a sigh.

"Dandy!" I said and nodded.

Smiling, Mrs. Sand got to her feet and removed the coffee pot.

"Let me see if I can find something I can show you," Mr. Sand mumbled as he went over to their bookshelf that filled the entire wall. He bent forward, searching across the spines of the books with his finger.

From where I was sitting I could see the piano. Only their daughter, Else, played on it which she had learned to do at the music conservatory. She had once played for us. Beethoven, Mrs. Sand had whispered. I watched Else's hands dancing across the piano keys and her feet that bobbed up and down when she stepped on the pedals. She moved her body with its rounded stomach which was at one with the music that pealed forth, rose and fell in volume. The child was bound to turn out to be beautiful when it was nourished with blood filled with music, right? Mrs. Sand whispered once again and closed her eyes. And she remained sitting like that until Else stopped playing. In the silence that followed the only sound that could be heard was the ticking of the metallic metronome. Else got to her feet, clutching her stomach. Then she turned off the metronome on the piano, brushed her hand through her light curls and once again placed her hands on her stomach.

Now as I was thinking about Else I remembered what Helle had said to Winnie. As always, we had been lying on our sofa bed, I had my back to Winnie who was lying in the middle and didn't have the least objection to us lying so close together. The warmth from her body and her sense of agitation spread straight to me, right under my skin. They thought I was sleeping.

Winnie *had* a boyfriend whose name was John and she said that he slept at her place whenever aunt Pavla and uncle Jafet were out at night. I thought that was very nice of him. Winnie didn't dare to be home alone even though she was older than Helle. Winnie was dying to get a ring on her finger, but it *had* to be John asking her, and she was worried that he would never get the courage to do it. I was just about to give myself away and advise her to take the initiative herself when I heard Winnie say that someone had gotten into trouble and had to get married in a hurry. Then Helle said that she would never marry for that reason.

That was what I had said to Else: that I would never marry just for that reason. Not until the words had escaped my mouth had I fully grasped their meaning and that she had to be the one whom Helle and Winnie had been talking about. But it was too late and a feeling of unpleasantness made the muscles in my stomach contract.

She had chosen to do it anyway, Else had said. Like her mother, she had a calm voice when she said, without the least indication that anything about it was wrong, that a child was a big reason. She was now living in Sydney with her husband and child.

Closed and so shiny that you could see your reflection in

it, the piano had kept its old place in the dining room along the wall toward the bedroom.

Early in the morning when Mrs. Sand and I lay whispering to one another under her blanket the policeman would snore loudly. Then we'd double up in laughter and let out a fart. And then we'd have to stick our noses into the smell under the blanket. Because if the policeman were to wake up all of a sudden, all hell would break loose.

Mr. Sand came back with a book in his hand, sat down in the armchair and flicked through the pages.

"Come over here and sit down, no one's going to bite you!" He pointed to a picture that filled two pages.

I went over to him. On the picture there were a lot of people standing and waving the Danish flag. The picture had been taken at the City Hall the day the War ended he explained and looked up from the book.

"But once, a long time ago, there had been another war and it had been called the First World War."

"Easy does it!" said Mrs. Sand, returning to the living room at that very moment and sitting down. She moved a little on the chair so that there was room for me. "She can make do with just one world war for now."

"Yes, the Second one!" I said and climbed up to sit next to her.

Mrs. Sand laughed with her whole body, took off her glasses and dried her eyes.

"No, you two gigglers! She must know our history! You understand that, don't you, you little fool?" Mr. Sand said with an affectionate tinge in his stern tone of voice.

"Yes," I said and got embarrassed.

Right then his face resembled that of a St. Bernard dog. The many folds and wrinkles gave his face a sorrowful expression, also when he smiled. The only thing missing was the barrel around his neck.

"But all of that happened long before anyone had ever thought of a little rascal like you," he added in his bass voice.

That was the first time I was ever told about the Second World War.

Everyone must meet their fate, Mrs. Sand said, she was sitting on the edge of the bed and talking with me about what she had read aloud.

Fate was a woman, or women, rather, she corrected herself as she took both my hands in hers. You could try to hide or run away from it, but fate would always catch up with you in the end. That was how it was with death, too. But death was a man, a man with a scythe. Mrs. Sand had been talking in her usual calm tone. Her blue-gray eyes looked right through me.

Her words sent shivers down my spine. I pulled my hands back. Was it also fate that determined whether you would be a Jew? Both a Jew and a little sister? Or was that God's punishment?

After Mrs. Sand had said good-night and I lay alone under the blanket, their words returned to me in my mind. Mr. and Mrs. Sand always referred to God as the "good one." It was the good one that gave them food on the table, Mrs. Sand said. Not the money for the household she got from Mr. Sand which she had told me about. And when visiting them, I had to be careful about saying the word "God." But "God" had tumbled out of my mouth when I had accidentally knocked over my glass during dinner. The milk ran all across the wax tablecloth, dripping on the carpet. Mrs. Sand fetched a rag. You weren't allowed to take the Lord's name in vain according to Mr. Sand. In my home we didn't talk about God in that way. Or about America. I was filled with warmth for the country that had done so much good for us.

The next day Father came to fetch me. I stood together with Mrs. Sand by the window and saw the Captain moving through the parking lot. Down on the street I turned and waved to Mrs. Sand who stood on the balcony. Then I got into the car.

Father sat down behind the wheel.

"Can we go to America?" I asked.

"I don't know, we've just gotten the car fixed," Father said, turning his head back and forth as hemaneuvered the Captain out of the parking lot and drove out to the road, "and money doesn't exactly grow on trees."

"But if we someday have enough money, can we go?"

"What's suddenly given you that idea?"

"Because American culture has put its foot in the door of our society," I said, "You know, the Marshall Plan, ketchup and chewing gum, that sort of thing."

He suppressed a laugh and said, "Let's play a word game. Name something that starts with the letter 'A'".

"America!"

When we got home Mom stood in the living room sprinkling the linen before ironing.

"There were absolutely no problems with her," Father said as he went to the book shelf and took out his bookkeeping folder, sat down by the desk flap and rustled with some papers.

Mother gave me a probing glance.

"Good," she said, patting me on the head.

"Where is Helle?"

"At Winnie's." Mother unfolded the ironing board. Set the iron on-end and plugged it in. She took a handkerchief and spread it out on the ironing board. Tugged at the corners and pressed the iron down across it. Clouds of steam rose when the damp cotton gave off a swishing sound that went straight to your stomach. She dried her forehead with the back of her hand and gave the other side the same treatment, folding corner against corner and ironing them in sharp-edged folds. If a fold was crooked she would start all over again.

I sat down on a chair by the dining table.

"Can't we go to America, Mom?"

"Mmm..." she said, placing the ironed handkerchiefs on the dining table.

"I'd really like to see America, it's God's own country."

"Hmm," she said, taking the last handkerchief.

"They helped us after the War."

"Mmm," she started on our underwear.

"The Marshall plan, and all."

"Mmm." She had reached the towels and checked the straps before applying the iron. She always said that you could separate the sheep from the goats by looking at people's towel straps. If they were wrinkled, or, even worse, torn, then she knew!

No one else, neither aunt Pavla, Mrs. Sand nor Nora, had ever said that about towel straps. But the same thing applied to rust stains in the toilet. It was always with a certain amount of trepidation that I would pee in a toilet with rust stains when visiting someone. And if the person had both things, I would grow dizzy and have to lie on the floor to keep from fainting.

Finally the entire dining table was covered with piles of clothes that smelled of soap and of Mother.

"Well, then!" she said in a joyful voice, "It's so nice having someone to talk to when you're doing the ironing."

She pulled out the plug for the iron and the wire fell lifelessly across the ironing board.

In our home children were never told about the World War. It was best for children not to know, Mom would always say when she was on the phone.

Still, I could sense the thing that wasn't mentioned to children. Without being able to prevent it, I was a little magnet for all the things that it was best children didn't know about, everything that was in the air and crackled mutely. It was there. But it was invisible and existed nowhere except within me. I was like the ship in the game where a little ship sails on a tumultuous sea laden with all the things that are never said aloud. The unspoken words were my blind passengers that were in the cargo just outside my navel, swaying in all the frightened feelings probably I was the only one who had within me.

Perhaps my little ship had other things in its cargo as well. Once Mother had placed a bowl with dough to let rise on a stool in front of the radiator below the kitchen window, I lifted a corner of the checquered kitchen towel that lay across the earthenware bowl and looked at the dough. Its yellowish surface reached all the way to the edge of the bowl and resembled a swollen stomach. With my finger I pricked a hole and took a chunk in my mouth.

The dough melted on my tongue but tasted so bad that I was forced to take a bite from an apple. I discovered too late that there was half a larva in the apple that rose and teetered on the red apple rind. I tossed the apple away and it flew across the kitchen, landing on the kitchen towel covering the bowl.

But now the half caterpillar was already inside and pupating. It would soon transform into a butterfly and fly out of the bellybutton and light up the world. At night the pupa lay in the stomach's soup of melted dough that made all the unsaid words and frightened feelings ferment and seethe and overflow.

*

Whether due to fate or God, I was born on the wrong side of the official cut-off date for when children could start school.

"Imagine, seventeen days too young to start school!" my mother said on the telephone. "Yes, dear Pavla ... she *is* ready for school!"

And since my mother knew best, she made use of her expertise to overpower the rigid nonsense of the law and wangled a spot for me at the Jewish school in the middle of the school year.

I ended up sitting next to Miranda. From the first day we were at home with one another and if one of us was sent to stand outside the classroom door the other one would go along. That was friendship.

In the schoolyard there was a boy who chased me, a boy

with curly black hair, who pushed me from behind or pulled my hair and who constantly bustled about close to me. Every time I turned around I saw the boy's same round face that lit up in a teasing smile. Miranda knew him well, his and her parents would meet for coffee, she said.

The school was in Nørrebro. Mother would accompany me there in the mornings. You had to take the trolley and get off at Runddelen Square. Cross Nørrebrogade Street and turn left at a side street. At the corner there was a haberdashery that always had yellow signs in the window. It was our father's.

At the Jewish school liver paste wasn't allowed to be included in my lunch box, only eggs and tomatoes bananas and that sort of thing. That wasn't so important when you were of the chosen people which the school taught us that the Jewish people were.

Our class teacher, who was named Bent, was nice. He wore a yarmulke and taught us the stories of the Bible: about Adam and Eve, the first two adults in the world that had a whole rain forest to themselves to romp about in. But they did the one thing they weren't supposed to: eat the fruit from the forbidden tree. They were punished by being thrown out of Paradise, which was Eternity, and sent into time. It was called Exile and meant homeless. that was why all people were homeless, Bent said. It was precisely the pain from this event that connected all of humanity in a community of which everyone was a member, like one big family.

He looked across the classroom, smiling, and reached up to his yarmulke and shifted it slightly. And the Bible was just like a family, filled with envy, enmity, and war; because there was nothing in the whole wide world that hadn't already been written about in the Bible. But Jews were a little more homeless than everyone else.

And then one, two. three and I was able to read and write, Mother said on the telephone.

One evening I got into trouble. I was setting the table for dinner and had also carried out two heavy bronze candle holders and placed them on the dinner table. Then I went into the kitchen to fetch some matches that lay next to the gas ring. Helle, who was Mother's right hand, was busy frying liver. Mom was standing next to her, slicing cucumbers for cucumber salad.

"What are you going to do with those matches?" she asked.

"I'm just taking them to the living room, so they're ready."

"Ready?" she raised her voice.

"It's Friday night and that's when we light the Sabbath candles!" I said, adding to emphasize my point, "That's what all the other homeless ones at school do, too!"

"Now, now," Father said as he stepped into the kitchen, suppressing his laughter, "The eggs do not teach the hen!" He pointed to the box of matches in my hand and, trying to sound strict, said, "Put that right back where you found it"

Christmas was approaching and, like all other shops on the street, Father hung red hearts, gold tinsel and spruce branches in the windows.

At school it was called Chanukah and the Jews lit candles for eight days because a miracle had once happened, Bent said.

When the bell rang signaling the end of the school day I said to Miranda that I was looking forward to Christmas.

She stared at me and said, "What kind of a Jew are you?"

I felt my cheeks getting hot.

At home I told them that Miranda had said that Jews don't celebrate Christmas at all. I was on the verge of crying.

Mom took me by the shoulders and asked, "Haven't you always gotten presents Christmas Eve?"

I nodded.

"And don't you want to continue getting that?"

I nodded once again. But like at school I felt a slight sense of shame.

"There you go! There's nothing at all to be upset about!"

"Yes, there is, because we never have a Christmas tree!"

Mother opened her mouth to say something but then she swallowed it. Instead she said that I ought to stop talking about what we did in our home because that was a private matter.

At school Bent told us about the time God freed the Jews from slavery under the evil Pharaoh of Egypt. That was how *Pesach* came about. And during *Pesach* you had to recline and recall the meaning of history. You were only supposed to eat unleavened food and you had to remember to open your door and await the prophet Elijah.

None of my classmates had seen him. When I said that the Prophet was my cousin and that my grandfather was Elijah, they all laughed. Bent did, too. He laughed so hard that his yarmulke fell off his head. But didn't the One above also have time for a little humor every now and then?

At home I told them about the things Bent had taught us: you were supposed to put an extra chair and glass out for the prophet Elijah should he come to say that the Messiah...!

"Certainly not at our house!" Mother sighed, turning the palms of her hands upward.

When I was let out from school I would go to Father's shop where Mom helped out in the afternoons. In the back of the shop, Grandmother sat sewing. I was allowed to help with the packing, if there were socks and handkerchiefs and those kinds of things.

Father would take care of the suits. Every time a customer entered the store he would remove his cigar from his mouth and place it at the edge of the cash register. There was a burnt mark where it was supposed to lay. He had genuine salesman's blood in his veins, everyone said. When a customer bought a suit he would always ask whether they wanted a shirt to go with it? And if the customer had his wife with him, Father always asked her. Then the client would take, in addition to the shirt, a tie, a pair of socks, underwear and, on top of that, a woolen coat which was the icing on the cake. And then Father always added an extra pair of underwear to the package.

Afterward he would look at Mom, grinning from ear to ear, and give her all the credit for the fact that women have purchasing blood in their veins. He would be in a good mood the rest of the day, rattling off juicy Jewish stories.

"Shy, di kleine," Mother said, practically without opening her mouth and clutching her head.

One day when I went to the shop there had been a robbery. The window to the door of the back room had been smashed to pieces. Father said a brick lay on the floor when he got there. And had his mother been sitting in her chair by the sewing machine the brick would have hit her right on the back of her head Mother said in the same tone of voice she had when it was her birthday.

The policeman had already been there and written a report, Mrs. Sand said who helped clean up. Piles of clothes lay scattered about everywhere in the shop even though they had spent most of the day trying to make the shop look normal again. And Father had almost not had any time to sell anything because the stock of goods had to be counted. Because this time the insurance company wasn't going to get away with dodging the issue he said, spreading out his arms.

"Anti-Semites, the whole lot of them!"

"Shy, di kleine," Mother said.

When we got home, I told Helle about the robbery.

She stared at me, "You're kidding."

"No, anti-Semites, all of them!"

Father suppressed a laugh. Mother shook her head and went into the living room. A little while afterward she said on the telephone that we were being showered with misfortunes.

"First the car and now the robbery. What'll be next?"

But then it was already summer vacation.

And then I could forget everything I had ever learned in that school Mother said. When you had vacation, you weren't supposed to think about everyday things, she added and smiled. Helle said that she didn't want to hear about Adam and Eve and the Israelites either and father didn't have any time for it at all.

"We're going to be summer residents now!" Father said in his vacation voice as he put the Captain into gear and turned at the curb.

"Yes, fortune favors fools," Mother said.

"That's not what we are!"

"It's just something you say," Helle placed a pillow at the back of her neck and leaned back into her corner.

But Lasse said it was foolish that we were going to spend the whole summer not playing. He stood by the window and saw us leaving. I waved until I couldn't see him anymore. All at once feeling both sad and light at heart. Just like we did every summer, we were going to spend the next several weeks in the Fisher house.

There were other children. Katrinn, who was Swedish and said "tant" to Mother even though we weren't related. Yvonne was Helle's age and lived in the house across from the Apple Girl and spoke in a deep voice. Was she lucky because she had been born a fool? But that was called retarded.

It was also foolish that Helle just settled down to sleep as soon as we started driving. She was already breathing deeply. Helle's and my room was on the first floor, we had each our own bed and the walls were slanted. When you lay looking at the flowered tapestry it was like having all of summer with you in bed.

"We're going to be summer residents now!" Father repeated when we drove down a new highway.

"Why is it called summer residents?"

"Because city residents move to the country in the summer to lie on the beach."

"Why aren't they called beach residents then?"

"Now, now, eggs don't teach the hen," he said, but he didn't sound the least bit angry.

"Look, there's the Stork's Nest!" our mother said, pointing at a restaurant behind the crash barrier where we had once had open faced sandwiches.

But we had already passed it.

Every summer everyone in the family rented a room at the beach town, a small fishing village in Northern Zealand. Father said we should appreciate the fact that we could afford to rent a whole house. He only had vacation on the weekends and not on the weekdays like the rest of us. Then they all came to eat dinner at our place, because our house was an open house, Mother said.

"But of course! We're family!"

The Fisher house was gray. Wild vine crawled up the wall and peered in through the windows. And when we moved in Mr. and Mrs. Fisher moved into their annex facing the courtyard.

Mrs. Fisher welcomed us, smiling. She was half as tall and twice as wide as Mr. Fisher who walked behind her at some distance. You could tell by the way he walked that he wasn't entirely normal, at least he wasn't like other people. With stiff movements he placed one leg in front of the other and stepped on the flowers in the grass with his gigantic clogs. He didn't look at people, either, just at the ground.

The Apple Girl was standing at the corner waving. I called her that because she had the same name as Grandma's favorite apple, Ingrid Marie. She lived around the corner, in the house next to the Fisher house. I walked over to her. She had gotten her braces removed and her blond braids reached down to the middle of her arm now.

We stood next to the moving van and watched the movers as they carried all the things into the house that there couldn't fit into the Captain

"What's that?" the Apple Girl asked, pointing.

"That's a refrigerator," I said.

"We don't have that at our house. And what's that then?" She pointed again.

"A television."

"What's it for?"

"For bicycle races and that sort of thing," I said.

The Apple Girl opened her eyes wide and stared at me. But, of course, she was from the country,

"Come on in," I said.

We went into the front garden of the Fisher house. Sat down on our knees in the warm grass and looked for four leaf clovers and soon it didn't feel at all like a whole year had passed since we had seen each other.

"Want to go to my place instead?" the Apple Girl asked.

"OK."

I got up and followed her into their garden. She had gotten a play house that had been arranged like a grocer's shop. On the shelves were packages and boxes, cans and empty bottles.

She went and stood behind the counter.

"What'll it be?"

I said that I wanted a little of everything because we had just moved in.

"Certainly!" With prompt arm movements she started taking down items from the shelves. Then she turned around and, leaning against the counter, said, "Jews always have to have everything!" She looked at me, smiling, "That's what my mother says!"

I looked at her blond eyelashes. Incredible that I hadn't noticed before. She was ugly. I itched to reach out and pull one of her braids. But I didn't, I just sailed right out of the shop.

"Leaving already?" she shouted after me.

Mom was standing in the garden.

"Coming so soon?" she said, pointing at my arm where the bracelet with the four-leaf clover normally sat, "Where's your silver bracelet?"

I touched my bare wrist with my hand and said that the pogrom must have taken it.

"Who?" Her eyes opened wide.

My head was spinning wildly.

She placed a hand on my shoulder and shook me.

I tightened my lips. She wasn't going to get a word out of me!

I could see from her eyes, that interchangeably grew hard and soft, that she couldn't decide what to believe. She lifted her gaze and looked up, her eyes asking, "Whatever in the world have I done?"

The sun was shining, and white flowers poked up their heads among the blades of grass where the Apple Girl and I had been sitting on our knees collecting four leaf clovers. That was when my bracelet must have fallen off.

We were lucky. We could thank Mr. Fisher for that. As he was walking and looking down, he found the bracelet in the grass.

Our father was also lucky, he often said. Because he had us. And on top of that he even had two kings: Frederik VIX and Victor Borge. He was the king of comedy and you couldn't live without that. And Mother also had two kings, he said, the other king was the telephone king, Bell.

"Isn't it true?" He looked at her and smiled.

Everyone who was vacationing in the beach town were summer residents just like us. The summer residents came from both sides of the Sound and filled the alleys, drying grounds, shops and restaurants, piers and beaches of the fishing village with colors, laughter and smells.

When we walked through the streets it was almost like being one big family, everyone stopped to talk with one another. Father used to say that we created high tide in the cash registers of the town as he and the uncles looked at one another with a salesman's' gleam in their eyes.

We went to the beach every day. Mother would rather not go in the water. She had overlaid toes that she had inherited from Grandma. When she joined the group of aunts on the beach she would, at a convenient moment when no one was looking, take off her moccasins. And she always made sure to dig her toes deep into the sand and keep them there.

One day Uncle Jafet took me way out in the water where I couldn't reach the bottom. On the way back on the burning sand (I was carrying my full bucket in my hand) he said tongue in cheek that he was 100% certain that the ladies also could use a little splash of water. I didn't waste a moment.

Mother and aunt Manja howled when a squirt of salt water landed on their sun-baked skin. And aunt Manja's voice sounded like one of those lemon drops she'd pop in her mouth after every cigarette to cover up the odor when she said, "Had that been my Jokke, he would certainly have gotten a slap on the face."

She was sitting up now and her facial expression, as she straightened the underwire of her new bathing suit, indicated that she wouldn't mind giving me one, too.

Slapping was not used as a punishment at my house. Father was a follower of modern child-rearing and used to say that you should ignore it when children are being disobedient. Then it would pass of itself.

However, at our house, punishments lasted much longer than a slap and I almost envied Jokke, aunt Manja would usually get over things quickly. But Mother's piercing eyes mutely expressed that if I didn't watch out God would punish me very soon.

In the evenings we would walk up and down the piers. We would get an ice cream waffle and pass the statue of Holger Drachmann and the benches where the locals would sit and stare at us. Then we'd go out on the pier where it smelled of fish, seaweed and tar and join the flow of pedestrians, a symphony of voices and laughter.

I caught sight of Katrinn who was wearing a loud yellow dress and ran over to her. Arm in arm we went out to the very edge of the pier. With our eyes we followed the sun that like a luminous gigantic orange slid down toward the horizon, making the pier let out a sigh that could be heard all the way to Sweden.

Afterward we found our families again and walked back along the harbor basin. It had started to get dark and flickering lights, one after the other, appeared on the decks of the boats. The flickering lights made the faces of the people on board look troll-like. The lights bobbed up and down and twinkled, competing with the stars.

You could hear slurping sounds in the harbor water where the yachts were bumping against one another.

"That's the harbor troll," Helle said. "He's bored and kicking the boats."

I looked down into the black water where sticks and other garbage was floating around. Even though I didn't believe in harbor trolls, I still felt my hair stand on end as the troll's fingers wrapped themselves around my ankles. I screamed.

Helle stuck her arm through Winnie's. A grown-up smile faintly played on her lips. "Imagine being scared of trolls!"

"You are my little winner," Winnie said, placing her hand on my hair, "You sang so wonderfully at the singing competition in the restaurant, imagine that you dared!" She turned around and looked at Helle, "Had it been you, you would have died from fear."

I couldn't help smiling.

Mother was walking arm in arm with aunt Pavla and Nora who was spending a few days of her vacation with us. With her free hand, Nora reached toward me. I grabbed it and calmed down, a shadow of shame passing over me as her fingers closed around mine. Aunt Pavla talked about Winnie's boyfriend. John was also a summer resident and she said that if he didn't soon prove that he was a mann with a backbone she'd kill him!

One day Grandma and Grandpa came to say hi. They were also staying in a summer house, but theirs was closer to Copenhagen.

"We just want to kill a joyful evening!" Grandpa said in his broken Danish, waving to us all in his straw hat which he always wore in the summertime.

"Just in time!" Mother said, embracing Grandma, "We were just about to sit down at the dinner table. Go in and sit down and I'll get a couple of more plates!"

"I'll take care of it," aunt Manja and aunt Pavla said all at once, looked at each other and shrieked.

Everyone praised Mother's food, helping themselves to plenty of roast beef.

"*Gott in himel*!" aunt Katja said, "It's so tender you could practically chew it with your eyelashes!"

"Hear, hear!" said Uncle Sem, "Maybe you can get the recipe?"

"That wasn't exactly the nicest thing to say," aunt Manja said, shaking her head. Helped herself to the meat dish that was being passed around and handed it on.

With a wry smile, uncle Sem stuck his fork into a chunk of meat and maneuvered it onto his plate

"I didn't mean to take the gas out of your balloon!"

"Jewish gas!"

"Shh, di...!"

"I must say, you're all very witty!" uncle Kam said speaking over my mother.

Especially Grandpa couldn't get enough and kept on filling his mouth with meat. He was Russian and ran a lot. I had heard the aunts talk about how he also ran after his female employees, men were so lecherous. The word was chivalrous, Father said, suppressing a laugh when I asked the meaning of the word. And Grandpa was the instigator of it all. I knew that an instigator was someone who made scratches on cars. But words could mean several things and I couldn't make out what it meant here. Maybe that was why Grandpa never got fat from all the meat he ate. An instigator like our grandpa who ran around as much as he did needed extra reserves.

I was given permission to leave the table. Went out and sat down on the step in front of the open front door. From there you could see the church tower rise above the houses on the other side of the road. The bell ringer had not come yet. When he had rung the bell and the grown-ups had finished eating, we would all go down to the harbor to watch the sun set. That was what everyone did, also the locals. It was like a lubricant for the sun to help it go down, Father said. Then it would surely shine the next day. But it didn't always work.

From the living room came the clinking sounds of forks and knives against the porcelain and all the talking and laughter. And Mother's voice that, like the sharp butcher knife, cut through the noise.

"Please help yourselves to more meat. There's plenty. I'll go out and cut more. Wait, Father, I'm coming..."

At that very moment Mr. And Mrs. Fisher turned around the corner to the front yard, both dressed in faded black. When Mrs. Fisher turned around to close the gate she caught sight of me and waved. They continued their walk in the direction of the harbor. I listened to their footsteps in the gravel until I no longer could hear them.

There was still no sign of a bell ringer in the bell tower and I was itching to get going.

Helle and Winnie had gone ahead of us. Winnie was all electric, pulled Helle along and couldn't wait a second longer to look for John. Down at the pier I had seen her and John kissing. The aunts had also seen it. Sun-tanned and dressed in light summer outfits from the city, which (in their own words) made the summer residents stand out so dreadfully from the locals, they had stood there, sticking their heavily made-up faces together. Wasn't it about time Winnie soon got an engagement ring while she still had that thin waist of hers? Aunt Pavla had the same expression on her face that our mother would get when the cat, Meshugge, came over and licked her bare leg.

I went over and pulled Helle a little to the side. Shouldn't we help Winnie? We could say to John that it was about time he showed that he had a backbone. She got furious, scowled like our mother and said how dare I interfere in things I was too little to understand.

But anyone who had eyes could see that Winnie needed help. And as we were walking back, Helle blurted out, just like when the lid on the spout of our kettle flew off, that the aunts ought to keep their noses to themselves. Mother shook her head and said that it was quite the contrary, that one should appreciate it when others show an interest in one's doings and, anyway, who else but the family would bother doing that?

Again, I looked toward the church tower. Normally after the bell ringer had rung the bells he would wave and make the bell give off one more clang just in my honor. But he still wasn't in the church tower.

There were still clinking sounds, talking and laughter coming from the dining room. And once again Mother's voice:

"Just eat! I have plenty more! I'll go out in the kitchen and cut more. Wait, I'll be right back..."

Why did she always say that? Why didn't she say what was *true*? What she always said when they were on their way to bed. That the family had once again eaten us out of the house so that Father would have to give her more money. Then he'd get angry, because she had just gotten money. One word led to another and she would say, expressing herself in no uncertain terms, that when it came to everything else he was a cheerful giver. Which was true, he gave money to the Jews in Israel, ice cream to me and playing cards wasn't exactly something you did for free. And when he finally did win something, he and the uncles would always end up fighting. On top of that he was the cheerful giver, no sponsor rather, for the pair number 7 when there was a bicycling race in Forum, he said. Someone had to pay for all the meat the bicyclists had to eat. They even put raw meat in their pants, I had heard, right against their bare behinds. I certainly wouldn't want any of that, no thanks...

Helle and I were upstairs lying in our beds. I asked her whether she wanted to go down with me and help Father. She hissed at me and continued reading her book, a romance novel. Maybe she had gotten a boyfriend, from one day to the next she had started using lipstick. I would have liked to say to Father that he might just as well get it over with right away, take his wallet out of his pocket. There wouldn't be any peace and quiet until Mother had gotten her way. But at our house the eggs didn't teach the hen and he must have finally figured it out for himself. At least their loud voices were replaced by affectionate sounds coming from their bedroom.

Mother's voice faded away to the back of the house. The kitchen faced the courtyard where I usually would sit whitening my shoes with a toothbrush and polishing paste in a saucer. That was where Mr. and Mrs. Fisher's annex was. Mr. Fisher's legs were so long that he had to bend them under the stool when he sat down in the courtyard to mend fishing nets. Meanwhile he'd mumble to himself over and over, "They're coming to take me away!"

"No, they ain't!" Mrs. Fisher said.

They spoke in a dialect, Father said, and a dialect was different from speaking a broken language. Perhaps all those years working as a fisher had taught him to understand what the fish said to one another below the water.

But I had heard that he had once transported something other than fish. Something that was dangerous to hide in the cargo. Then he got obsessive thoughts. There was no way of knowing. There was always so much you couldn't be sure about. You could get scared of him. I sided with the story about the fish.

Meanwhile Mrs. Fisher bustled about at the gas ring behind the half-door to the annex and was frying some flounders that Mr. Fisher had been lucky enough to catch in his net.

The smell of fish attracted Meshugge. Father was the one who had thought of its name, which was Yiddish and meant crazy. In reality its name was Missy Cat. Sniffing, with its tail straight in the air and its snout lifted toward the doorway, it stood still for a moment. But it didn't have to trouble itself jumping onto the half-door because at that very moment Mrs. Fisher entered carrying a bowlful of fish in one hand and a bowl of milk in the other. She placed both bowls on the flagstones in the corner where there was shade.

Meshugge immediately began devouring the contents. Lapped up the milk with its pink tongue that was like wet silk on the skin. But I didn't want him to lick my newly whitened shoes with his fishy tongue, so I pushed him away every time he came over to me after eating.

"They're comin' to take me away!"

"No, they ain't!"

Helle said it was his kidneys, tapping her finger against her temple, That also meant crazy. But it was called obsessive thoughts. Could you get obsessive thoughts from fishing? No, it was probably the other thing. The thing that had been dangerous. What were obsessive thoughts?

Again, Mother's voice came from the house, "Eat up now! I'll go out and cut some more meat. Wait..."

I decided I would go inside and help her to say the truth. But at that very same moment the sound of the bell interjected itself in between the sounds coming from the dinner table. At first hesitating, as though it couldn't decide on what it wanted to do. Then it burst through at full strength, drowning out everything else.

*

When the summer vacation was over I almost couldn't wait to get back to school again to learn more about the chosen people. But then I heard Mother say on the telephone that I was to change schools and take second grade at the public school, where Helle was taking the 7th grade.

"*That* school was much too Jewish, yes, dear Pavla, it *was!*"

My heart sank to the very bottom of my stomach. Why was it wrong to be Jewish when that was what we were? Furthermore, no one had asked me whether I wanted to change schools. From one day to the next, my life was turned upside down, so to speak.

When my new class teacher, Mr. Jensen, shook my hand and bid me welcome, he said that school was for life. And when something as significant as choice of school went over my head like that I would have to be on my guard. The same could happen with other things. It made me more alert.

There was nothing strange in feeling different when starting at a new school, everyone did. But there were things that occurred that I didn't like. Already on the first day someone pulled my hair and said silly things. "Hey, Afro-hair, shouldn't you be somewhere else?" or "Have they now started making *white* negroes?"

I missed Miranda. And *him*.

That night, I pushed my plate away. "I won't eat if I have to go to that school!"

"There'll be no discussion!" Father said, making a sweeping gesture.

"I won't do it!"

"It's much more refined to go to public school," Mother said, "Isn't that right, Helle? Plus..."

"I won't do it!"

"Ignore her," Father said, looking at my mother.

Inside me someone had put out the lights.

At the Danish public school girls and boys weren't allowed to play together during the breaks, but were kept separated in each their courtyard by a yellow stripe painted on the cement. A teacher on playground duty was constantly on patrol, marching back and forth along the stripe and turning his or her head from one side to the other. The school building also seemed much too big to me, it was dark and had long hallways which made it difficult to find one's way. The only advantage was that it was close to where we lived.

I noticed that my new classmates had last names like Hansen and Petersen because one of them shouted, "Jew face" at me. I told Mother so that she would finally be convinced that it would be much better to put me back in the Jewish school. But I had probably been asking for it myself, she said, because that's how these things always were. And anyway, I wasn't supposed to talk so much about it, for Pete's sake, we were just like everybody else!

I don't know why it happened. It just happened. In the middle of class I jumped up, grabbed my school bag and ran out of the classroom. Found my windbreaker on the coat rack on the wall, spurted down the long hallway, down the stairs and out of the school building filled with only one thought: I had to go back and make sure that our house was still there. Mother? I ran through the park, past the ice cream booth on the corner and across a big street. Stopped at the fire station right next to our house and checked to see that the gates were closed. Then I ran past it. My heart was throbbing all the way up in my throat because what if there was suddenly an emergency call-out?

When Mother saw me she pursed her lips. I said I had a stomachache. She studied me.

I saw my reflection in her disapproving eyes and with a slight sense of shame, calmed down. Exactly there.

But if the stomachache had passed I could go with her to Wama and buy coffee. Now she was smiling and put out her hand, "It's nice to have company instead of always doing the shopping alone."

Above the entrance door to the shop there hung a neon-sign with a black girl in a grass skirt and letters that turned on and off in time with the rhythm if you said the words, "Umbadulla-mama- the coffee is from Wama."

Mother opened the door and the shop bell let out a tinny ring. Inside the shop smelled like many different kinds of spices. On the floor at the end of the counter there were big barrels filled with herring in brine. Coffee beans were poured into a chromium-plated electrical coffee mill. Underneath there was a drawer, and when that was open the smell of newly-ground coffee would waft across the counter and right into your nose. The smell of the coffee and Mother's smile was like holding a balloon in your hand, floating and at the same time present right here.

On the way back, we met Lasse and his mother and walked together with them into the hallway.

"Why don't you come up with us?" Lasse's mother stroked my cheek.

My mother said she didn't want her to bother with that.

"No, it is not a bother at all, it would be cozy, right Lasse?"

Lasse had had polio and wore boots that had metal braces that went up his legs, so it took him awhile to get upstairs. They lived on the fourth floor, right under the drying loft where I always would sneeze by accident whenever the neighborhood kids played hide and seek behind the newly washed sheets hanging on the clothesline. It said "Christensen" on their nameplate. Like his father, Lasse had brown bangs. But his father had a beard, was a teacher and had dark circles around his nails.

Lasse had gone to the bathroom and I tip-toed around their living room looking at the paintings that Lasse's father had painted. They hung everywhere on their walls. The subject of most of them was a naked woman with blue hair who looked like Lasse's mother. Her skin was like cream or cream-colored silk, and she was either sitting at their writing desk with her hands under her chin or lounging on an armchair. On one picture she lay stretched out on a red carpet with her eyes closed. I imagined paintings with a nude woman that looked like my mother hanging on our walls in our apartment. But the picture of her dissolved before it ever got a chance to materialize. Perhaps it had to do with the fact that I could never envision my father with a paint brush in his hand. Mother often sighed over the fact that he didn't know how to hold a hammer.

Lasse's mother didn't sigh but moved about in the kitchen, humming as she took things from the cabinets. I stood at the doorway. Their apartment looked very different, but then their apartment was opposite to ours.

When she caught sight of me her face lit up in a smile.

"I'd like to have a little girl like you," she said, "we don't have any little girls in the house anymore."

"You can just borrow me," I said.

She came over and gave my hand a squeeze. It gave me a bubbling sense that what I had said meant something.

Then she went over to the kitchen table and cut up a piece of pork into slices. Turned on the gas and placed a pan on the flame where the pantry was at our place.

The smell of the sizzling meat made my mouth water and I said that I also loved fried pork.

"With parsley gravy!"

She studied me. Then she asked if I was entirely sure that that was what we got at my place.

We often got fried pork. But it still seemed as though I had said something wrong. My tongue got stuck to the roof of my mouth and I asked for something to drink. Took the glass she held out. The water went down the wrong way when I swallowed it and I started coughing. She was now smiling again.

Lasse peeped at us from the door and sniffed.

"Yum. Fried pork, I can barely wait."

His mother pinched his cheek. "You'll have to. We won't be eating for another hour. Why don't you sit out on the balcony in this sunny weather?"

We walked together through the living room out to the balcony. Lasse opened the door and I let myself fall onto the stone floor that was covered by the red carpet I had seen in the painting. It itched, but the sun warmed me.

Then Lasse said I should stay on the balcony while he went in to get something, and he went limping back inside.

I got on my feet. Climbed on a chair and leaned over the railing. Up from here you could see much further than down from our balcony. All the way out to the open fields where the circus usually was and where we would go sleighing in the winter. On the big lawn next to the playground Long Torben was playing soccer with a group of boys. I waved but he didn't see me.

With his thin polio legs Lasse was unable to play soccer with the boys in the courtyard. He was, of course, upset about this, but not as much as you'd think. Lasse didn't have the kinds of toys that the healthy boys played with but a library instead. When his grandpa died, Lasse inherited his books. Lasse's father was the one who would read together with Lasse and Lasse beamed with pride of knowing what it said in all the books.

After a little while Lasse returned with two books. Placed

them on the carpet, sat down and skimmed the big book which was about the constellations. I knew of the Big Dipper which Mrs. Sand had shown me. But Lasse was familiar with all the constellations, they always looked at them whenever he visited his grandma and grandpa, he said. Out in the country the night sky was so dark that they were practically falling on your head. When he read about the stars he would hear his grandpa's voice in his ears. Did I know that the Milky Way consists of thousands of billions of stars?

"Thousands of billions."

We sat for awhile not saying anything, just letting ourselves being sucked up into the tufts of white that sailed above our heads.

Then he took the other book. Leafed through it and pointed at a picture of a black-haired man whose eyelids hung heavily over his big, dark eyes.

"That's Proust."

"Who Pr...?"

"Marcel Proust! He's French. A famous author. *A Remembrance of Things Past*. A quarter of a million words! You must know him!"

I shook my head. Lasse frowned and looked thoughtful.

"My father says that you can always tell by the eyes."

"Tell what?"

"If someone's Jewish!"

I winced. "I'm not allowed to talk about that!"

That night Father came home from the shop, lifted me up and asked who was the best in the world.

I grabbed hold of his nose. "Jew face!"

"Little anarchist." He put me back down and looked at me with an implicit smile. And then I knew that he loved me.

When the others had finished eating, Mother remained sitting next to me. She pointed at my full plate and said, "Eat!"

"Up at Lasse's they know that we're Jew--"

"Keep quiet and eat!" she sighed.

"Lasse said, that you can always tell by the ---"

With impatience and subdued anger, she said that I was to stop thinking or talking about it. If you didn't talk about something it wouldn't be there at all. She raised the fork with the food toward my mouth. "Open up!"

I knew she was doing it out of love. But my throat constricted and only reluctantly made room for the pieces of pork and the congealed parsley sauce. But I wouldn't be allowed to play with Lasse anymore. If I didn't finish my food.

So I swallowed it all. Together with the pork I swallowed my mother's love and had to swallow her impatience and anger along with it.

Despite that I loved them both all the way to the moon and back. Mostly because I couldn't distinguish one thing from the other, but also just as much because I, like all the other children I knew, loved to be loved and in my own way did everything I could to make love last.

But behind my own face another face had turned away.

*

I had gotten my own key which was suspended from a string that I wore around my neck. Still, I wasn't a real latchkey kid. Real latchkey kids didn't have parents who owned cars. They didn't have electrical refrigerators at a time when everyone else had a block of ice delivered for their ice box every morning, they may not even have had two parents.

Nora was the one who had told me about latchkey kids. She said there were a lot of them on Vesterbro where she lived after she had gone ashore and she took me with her there one day.

We were going to visit her sister. In a narrow street we stopped in front of a gate. Nora pointed to the mailbox that was hanging from the wall next to the gate. The "b" was missing, so it said "ox." We writhed from laughter and walked in through the gate.

In the backyard a group of latchkey kids were playing ball. A couple of men were standing drinking beer next to the garbage pails. One of them whistled at us. Nora turned around, put two fingers in her mouth and whistled back.

The hallway smelled of mold and cat pee and I held my nose as we walked up the stairs. Nora said that Tove lived all the way up in the garret and had a girl my age whose name was Birgitte. We were to play together in the bedroom while Nora talked with Tove.

Birgitte wore glasses and had a band-aid across her one eye. She stared at me with her other eye. It was so frightening that I got a stomachache.

On the way back home Nora called me a wimp and continued to poke me. I certainly had nothing to be worried about. We belonged to the privileged class of society, she said, which was a fancier word for refined.

When we got home to our place she said that she would just take a bath. In the bathroom she turned on the faucet and poured a drop of the pine needle liquid soap we used for bubble baths into the bathtub. I was allowed to stay in there while she undressed. She placed her clothes on the laundry bin in the corner, tiptoed across the terrazzo floor to the bathtub and swung one leg over the edge. Slid down below the foam and let her neck lean against the edge of the tub.

"Aaah!" she said, smiling at me. "Can you hear the angels sing?"

After a little while she sat up and asked me to scrub her back. Then we could talk while she became a new person, she said. Afterward she dipped her entire body into the water. When she sat back up she rubbed her face with both hands. I stuck my hand in the bathtub, put a blob of foam on her head and said, "Queen Nora!"

She laughed and sprayed water on me.

"It's also darn well about time that you open your eyes to the inequalities of society!" she said.

When we had eaten dinner Nora helped undress me and tucked in my blanket. Then she and Helle went into the living room.

I turned around on the other side as Nora's words kept sliding back and forth inside my skull.

"If you don't have any candy drops, you can't suck them!" she had said. And that she had neither a bathroom nor a kitchen, not even her own toilet. But you didn't get those things when you were renting a room, she had said. And we had everything and could also afford a housekeeper for cleaning and babysitting, right? I didn't think she looked all that poor, always wore skirts and knitted cardigan sets and had a steady job on land with DSB at Copenhagen Central Station. I turned again. But why did Nora think that just because you had everything you had nothing to be scared of?

I ended up finally falling asleep. When I woke up it was still dark and Birgitte's eye was staring at me. I screamed.

One day it became too much for Mother and she took me to see the doctor. He looked at me over his spectacles and helped me up on the examination table. And with his big hands he pressed my bare stomach. There was absolutely nothing wrong with it, he said, scratching the elongated sun freckle on his forehead. Then he took out a prescription pad from his white coat, leaned across his writing desk and wrote down the name of a medication I was to take before going to bed. A half a pill dissolved in some water. That would work against nightmares.

But I was scared of being helped and tightened my lips.

Then Mother asked the Giant Angel, who did the housecleaning, to help. That in itself was a nightmare.

"Oh, you're an angel," she always said when the Giant Angel put on her coat after a full day of working with soap and ammonium chloride.

Father always said that a potentially great vaudeville singer had been lost in her.

I looked at her stomach. Further up. Across her bosom the smock was gaping. I shuddered when I saw her drape her scarf around her broad cheeks and tie the knot on her forehead. You could see in her eyes what she was thinking: It was such a shame that my mother had me!

The next moment I lay in the grasp of her angel arms. She pressed the glass between my lips and tilted it. I coughed, sputtered and writhed. Clenched my fists and fought with all my might. But the angel was as strong as a giant. My hands constantly got caught under her wings which were everywhere on her giant body.

That was how she got her name. I was the only one who called her the Giant Angel. But I never said it aloud.

"Oh, you're an angel" was always the last thing I heard when, after the battle, I lay in my bed. That night, a fear of death rushed through me while a dullness, as when one has a fever, overwhelmed me, making me unable to so much as lift my arm for a last goodbye.

But I didn't die, I was awakened by the siren of an ambulance and told Mother that I didn't want to go toschool. Because I had a headache.

She studied me. Then she turned toward the Giant Angel and asked in an anxious voice:

"Headaches? Can children get those?"

"That's a good sign!" the Giant Angel droned, "At least then you know that she has a head!"

One evening, after dinner, just when I had carried my plate into the kitchen, the phone rang. Mother was doing the dishes. Helle was drying them and Father had just gone back to the shop to get something he had forgotten. So I placed the plate on the kitchen table, ran into the living room and picked the telephone off its cradle.

"Hello?"

I immediately recognized Winnie's voice that had completely dissolved into tears. But before I had a chance to console her, Mother wrenched the telephone out of my hand.

When she came in to say good-night to me, I asked her about Winnie.

"Winnie?"

"Winnie!" I nodded, "She was crying."

"Oh, that," Mother said, bending down to pick up some clothes from the floor. "Don't you worry your little head about that." She smiled, giving me a wet kiss on my forehead. "Go to sleep, now. Good-night."

*

We were at the doctor's again. And once again I looked into his blue eyes above his spectacles as he helped me onto the examination table.

"Do you think she might have contracted a tapeworm? I've heard of a case with a 16 meter long..." my mother made an unexpected pause.

He pressed my stomach and twisted my knees from side to side for a very long time. Then he once again placed his big hands on my stomach.

And every time my inflated intestines responded in the only language they mastered, or rather didn't know, he would mumble, "Now, now" or "There, there" or long words in Latin. Finally, touching the sun freckle on his head, he said, "No, I don't think it's tapeworm...hmmm...but..."

And while the smell of intestinal gasses permeated the room, making mincemeat of the smell of alcohol disinfectant, he, very hesitantly, pronounced his definitive judgment.

"We'd better let the hospital examine her tummy this time."

"No!" I shouted as loud as I could.

But it was always the parents who made the final decision. And the ones in white coats. Unfortunately, they were almost always walking around holding a needle in their hand.

While Mother helped me get changed into a hospital gown I remembered a time once when we had been to the eye doctor with Helle.

Her eyes were watering and her face was completely pale with fear.

We had been sitting in the waiting room and I said, "He'll probably stick a needle in your eyes!"

Mother placed her hands on Helle's shoulders and told her not to mind what I said, what did a child know about such things anyway?

But what had the giant in the white coat done? He took out a flashlight, shone it in Helle's eyes and came up with some stupid explanation about her tear ducts being blocked. Then he turned his back to us and started rattling with some instruments.

Helle grew more and more pale. I held my breath. I had only said it for fun, plus I was just a child.

When he turned around he had a needle in his hand. He pulled down Helle's cheeks, first one and then the other, and stuck her in the eyes!

Helle kept saying that it had been my fault.

Now I was getting what I deserved. Christmas and New Year's came and went, while one white coat after the other stuck needles in me, took samples of my bowels and crammed tubes down my throat. Even though Mother had promised me that that was something they would never dream of doing to a child, but the other sick girls had been right!

They didn't find anything in me that wasn't supposed to be there, neither tapeworms or anything else. I just needed glasses. Other than that there was absolutely nothing wrong with me. At least not anything that could be measured by their instruments.

"It's psychological" Mother said when she with as much concern as pride in her voice told aunt Pavla and Mrs. Sand and Nora about me.

Then I started seeing a psychologist. Her name was Louise and she lived close to the Copenhagen Lakes. From her window you could see the swans sailing on the water. Louise's gray hair was gathered into a soft bun and her smile reached all the way to her eyes, like Nora's. But her voice was deeper than Nora's.

I was to sit at her coffee table and draw, she said. Tell her about myself and say whatever came to my mind. Sometimes Mother would interrupt the conversation, but I was the one who had the floor, Louise said.

We spent three hours with Louise. She didn't think there was anything wrong with me, either. But I had a lively nose, she said to my mother. It could sniff out when the things that were said aloud did not agree with the things that were left unsaid. And in my case, my nose was in my stomach. She gave me an encouraging smile and added that contrary to what you'd think, a child was able to understand that sort of thing. Because in reality a child could only express in words the things it had always experienced.

When we left, Louise gave Mother one of my drawings which was of a swan and said that she should think of me as an opening into the family's self-perception. A tiny "crack" letting light seep into the darkness of the family's history.

And in her experience, it could be very beneficial to listen to what such a "crack" had to say.

Mother smiled and nodded and nodded and smiled again and put the drawing in her purse.

Louise concluded by saying that it would be good for me to learn how to play an instrument.

My nose made a few somersaults in my stomach.

My mother held out her hand and thanked Louise for her kindness. As we walked down the steps she studied me several times. I had been pestering her for a long time about getting a guitar.

I was certain, as certain as you could be about anything, that it would also be good for Mother to tell Louise about herself. I had heard her say on the telephone that she had gotten some new pills. They were called Librium and when she had to take a pill she would place it on her tongue, take a gulp of water and toss her head backwards. Sometimes she had to do it several times before she managed to get the pill down.

But I should never have said it aloud. That it would be good for Mother to tell Louise about herself. Because it helped Mother if she could believe that sort of thing was really only good for me. I wanted to help her, even though it sometimes became too much for me. But it became too much for her, too. I had heard her and the Giant Angel talk about how there were family relief care centers, which was always good to have as a backup.

At first I was sad that Mother wanted to leave us because I knew I would miss her. But then I heard the Giant Angel say that as far as she understood, they were willing to take kids already from the age of eight.

My stomach turned to ice!

No one could help me now, neither Lasse or his mother. Mrs. Sand or Nora, Winnie, aunt Pavla or uncle Jafet. The parents had all the power and Louise had been an acute mistake, my mother said on the telephone.

Helle wasn't able to prevent my being sent away either, she had her own problems to think of. She had gotten a boyfriend at school and he wasn't Jewish. Our parents fought over it. It was unheard of, Father said, and forbade her to wear lipstick at school. She was only allowed to do it at the Jewish Youth Club in which she said she would never set foot. But she did it anyway. She had let me see her new lipstick once when Winnie was sleeping over. We lay on the pull-out bed and Winnie poured a whole bag full of make-up samples from Magasin onto the blanket.

No, I should never have said it aloud!

Mother and Father drove me over there, it was on Zealand because we didn't have to go by boat.

"Something with 'A'" Father said in his vacation voice when we turned at the corner.

I didn't answer. To the very end I had been clinging to the hope that they might change their minds. We could never dream of sending you away from home, they should have said, did you really think we would? But they didn't.

In front of a building that was surrounded by a forest of

birch trees Father stopped the car and pulled the hand brake. Birch Home it said with big twining letters on the wall.

A man with a beard came out to us, bid us welcome and showed us around the house. His name was Søren. His wife had dimples and was named Kate. She went with us up to the first floor where the dormitories were. Pointed at the bed closest to the door. That was where I was to sleep.

I looked at Father and tried to catch his eye, but he looked away. A little while later he followed Søren down the stairs. Then I stood watching as Mother placed my things in the closet next to the bed.

"There!" she said, sounding like she had just finished the ironing.

Søren stood with me in the parking lot and watched as the Captain drove away. We remained standing there until the sound of the wheels on the gravel had faded.

All the other children looked up when we stepped into the common room and Søren asked us to sit down on the floor in a circle. Then he also settled down and put the guitar strap around his neck. Struck a couple of chords and began singing.

"Are you unsocialized, too?" the girl next to me whispered when we were done singing. She had a ribbon in her blond hair. And when I didn't answer she said that we all were. I was among friends.

No one had said anything about how long I was supposed to stay there. When Kate had finished reading a good-night story to us, she came over and sat down next to me. Her hand was warm when she took hold of mine that was so cold I could hardly feel it.

I started to cry. She held my hand tightly and whispered that that was normal and that it would soon pass.

For every day that passed I made a checkmark in the pocket diary that Helle had given me as a going away present. But like the other anti-social kids I partook in the meals and slept during the nights. Every day before dinner Søren would play his guitar and sing with us. I was allowed to borrow his guitar and practice the chords that cousin Ralfi had taught me. Søren taught me more chords and said that I had gotten very clever at playing the guitar.

One day we got something as a first course which I had never seen before. It was porridge made with water, we were told. I froze. The other children had already started eating but I remained sitting still, unable to move, looking at the colorless enemy in my plate. Mother had often threatened to send me to an orphanage where I'd get porridge made with water. Her facial expression, when she said it made it very clear: Of all the things in the world, porridge made with water was the most atrocious thing you could put in your mouth. And beyond what any person could possibly imagine. But I thought that was just something she thought up to make me eat.

Søren came over. "If you don't eat the first course, you won't get the second course. No excuses!"

Since I still hadn't taken the spoon in my hand, he asked me to leave the table and go up to the dormitory. Weak from hunger and homelessness, I went up to the dormitory and fell onto my bed.

Shortly afterward I heard footsteps coming closer. Søren

stepped in holding a tray in his hands upon which there was a plate with potatoes and meatballs.

"It's only because you're such a little skeleton," he said, winking. But first I had to swear not to tell the other kids, or else they'd start getting ideas, he said.

I crossed my heart and devoured the food.

The day Mother and Father were supposed to come get me, I counted the number of checkmarks in the pocket diary. There were forty. They had a present for me, a long package. In it was a Spanish guitar.

Shortly afterward I performed at a singing competition at a neighborhood party nearby that my father had entered me in. I felt like my heart would jump out of my throat when the winner was announced: I had won first prize.

When I walked off the stage Father helped put the guitar in its cover. The Giant Angel came over to us, it was in her courtyard that the party took place. She smiled at us and said, "It is an ill wind that blows nobody any good, right?"

Lasse and his mother had also come over.

"You certainly kept that quiet!" Lasse's mother said, stroking my cheek. Father looked at me and smiled his "the apple doesn't fall far from the tree" smile.

"Are you going to be a star, now?" Lasse asked.

"No, I'm just saving up. I'm going to go to America!"

Back home in my room I put the money in my piggy bank. Looked at the mottled carpet as a strange feeling spread through my body.

I was back home. But I felt the sense of homelessness right to the very bone.

One night, when everyone had forgotten that I had been away from home, the Aid for Hungary was on television. It was because of the Russians. The announcer talked and talked. Money was pouring in from all over Denmark. But Russians? Our grandma and grandpa were born in Russia, what was it with those Russians?

They were visiting and I looked over at Grandpa. But he just sat there taking a bite from a slice of orange Mother always put out whenever we had visitors. His chewing jaws gave no answer.

Grandma sat in the sofa crocheting. She could both crochet and follow what was going on on the screen, just like Mother. She and the aunts would often talk about how much one could get done while doing something else. Men were more impractical in that sense, Just one thing at a time. It was something in the brain. But Grandma didn't show any sign either that could explain the Russians' behavior.

"Stalin was a criminal, Khrushchev is a criminal, criminals the whole lot of them!" Grandpa said in his broken Danish. Then he reached out with his big hand again and yet another slice of orange slid between his fingers. This time he stuffed the whole slice into his mouth and dried his hand in a napkin. He chewed for a long time without turning his head from the TV screen.

I also took a piece of orange. The juice prickled in your mouth, like fizzle.

We had also given money, Father said.

"And every little thing helps..."

Part II
The Angel of Light

A new chapter in our lives began. We were moving to a residential neighborhood. 85 000 DKK was what our house cost, I heard, and became dizzy at the thought of all that money. But Father had kept his cool he said, and had haggled and gotten the price down to 79 000 DKK. It was still a staggering amount.

"From now on we're going to save!" he said.

That meant that the bicycle races were all over and done with. As well as the Fisher house.

"Now that we have a backyard, we don't need to ... yes, dear Pavla, there is both a terrace and a nice big lawn," Mother said on the telephone.

That was how it was, those kinds of decisions were made over my and Helle's heads. But she had had longer time than me to get used to the idea.

"You'll probably make new friends quickly" Lasse's mother said when I went up there to say good-bye, "but do come and visit us!"

In our new house we had a lot more space.

Mother said on the telephone that our furniture was given its proper weight in the new house, it looked brand new! And the ceilings that had stucco and everything were made for our bronze chandeliers, she said, knocking on the wood under the telephone table. Not that she was in the least bit superstitious...!

She said to the Gigantic Angel that she hoped that we also would get more peace in the house now that Helle and I had our own rooms. The big age difference made us seem more like two only children.

I had changed schools again. But this time I was much better prepared for it. I had gotten older, almost 11 now. And one public school was just as good as another.

There were children living in almost all the houses in the residential area and most of my classmates also lived in their own house. In the house next to ours lived Agnete. She was one year older than me and had painted her own room yellow.

I also wanted my room to be yellow, and Mrs. Sand, who came to give us a hand when we moved, helped me paint it, She asked me whether I liked my new school.

"You've chosen a real sunshine color!" she clapped her hands and examined the wall we had just painted, "You just have to watch out for holidays."

I knew that, I said, but now I wasn't going to the Jewish school.

"There's a spot," she said, pointing, "that needs more paint, do you see it?"

"Oh," I said and quickly dipped the paint brush in the pail and gave it an additional coat.

My new room had two doors. One led to the living room and the other to my parents' bedroom. One evening they were talking in there about a letter that had arrived with the mail that same day, an anonymous letter!

I held my breath. It seemed that there was something about our family in that letter. But it was malicious gossip and was utterly unfounded, Mother said. Malicious gossip of the worst kind!

What could it be? Who would want to do something malicious to us? Something so evil that the writer of the letter hadn't signed their name? I pulled the blanket way up above my shoulders and turned around on the other side. It rustled behind the walls like the sound of a thousand mice and down from the cellar rose the subdued moan from the boiler up through the floor.

We hadn't heard from Nora for a long, long time. I was certain I had heard Mother say several times in the telephone that Nora had caught fire. Even though her voice didn't sound alarmed it filled me with unease. So much so, that I ventured down to Helle's room without being invited. She went to high school now and had a lot of homework to do.

She sat at her writing desk with an open book in front of her and lifted her head all at once when I stepped in. I was so surprised that she didn't immediately tell me to leave that I forgot why I went down there in the first place. She had painted her walls white and in one corner there was a standing lamp whose lamp shades had different colors. I glanced at her and searched for a sign in her face. Did she know anything about the anonymous letter?

She cleared her throat and asked, "Sorry, but what exactly did you come down here for?"

Quickly I said, "Have you heard anything about Nora, I mean, has anything happened to her?"

"What would have happened to her?"

"I don't know, was just thinking."

In one of the rooms in the cellar we had practically gotten a grocer's shop. On the shelves of the plastered walls there were boxes, packages, cans and glasses with all sorts of pickled and preserved goods. Everything had been thoroughly stacked in tall piles according to size and shape. There were also bottles with liquor in all colors and at the end wall there were piles of beer and soft drink bottle cases from floor to ceiling.

"There's enough for a whole regiment of soldiers" said Mother whose eyes lit up when I asked what in the world we were going to do with all that food.

Maybe it was just something she said. But in our larder there was enough food and beverages for a family of four to survive for at least five years.

*

Already on the first day of school I had especially noticed Marianne. Not just because she wore nice clothes, chequered pinafore dresses in Black Watch and Prince of Wales and had a certain equilibrium with a natural sense of self-confidence. But we had almost the same color hair. And I kept thinking about how I could get to talk to her in private. She always walked arm in arm with Agnete during the breaks. Or Laila. Always two and two.

Whether it was due to God or destiny, I couldn't say. But one day something unexpected happened.

The day had started like it always did. Father opened the door to my room and said that it was 6:30 am. I got up and went to the bathroom. Got dressed, had some tea, ate two pieces of white bread with marmalade.

When I sat at my writing desk to pack my school bag with my school books, I froze. During our last Danish class my new class teacher, Mr. Ovesen, had explained the political parties and tested us on the government. What was it he had asked us to remember as the bell rang at the end of the day? I closed my eyes and saw Ovesen before me holding a piece of chalk in the hand he had lifted as he scanned the classroom before turning around to write the names of the Prime Ministers on the chalk board. Everyone of course knew the name of the Prime Minister, which was Viggo Kampmann.

But when he asked me for the names of two ministers, the Minister of the Interior and the Foreign Minister, I said the wrong names twice in a row. I mumbled that I knew the names from television.

"Well," Ovesen said, folding his arms, his smile as sweet as candy. Take for example the Minster of Foreign Affairs Jens Otto Krag. I now ask you, do you know Jens Otto Krag?" And then answering himself, "'Yes, but of course I know Jens Otto Krag!' Is that how you know the names of the Ministers?"

Laughter broke out from the rest of the class, making me wish I had never been born.

The idea was for us to learn the basic values of the various political parties and acquire a sense of what Ovesen called, a political standpoint.

"Go home and talk about it with your parents!" he said when the bell rang. That was *that*.

I ran into the kitchen but Father had already left.

"Who do you vote for?" I asked my mother instead who was busy measuring coffee with a spoon to make another pot for the Gigantic Angel.

"…three, four…oh, now I lost count, did I say three or four?"

"You said four!"

"It's just because you came barging in like that."

"You said *four*!"

Still, she turned the coffee filter upside down and poured the coffee back in the coffee jar. Stuck the measuring spoon into the coffee once more and started all over again.

This time I waited until she was finished counting.

"So, who do you vote for?"

"Vote?" A shadow crossed her face.

"Yes!"

"For the armchair!"

"No, tell me! I said, "We're supposed to talk about politics with our parents as a class assignment!"

"I just told you!"

I kicked the leg of a chair. It flew, rattling across the floor.

"You want to talk politics and you don't even know…" She paused and smiled to herself. Reached out her hand to pat my head. I pushed her hand away.

"Get out of my kitchen!" She shouted laughing as I was leaving.

I was late. Agnete had already left her house.

I got off my bike at the corner and wheeled it across the street. When the crossing guard wasn't there the cars would rush by. Ovesen had also talked about being unmotivated and … armchair voters! I choked on some saliva and coughed.

"She's coming now!" could be heard from the classroom. "Get rid of it!"

When I stepped in I saw it. There was a big swastika that had been drawn on the chalkboard. The classroom was deathly silent. The others were already sitting in their seats. I stumbled over a school bag and sat down.

From the corner of my eye I saw Marianne go up to the chalkboard and rub out the swastika with both hands. Was she then also...? I didn't let myself think the thought to its end. If I just dared to ask her. Walk over to her even if she was in the middle of talking to other kids, and tell her that I wanted to talk to her. Or suggest that we go home together, she lived close to the stream not far from my street.

She just managed to sit back down in her seat when Ovesen's tall figure appeared at the doorway. He had forgotten to remove his bicycle clips.

I ducked. But then I got to thinking that that would be the same thing as shouting to Ovesen to pick on me. My heart was pounding so hard that it practically tore through my shirt but I forced myself to sit straight. To pay attention in class and take down notes in my notebook.

I was let off easy! I sensed Marianne's gaze several times for the rest of the school day. When the final class of the day was over she came over to me. Smiling, she asked, "Want to go home together?"

We went for a bike ride, past the post office and the dairy at the corner. The train station. Further, all the way out to Søborg Hovedgade Street where we turned around and biked back. There was still not a word mentioned about what had happened at school that day. Marianne pointed toward Ewaldsbakken. Tove Ditlevsen had lived there! Had I read anything by her?

Wasn't she soon going to get to the point? I thought.

We turned and rode through the park, biking along the stream below the tall chestnut trees that grew along the banks.

Marianne kept running her mouth. She had two younger sisters. Malene was in the class below us. The youngest was called Anne-Marie, like the youngest princess of the royal family, and was in kindergarten.

Wasn't she soon going to mention the other topic?

Her mother was a nurse, her father a judge. In the summers the whole family would travel to Italy. They had three floors in their house, they didn't have a television.

Still no mention of the other topic. Then I would just have to myself ... at that very moment I became breathless and my bike started wobbling. I had to get off it.

Marianne got off her bike, too, placed her hand on my handlebars and steadied both bicycles.

"You're all pale, you should put your head down."

My knees were shaking so I did what she told me. Bent forward with my hands on the gravel.

Shortly afterward, when we leaned our bikes against the fence, I summoned up my courage.

"I was wondering…are you also a Jew?"

"Why, of course!" Marianne turned around and looked directly at me. "I'm from Jutland, too! I'm from Himmerland, where are you from?"

One afternoon when Mother wasn't going to the shop she asked if I would go with her to the grocer's. Then I could help her carry a few things, we needed more soda. And malt beer for Nora.

"Mom, what was I like when I was little?" I asked after we had walked for a little while.

For a moment she looked very thoughtful. Then she looked

at me and smiled. "You were so eager to get out that you gave me seven stitches. And then I got a violent hemorrhage and we both had to go to the hospital."

I visualized a heavy sea of blood and shuddered.

"But it wasn't your fault," she added, smiling again, "You mustn't think that."

On the way home we saw Tall Torben's mother, a tall woman with an erect posture. She came walking toward us with her big dog. Its fur was long and had the color of a floor mop.

We stopped. The grown-ups talked about how nice it was that we again had become almost neighbors and about the joys of this lush green area,

With my free hand I tried to scratch the dog behind its ears but it kept running back and forth, pulling at the leash and sticking its wet snout in between our legs. Then it turned its behind toward us, lifted one of its hind legs, sending a spray of piss shaped like a bow toward the bottom leaves of the hedge.

I also wanted a dog and had asked Mother about it several times. She said that I already had a bird. But I couldn't take Birdie for walks.

"So, do you have any nice teachers?" Tall Torben's Mother asked, smiling.

"Yes!"

But when she asked whether I had gotten Mr. Videbæk for Christianity classes, before I could open my mouth my mother explained that I had been excused from taking classes in religion. Then she lowered her tone of voice and, keeping her words on a tight leash, said, "We're Jewish (and as though it were contagious) but we're not orthodox! We're assimilated, as they say."

The words stung me like needles. But Tall Torben's mother merely nodded, as though she understood perfectly and tugged on the dog's leash.

"Come on, Rudolf!"

We continued walking in silence. What Mother had said. That she said that about us to other people! That she said it in a way that emphasized what we weren't! It enclosed us in something shameful. Or at least it increased the feeling I had that there was a certain amount of distance between us and everyone else.

Even though I was able to grasp that when she used the word assimilated about us, it was to soften the two previous words, "Jewish" and "orthodox." But I found that word to be worse than the other two. It made the outside world even more inaccessible.

I said assimilated to myself and the "s's" in the word were like the sound of a poisonous snake on the verge of creeping up on its prey. Could the word mean that we had been poisonous but had been detoxified with an assimilating liquid? But that word was disinfecting.

"What does assimilated really mean, Mom?" I asked.

She looked at me and straightened the collar of my dress a little. She said that what it meant was that we were just like everybody else. But that didn't make it clearer or explain it. "Like everybody else," except we weren't!

When we got home I went out to the sun room to say hi to Nora. She had had a baby and was living with us. But only until she found a place where she could live with the child, Father said. She lay on the couch with her back to us, the boy was sleeping in his baby lift.

One night Nora had come to our house, I was the one who had opened the door. She didn't seem to have been burnt anywhere, neither in her hair nor anywhere else, but she smelled of something strange. Without saying anything she kept her coat on and with mechanical steps walked right past me into the living room. She said to my mother that she had wanted to bring her a plant but that the flower shop was closed.

"So I took this, instead!" She held out a bottle.

Mother accepted the half-empty bottle and placed it on the coffee table.

"It's always the thought that counts, dear Nora!" she said as if holding the bottle with the very tips of her two fingers.

Father left the living room. I heard his footsteps running down the cellar stairs. I was sent to my room. Went to bed and tried to read. But I kept seeing Nora's eyes before me. It was as though her gaze had acquired several new levels.

I was sitting in my room and had just stuck a fresh millet cob through the cage to Birdie when I heard Helle's key in the door lock and ran out to the hallway. Asked her whether she could explain what assimilated meant.

She stared at me. Then she said she didn't have time and took hold of the door knob to the cellar. Instead I went out to the kitchen where Mother was peeling the potatoes. When she saw me she asked me to set the table.

A little while after Nora came into the dining room with the boy in her arms, she was holding a lit cigarette in her hand. "Do you think that's good for the little one?" Mother asked, frowning. Then she turned toward the boy and smiled. He yawned and stretched his little body.

"There's malt beer for you in the fridge, dear Nora!"

"I could use something a little stronger, actually" Nora said.

"But it's not good when you're nursing."

That night, when they had gone to bed, Father and Mother fought over Nora. Mother expressed in no uncertain terms that she would not go along with throwing Nora out until she had gotten a decent place to live. The boy's father was married to someone else.

We walked up and down the street with the baby carriage. Nora sighed and said that becoming a mother had stripped her of her good spirits. Aside from her sister, Tove, she only had us and a few distant relatives in southern Jutland where she was born. But she not had seen them for years. Their parents were dead and her longing for them gnawed within her with new strength, she said.

"Especially after I've gotten this guy here!" Nora tipped the baby carriage up on its front wheels so that we could better look inside. The boy lay completely still with his eyes closed, the only thing moving was the pacifier in his mouth.

She turned the baby carriage 180 degrees and sent me a shadow of a smile.

"I'm afraid your mother thinks that I'm..." she turned her thumb down. "Has she said anything?"

I immediately shook my head and waved at Helle who was coming toward us with her new linen school bag that hung from a strap on her shoulder.

"And what about...?" Nora paused, nodding toward Helle when she had turned her back and was on her way down the path of flagstones. I shook my head again, feeling more and more ill-at ease.

"I thought your sister seemed rather curt, but maybe that's just me. I think I myself may have become somewhat of a wimp!" She laughed and held out her hand.

I took it and gave it a swing.

*

It was Sunday, I was sitting at my writing desk and was thinking about what I was going to write in an essay about my grandmother. Later that day we were going to visit her and Grandpa.

But not Nora. She had made a call to her sister and said that they were going to take a long walk with the baby carriage and lie on a blanket in the park, now that the weather was finally good.

I was the only one in the class who had a grandma and grandpa who could speak three languages all at once. Some of the words they made up themselves. I had once been to the grocer's with Grandma and she had said that she wanted a "Colle-Drolle."

"Certainly," the grocer had said. "Hmm ..." he then said as he turned around, "What was it you said you wanted?"

"Colle-Drolle" Grandma said again, slowly this time and emphasizing every syllable.

"Sorry?"

But then I translated it for him and asked for a "Coca Cola." the new American soft drink. Now I had another good reason to go to America. I loved Coca Cola.

Grandma also switched the nouns in compound words and

called a "bicycle rider" a "rider bicycle." Everyone was able to understand her, but people still smiled a little when they heard her say it. And when there was the 6-day race at Forum on TV, Grandma would cheer with the rest of Denmark for her hero, which in her mouth became "Kalle Vajne."

So my ear for languages was in sharp training to begin with at the new school and the power of language was reconfirmed to me. Being able to spell and express oneself in flawless Danish was the most important thing of all, Ovesen said. Otherwise you wouldn't be taken seriously and then you wouldn't amount to anything. And if there was one thing you had to do in this world it was to amount to something. That sharpened my ear for languages even more.

In the previous essay we had to write about a country that we admired. I had, of course, written about America and concluded by saying I had been drawn to their racial problems. Ovesen said I had to learn to apply my words carefully, that you shouldn't point out problems to someone with whom you wanted to have a good relationship. What I had written wasn't wrong, but it had still pulled down my grade. "And that's a shame" he said, holding my gaze, "When your spelling and everything else is worth an A+."

This time we had to write about a person we admired and I had asked my mother about it.

She was out in the yard hanging the laundry to dry on our new drying rack while my father was raking weeds off the garden path. When I waved down to Helle, whose windows faced the garden, she jumped out of her chair and drew the curtains. Nora had already left.

I bit the pencil, there had to be more, also something that dug a little deeper. Why did they come to Denmark in the first place? What was it Mother had said?

"It's nice that you've started taking an interest in Grandma. She's the only one who gathers the family for the Jewish holiday meal."

"So does my mother!" my father said.

She didn't answer but continued hanging up the clothes to dry.

"Grandma has always been very good with her hands and she's crocheted this herself." Mother held up a wet blanket with a laced pattern before fastening it with the clothes pins on the clothesline. " In Russia Grandma had an embroidery shop, couldn't you write about that? By the way, did you know that she can write in Russian?"

"Yes, and Grandpa is illiterate," Father said, "which means that he can't sign a business check. Everything has to be done in cash."

I had once seen Grandpa take a few bills from his wallet, fold them and wedge them under the golden frame of one of their cattle paintings. Luckily, he was just as skilled at earning money as Grandma was at spending it, he said. She had once been *a good cigar*, a "dronnik.." Grandpa's eyes glazed over and he patted my head.

But even though Grandpa could neither read nor write, he was good at arithmetic and had his own methods of running the business. Our father was now in home territory and the rake in his hands was moving swiftly. Things could go up and down with the shop but no matter what there had to be proper financial conditions that could withstand the light of day. When he himself signed a check there would always be coverage. But a certain someone tended to change employees at the rate that others changed their shirts.

"Shy, di kleine!" Mother said in a low voice.

Normally Father would have stopped talking when she said that. She was usually the one who would utter a string of words, one after the other, and he who would, with the lift of an eyebrow, get her to stop talking right in the middle of a sentence. But he usually wasn't holding a rake in his hands. So he just continued talking while she, looking in every way surprised, stood still, looking at his hands that continued to scrape the ground with the rake. Back and forth it went, as though the movements of his teeth and the movements of his hands glided directly up through his arms and loosened something or other in his mouth. Something or other that must have been stuck there for a long time but which had now been set in motion. Dirt and weeds flew from right to left as he was talking away about Grandpa, his shop and all his employees.

And he lifted the rake above the ground as he briefly paused before "the employees" and you'd have to be a slowpoke not to register that there was something wrong about it. And he used the word uncouth. It sounded a little bit like Grandpa dealt in diamonds.

"The apple doesn't fall far from the tree," Father said, planting the rake violently on the ground.

"Shy, di kleine!" she said again, this time more forcefully.

But he wasn't listening. He took a big step toward house, placed a hand on the wall and patted the bricks.

"2-9-0-0, now that's a zip-code that proves there's still a

little justice in the world!" he said. "And what do your brothers live in today? In two-bedroom apartments in Nordvest!"

For Mother's sake I ignored it and didn't ask any questions, anyway the essay was supposed to be about Grandma. At that very moment the phone rang.

Father let go of the rake and ran into the house. Now that Mother was in a talkative mood, I took the opportunity to ask her whether Winnie would also be coming today. But either she hadn't heard me or she pretended not to have heard, either way she didn't answer. The last time I had asked about Winnie, Mother had started talking about something else. But in the telephone she said that aunt Pavla had said that she would strangle John with her bare hands which was understandable since he had kept Winne dangling for all these years. Helle didn't want to talk about it, either. So I could figure out myself what had happened to Winnie and John. I wanted so badly to show Winnie my sympathy but on the other hand I didn't want to make matters worse now that she had been crying for an eternity as my mother had said in the telephone. No, she hadn't said cried, but bled.

Instead Mother talked about Grandma's illness. Saying that I mustn't think it had been easy having a mother who had always been sick, no, it certainly hadn't. She sighed as she threw a duvet over the clothes line. Spread it out so that it hung without creases. Then she said once again that it was nice that I was showing such interest in Grandma and asked whether I had enough material to use in my essay.

When Father came back outside he was grinning from ear to ear and could barely get a word out of his mouth. But once again he grabbed hold of the rake and continued from where he had left off. It was his mother. She had wanted him to call an ambulance because she was worried that she had had a stroke, he placed his finger on his temple, tapped it a few times, laughing again.

Recently, when he was going to pick up his mother so that she could sit outside in our yard, he had asked me to ride with him just so he could avoid her reproaches. It was true, our Nanna was rather surly and she didn't say a peep while we were driving. It had to do with her becoming a widow rather early with four kids. Her husband had died of cancer when Father was a big boy. He often said that he had tried being really poor and had to help support the family from the time he left school.

But the whole story just went to show that Father was also a human being just like the rest of us which was something you might forget every now and then.

I corrected the commas and misspellings and put the exercise book in my school bag.

Unfortunately, there were none of them that said anything about why all of our grandparents had left Russia.

We drove in the Captain and were on our way to Grandma and Grandpa's summer house which they lived in for 6 months out of the year. It was on a side street to Strandvejen Street on an L-shaped lot and a long tiled driveway led to the garden. All the way along the lath fence flowers would bloom in the colors of the season. Grandma was proud of her long forest of flowers but still always let Mother and the aunts cut a few flowers to take home with them when they had pestered her enough about it

We played word games and I had just said Russia for a word starting with R. But then Helle had said that she was tired. Put the pillow behind the back of her head, leaned back and fell asleep.

"Why did you leave Russia?" I asked.

Grandpa didn't answer right away. He blinked with his deep-set eyes that vanished into a net of wrinkles when he smiled. And then he started talking about Russia. Their town had been called Vitebsk. It was the same town that the great Chagall had grown up in, he said. He and Grandpa, who were sons, one of a herring seller and one of a window polisher, were almost the same age. One time when Grandpa had helped his father polishing the windows at the Chagall's he had broken a window by mistake. Then I think he had to go inside and was posed on the carpet.

No, I wasn't sure about the last thing he said. When he got to that point he got shivers down his spine which made it hard to hear what he was saying. Or it was because he started speaking Russian. But while Grandpa was talking I closed my eyes and saw the whole scene in front of me.

But just like Chagall had found his own path in life, Grandpa could use his hands for other things than "putse" windows he said and smiled. He held out his big hands, turning them in the air. The skin looked a little worn. They were hands that had tried things! Again, I closed my eyes and saw it all in my imagination.

Aunt Manja always rolled her eyes whenever he placed his hand on her knee. Or when he patted her or the other aunts on the back of their dresses and praised the weaving of their worsted. Then their cheeks would turn red. The uncles would tilt their heads back and guffaw, Mother would give a scolding, yet still not sound angry when she said, "Dad!"

Recently he had entered our door and put out his closed hand.

"It means luck," he said, pronouncing the "u" like in "mute." Then he opened the palm of his hand and laughed. It was a splattered bird dropping.

"You are quite the life artist, Mr. Elias," said Mrs. Sand who had come to give a helping hand.

"Yes, the old man is absolutely priceless," Nora said, giving a skewed smile, "even if he is a bit of a dandy. She had gotten color in her cheeks. She let it come out that while she had been nursing the boy, Grandpa had come over to playfully poke. "Akkuratnik!" he said with a glow of laughter in his voice.

It had taken her awhile to figure out that it had been the boy's ears he had been referring to.

But then Elias had also probed into whether it had been more fun for Nora to get him in than to get him out again. Nora wasn't peevish. But she said that giving birth had been more painful than getting all her teeth pulled out. She laughed, "And at least that was under sedation!"

Despite what Father had said, Grandpa had become something, he was a life artist and priceless. He made people happy. And when people were happy the world was a better place to be in. Erect as a king, the life artist ran around leaving traces of scent from his hair lotion wherever he went. Whenever he spoke it was almost always with a small laugh.

But despite what he said, it wasn't certain that those two had ever been close to meeting one another: the artist Chagall and the life artist Elias.

I opened my eyes: where was Grandpa?
But that's how it always was with him. One moment he was there and then he wasn't there after all. Then he'd either be out collecting bird droppings or he'd be lying in a snowdrift sleeping after having overeaten.

Several times that day I heard the aunts whisper about how good Winnie looked. If she was as upset as Mother and Helle said she was then she was hiding it well, there was no sign of redness in her eyes. She and aunt Pavla looked at one another and smiled as though they were keeping a secret between them.

After the meal, Mother, Grandma and the aunts went into the kitchen. The rest of us went into the garden. Father and the uncles, who agreed that stretching their legs and getting a little fresh air could do no harm before a game of cards, went out to stand on the terrace. They asked about one another's businesses and fingered each other's jackets. As they took out their cigars and Ronson lighters, Father said:

"Listen to this. Herschkel meets Mershckel on the street and says, 'Have you heard, old Lieb is dead! Oy, Mershkel says, you don't say! What did he die from? Well, Herschkel says, he was old so it was nothing serious!"

The uncles tilted back their heads, Father buttoned up his jacket and looked at them with a double-breasted smile. But soon their heads were surrounded by a cloud of smoke so that you couldn't distinguish one from the other.

Jokke and the Prophet were sitting in the swing sofa smoking cigarettes. If cousin Ralfi had been there we could have sung songs and played music on the guitar, but he had been hospitalized again. I circled about listening to the conversation. Grandpa stood talking about his new car, a Lada. With a glow of laughter in his voice he said that he only used two shifts. First and fourth. Jokke and the Prophet, who had gotten their driver's licenses, laughed and offered to give the car a spin. Then they could also see just how fast a Lada could run on a highway.

Winnie took Helle by the arm, they were going to go for a walk. At that very moment, Mother came out insisting that they take me with them. Helle lifted her hand, looking tired. I made a gesture to her, indicating that she had no need to worry.

I went over to the Prophet. I had heard that he was busy inventing something great. He nodded, yes, I could join them.

"Shift gears!" Jokke shouted, "This crap is about to fall apart!"

"It's going to get full throttle!"

We turned down at the highway. I stood up, clinging to the front seat.

The Prophet, who was sitting at the wheel, cast a glance behind his shoulder, "Are you kidding? We're going 120 kilometers an hour!"

The car careened and I fell down. But I didn't get hurt. I sat down on the seat, moved all the way into the corner and looked out. The trees rushed by, I had a tickling feeling in my stomach. I moved so that I could see the Prophet's eyes in the rear-view mirror.

"What are you inventing, anyway?" I asked.

"Can you keep a secret?" he said, rolling his eyes.

I nodded.

"It's a small telephone recorder. It can take messages when you're not at home. Then you can hear who's called when you come home. I just need to get a patent for it."

"Man, what made you think of that, a telephone recorder?" Jokke asked.

The Prophet looked thoughtful and after we had been driving in silence for a little while I asked,

"Why did Grandma and Grandpa come to Denmark?"

Jokke turned around and said, "That has to do with our history. Aren't you going to the Jewish school?"

I shook my head.

"Pogroms!"

"*Pogroms?*"

"Yes, the Jews were getting persecuted in Russia and so loads of them fled the country! You're staring like you just saw a ghost, did you really not know that?"

I shook my head once again.

"Listen!" the Prophet said, "The Czar had started to draft the Jews for 5 and 20 years of military service. But Grandpa refused to get recruited into the Russian army. In 1911 he managed to leave the country and he went to Copenhagen. His plan was to go all the way to America. That's what a lot of people did, your Grandma's sister went to South America, Uruguay. And the Danish Jews in the congregation were more than willing to pay a ticket to get the Russians out of Denmark in a hurry."

"Why?"

"They stood out too much and most of them were dirt poor. But then Elias met someone from Vitebsk who told him that it was safe here for Jews and that there was work. He got started on buying and selling and found a small apartment in town where immigrant Jews had settled down, it was an entire ghetto." The Prophet smiled and said, "The old man has always been creative and he got into a jam that involved the police. But he sent money to your grandma and my father, your uncle Sem, who was born in Vitebsk. And the following year they came here." He looked quizzically at Jokke, who nodded. "But the old man put down another kind of root: there's one more uncle!"

The Prophet looked at me through the rear-view mirror.

"Your eyes look like they are about to fall out of you head!" he said and smiled. "But it's true. The old man is Russian and he's the most Russian Russian walking on two legs. Do you know what he usually does? He celebrates birthdays with his *shikses* in the shop. His party clothes and straw hat always hang in the back room waiting for him. Because, to shield his "*dronnik*" he always leaves home in his work clothes. Then he changes clothes when he has to go back home. And he always puts the key in the lock before sunset."

"How do you know all of that?"

"From my father, of course! Don't you talk about it at home?"

I shook my head.

"It's true," said Jokke.

"Does Grandma know that?"

"Does Grandma know that?" the Prophet mimicked my tone of voice, "Half the congregation knows!" then he swung into the driveway.

In the moment of clarity that followed there was one thing that was crystal clear to me: it annoyed me that Mother, who was the only girl in a flock of brothers, hadn't been born a boy.

"Look at how red your cheeks are, it must be all that fresh air!" Mother said when we stepped into the sun room at the same time as Helle and Winnie. The table had been set with tea glasses.

Jokke took me by the arm. I looked up. His eyebrows had started to grow together above his nose. He put his index finger to his mouth. I nodded.

Shortly afterward we all had something else to think of. The samovar and the tea pot had been placed on the table, Grandpa clapped his big hands and bade us come to the table.

Everyone sat down. Only Winnie remained standing in front of her chair and said that there was something important she wanted to announce. She straightened her headband that was the same color as her light tailor-made suit.

"It's fan-tastic!" aunt Pavla said, putting her hands on her mouth.

"Quiet, Mother, I haven't said anything yet." And with a telling movement Winnie lifted her left arm which she had been hiding behind her back, held her hand out across the table, sticking her fingers out.

Then I saw it: sitting on her ring finger was a smooth, gold ring. And as usual she put all her heart into pronouncing every syllable when she announced that she had been engaged. His name was Ben and he was American.

"What do you say to that?" she said, looking from one person to the next all the way around the table. "Right now

Ben is visiting his brother in Israel but when he comes home we're going to get married. And the greatest thing of all: We're going to live in America!"

For a moment no one said anything and in the silence it was as though the air moved in waves, expanding itself.

Then Grandpa sprang out of his chair, flung his arms out and was close to knocking over his tea glass: "America!" he bawled in his broken Danish. "This calls for a little kasatske!" He took a few steps away from the table, folding his arms across one another. Then he crouched down and started kicking.

Uncle Sem and Uncle Kam got on their feet and with powerful voices began singing "Kalinka." Jokke and the Prophet went over to Grandpa, laughing, and danced with him. And Uncle Jafet also went over to see if he could dance the Kalinka. But he fell over backward, sat on the carpet, kicking his legs into the air. The aunts shrieked and soon everyone was standing around the table, also Grandma, singing and clapping in time with the rhythm.

Only Winnie sat silently. Clutched the ring with a small smile on her lips, looking as though she wanted to take it all in one last time.

*

I sat in the school library with a book in my hands, It was written by Tove Ditlevsen and called *Man gjorde et barn fortræd* (*A Child Was Betrayed*). It was the book Marianne had suggested I read.

A ray of sun fell in through the pane of glass, making the floating particles of dust glisten. I sniffed in the air, the smell of the books did me good, but the letters jumped and danced before my eyes. The rest of my class was having Christian studies and the principal of the school had agreed that I could sit here in the meantime.

Even though Mother and Helle, chuckling, had said that a free period was much better than "Joschke" I didn't feel free at all. Why did I have to go to a school where I felt different and didn't feel like I was a part of the social life of the class?

But the morning assembly in the school's assembly hall *wasn't* something I could be excused from. In the morning I had stood next to Agnete, singing "On your way! be brave and true.". But although I tried to sing with force, I just didn't feel that the words had anything to do with me. Afterward I walked with Agnete back to the classroom.

"That's my favorite song," she said, bravery glowing in her eyes.

I tasted the word "brave" and thought of Winnie. She had also looked brave when she had said that she was going to America. Brave and happy. She had now left. But she had taken both my hands in hers and said that I would have to visit her someday in America. Helle said, with a tiny, knowing smile, that I could just get that out of my head, I would never get permission to do that.

The librarian sat behind the counter with a stack of books in front of her, writing on the check-out slips. My gaze was drawn to the library pencil with the eraser in her working hand that bobbed up and down as she wrote. She turned the pencil upside down and erased something, looked up. Our eyes met for a second. Then I forced my gaze back to the book and continued reading.

Was I the only one who had a premonition that when God floated way up high, high above everything, then it wasn't as a stellar light that could show the way when you didn't know what to do. That only applied to those who were brave. And chosen. But I no longer felt I belonged anywhere. To me, God was a dark and threatening thunder cloud that was almost always just above my head.

This being watched over from above turned into a gnawing form of self-monitoring that followed me in almost everything I did. Just thinking like that made my stomach feel heavy. But it wasn't God that looked down on me. It was my mother.

What she had said to Tall Torben's mother was still within me. Mother turned her palms upward and didn't want to talk to me about it. Said I should think about something else, we lived just like all other Danes. No, we didn't! None of my classmates had a burglary alarm that howled like a siren if you forgot to turn it off. And none of my classmates had had all their possessions in their house marked so that they could always be recognized when they someday got stolen, as Mother said. They didn't have a stockpile of food in the cellar that could last them through a whole world war.

But I didn't dare do anything but obey when she told me, for God's sake, not to open my big mouth in the new school about us being anything other than Danish.

The ban on mentioning our background thrust itself between me and the world like an insurmountable obstacle. That which I wasn't allowed to say was there, yet wasn't, since I couldn't tell it to the others. And what would happen when I went back to the classroom? If my classmates were to start asking me questions?

Mother said on the phone that I was impossible. But in

front of me she just brushed it aside and said I should just act like there was nothing unusual. After a while I had become a master in acting like there was nothing unusual. At least on the outside: but I used all my energy not to say the wrong thing: which was the right thing.

It moved up my spine, and a light illuminated my brain! I got up, put the book on the table, and ran over to the counter.

The librarian looked up and smiled when I told her what I wanted to do. She immediately put down her pencil. Then she got up, pulled down her knit skirt and asked me to follow her to one of the book shelves. Searching with her finger across the book shelf, she placed a red book in my hand.

"This one's instructive," she said, smiling.

I slipped back to my seat and looked up in Gyldendals' Foreign Dictionary where it said that "assimilation" was a Latin word and meant "to make equal." Everything was clearly explained here: We had to make ourselves equal to other Danes because we weren't Danish. Had we been like everyone else, we wouldn't have had to make ourselves like them. Then we could have made do with just *being* it. In other words, we were different.

The previous Sunday at the breakfast table I had asked Mother why she didn't just admit that we were different. She got red blotches on her face. Flew up from the chair and left the room. From the bathroom you could hear a little wet click from the medicine cabinet that was then closed. Then we heard the water running.

Shortly afterward she came back in and sat down. She said that I was asking all sorts of unnecessary questions just to drive her crazy. Then she put a roll on her plate. Father said as he usually did that she should ignore me and Helle was tired of the fact that I always had to ruin our meals (she should talk!) she certainly didn't want to talk about it.

Nora sat silently looking down at her plate as she slowly chewed her roll. Just before, Mother had vented her spite on her. She said that Nora had ruined all the Sunday rolls that she had been looking forward to all week. Rolls had to be cut so that they were smooth on the side that was cut, she said, swaying her hands in the air, mimicking Nora's hand movements as she cut them in half the wrong way. Now there were lumps and holes inside.

Father smeared a thick layer of butter on his, put a slice of cheese on it and said, with glowing laughter in his voice. "Look! You can't even see it now!"

But I didn't get a chance to say that I wanted for us to talk about *how* we were different, we had been persecuted and everything. The word "assimilated" merely cast a confusing veil over the whole thing so you couldn't tell what was what. *That* was what it was!

I gave Nora a sidelong glance. The rolls had put us in the same boat. I felt for her and decided to get back at my mother a little. So I said, "We have another uncle! Grandpa...!"

Nora blushed deeply and Father sprang from his chair and came over to me and grabbed my arm, interchangeably pulling and pushing me all the way to my room.

Shortly afterward my mother came in. She moved a pile of clothes from the chair to the bed. Sat down and looked at me. One of her eyelids was vibrating.

"You can't go around saying things like that. It's malicious gossip! Who told you?"

I didn't answer.

"Answer me!"

"Shouldn't we go to Uruguay and visit...?"

"No, don't you change the subject!" She got up and smoothed her dress with impatient movements. Then she looked at me again and changed her tone of voice. "There is nothing to those rumors! You have to understand that!"

One day Agnete and I were biking along the stream that, like a black and shining snake twisted past all the yards. Agnete pointed at an apple tree, whose branches reached above the hedge, heavy from apples that were ripe for picking. Pick me! Pick me! the luscious Ingrid Marie apples tempted us with their scent that the wind sent right into our noses.

"Should we?" We looked at one another with hungry eyes.

You were not allowed to steal. No, you weren't allowed to do that, but scrumping was something everyone did, she said. So we stopped and parked the bikes. Took whatever we could reach. We were in the middle of filling our pockets when someone from inside the house came out.

Quickly we ran and threw ourselves on our bikes. All at once I felt how the pedals became more and more heavy as I stepped down on them. I had to put all my energy into it and not until we had turned the corner did I hop off the bike. My heart skipped a beat when I saw what had happened. My sweater, which I had tied around my waist, had rode up and one of the sleeves was stuck in the bicycle chain. I coaxed and pulled the sleeve loose. It was black from dirt and bicycle oil and some of the threads had been torn in half. A sense of misery swept through me and there was only one thing I wanted to do: lie down on the cement and die.

"My mother knitted it," I said, "Should I throw it in the stream and say that I lost it?" (I wouldn't be able to answer for the consequences if she ever got to see the ruined sweater itself).

Agnete gnawed at an apple and looked at me with sympathy in her eyes.

"You just need to tell the truth and repent," she said. "Then you'll be forgiven, you always are when you repent!"

"You don't know my mother."

"You also have to include it when you say the Lord's Prayer" her voice was gentle as she put her hand on my shoulder. "And Jesus is always there for everyone," she added.

"Please don't tell anyone...?"

"What?"

"I'm not allowed to talk about it!"

"Cross my heart!"

"Jews...well...I don't think we believe in Jesus."

"Is that what you are?"

I felt my cheeks blushing deeply.

"You won't tell anyone will you?"

Agnete shook her head. "But don't Jews say the Lord's Prayer?"

"No, we don't."

"What do you do then?"

I shook my head and was close to crying.

Agnete pulled back her hand.

"Then I don't understand. I mean, that they couldn't just as well believe in Jesus."

"It's also hard to..." I searched for words, "It's hopeless!"

"But that's the whole idea! When everything seems hopeless, Jesus is there for you, can't you see that?" Agnete's eyes shone with a triumphant radiance.

I got transfixed by her hair that seemed to form a halo around her head. And when I still didn't say anything she continued on her own accord. "Go home and say you're sorry! Say that you'll repent, then you'll surely be forgiven. You always are when you repent! Jesus is there for everyone!"

It sounded so convincing, so seductively beautiful that I decided to plunge into it.

"I repent!"

But Mother tore her undeserved calamity from my hands. Held it forth above her head as though to show her ally above just how bad things were down here. "I knew it!" she said.

But those three words said everything. Those three words sealed the only world order I knew: an expectation of disaster that, regardless of what I said or did and in complete accordance with its nature, would ultimately be fulfilled.

I felt my tongue curl up. From the corner of my eye I saw Nora walking along with her little boy in her arms. I dragged myself back to my room. Had it been in my power to undo what had been done, I would have done it! I felt evil and hated myself just as fervently as Mother did who had been proven right once again. There would always be a next time.

I took the guitar and sat down on the bed. Struck a chord and looked up at the poster of Cliff Richard which I had hung with thumbtacks on the wall above the head of my bed.

Just recently the fingerboard had fallen off while I had been biking with the guitar hanging from its cover on the luggage rack of my bike on my way home from guitar practice. I discovered it when I was about to start practicing. Father forbade me to get it repaired. He shouted so loud that Helle came running up from the cellar. And even though eggs weren't supposed to teach the hen, she protested loudly. She had her own reasons for doing that, she was the one who had taught me to sing Tom Pillibi, the winning song of the Melody Grand Prix in flawless French. I had sung at a competition at Dyrehavsparken, the amusement park near Copenhagen, and had won. When I was to go on stage to receive the prize of 50 DKK I was asked what I would use the money for. I said I was saving up money for a trip to America. Roars of laughter rose from the audience and then the entire tent applauded me.

Once outside Helle had said she was proud of me. Mother placed her hand on my head and said, "You're a real rascal," which was her way of saying that I had done well. I thought it was because her mother had always been ill and she had gotten certain things confused within. But then she said an expression in Yiddish which was supposed to mean that you were to beware of the evil eye. Not out of superstition, oh no, not at all, she said. And then she patted me once again on the head, repeating that I was a real rascal.

I looked out into the garden. The leaves had started to turn a golden brown. They always did this time of year. It was the natural order of things. And according to the natural order of things even the wildest of storms would at some point pass. That was only normal. That was how things worked outside. I sighed, placing the guitar on the bed. Got up and opened the window. Strong winds hit my face. How I envied Agnete's pure, simple world. Mine was tied to destruction and evil. Guilt and eternal damnation.

Someone rang the doorbell and I ran out to the hall and bumped into Helle who was just coming up from the cellar.

"Watch where you're going," she said, slapping at me.

Aunt Pavla and Uncle Jafet stepped inside and were all smiles. They had come to tell us the big news, no, we were to hear it from Winnie herself. She had sent something from America.

"It's fan-tastic!" aunt Pavla said.

Uncle Jafet tilted his head back and guffawed, saying it was 1000 times better than a letter, it was a tape. And the Prophet had devised a way to copy it so that everyone in the family could hear it.

We went into the living room. Uncle Jafet ran out of the car and came back carrying a tape recorder in his arms. He placed it on the coffee table and pressed a button.

"It's fan-..."

"Keep quiet, woman, and let them hear for themselves."

Aunt Pavla immediately put her hands up to her mouth.

The device whistled. And then came the sound of Winnie's voice:

"Hi, everyone! Heee!"

She was just so *happy* to be in L.A. They had two cars and lived in a castle. Their neighborhood was almost like at the beach town, all Jews. Everyone knew everything about one another and invited each other to cocktail parties.

"It's just so me! Heee!"

And then she had a piece of *wonderful* news to tell. She was expecting a child. She concluded by sending her love to all of us.

"What do you say to that?" Uncle Jafet laughed, sounding like a pig.

Aunt Pavla smiled, her eyes were shining.

Father opened his mouth. But instead of saying anything

he let his hand glide down across his face a few times with rapid movements as if to help it find its proper expression. Then he gave a little persuasive nod to Mother who had gotten red blotches on her face, and went down in the cellar. She immediately ran into the living room and opened the tall cupboard with the coiled wooden columns. Reached in with both hands and took down the gold rimmed glasses from the shelf.

Helle and I got Coca-Cola. Nora had to toast in malt beer even though she looked longingly at the cognac bottle that Father had placed in the middle of the table. But Mother had had the final say: nursing and cognac were incompatible!

Then Aunt Pavla signaled to Uncle Jafet. Staggering somewhat, he managed to get on his feet, stuck his hand in the inner pocket of his jacket and said, "And we have now made the decision of our life! We've sold the shop, terminated the lease of our apartment, we have sold everything!" He made a long, significant pause, pulled forth his hand again, waved two plane tickets in the air, shouting, "We're moving to Winnie in America!"

"Can't you play a number for us on the guitar?" Mother asked when they had gotten one more cognac for the road. She was now smiling at me. "The one with Cliff Richard, *Traveling Light.*"

That night I woke up to the sound of a crying child. I got up and went out to the sun room. Nora's face lit up when she saw me. She sat smoking while the little one lay at her breast. He coughed and screamed. That was just because he couldn't keep up with the milk she said, lifting him up so that he could breathe again. A jet of milk spurted from her breast and right into his mouth.

She nestled him against her breast again, took a cigarette from the pack lying on the table and asked me to hold the cigarette she was smoking so she could use it to light up. Said she was pondering whether to write about her life but, unfortunately, she had dyslexia and couldn't even spell the word itself. She blew out a mouthful of smoke and laughed. There was certainly enough material to write about, she said. She was trained as a children's nurse. But from one day to the next she had had enough of screaming children and signed on as a young innocent stewardess on a ship. Now the part about being "innocent" had to be taken with an extra grain of salt, she said, laughing again.

She took the cigarette in her mouth and lifted the little one over her shoulder. Clapped him lightly on his back. When he had burped she put him on the other breast.

"I've learned that you have to listen to yourself and not be too concerned about slipping up a little," she said. She had once done some smuggling. She had tied a skirt made of gin bottles about her waist which she concealed underneath her coat and walked right past the customs officer. She laughed once more.

But here she was sitting with a screaming child of her own. When she had found a decent place to live she could start work again. She had found another job from which she was waiting for a response and then the screaming child would be put in day nursery.

"But your cousin's sure hit the jackpot, a rich American! It almost makes you feel like running away with your aunt and uncle to America, doesn't it?"

I nodded.

"When did you start coming over to our house, Nora?"

She sat for a moment, thinking. Then she said, "During the War i used to go to the Christensen's a lot. but your mother needed me and I wanted to do something for a family like yours." Nora paused, looking directly at me. "Yes, I have both eyes and ears. But you have to know that it hasn't always been easy for your mother. Your grandma and grandpa lived with you in the first hard period after the War. The whole ordeal was hard on your mother. She had a nervous breakdown."

I had moved all the way to the edge of the chair.

"Yes. There's a lot you don't know, your family's got quite a lot of baggage. You weren't born until after the War, but your sister was there back then." Nora continued, lowering her tone of voice. "You should know that I have often said to your parents that I think they're betraying you by not telling you about what happened during the War. But your father has his principles, and your mother…"

"Aren't you sleeping?" Mother entered the room, placed a cup of coffee for Nora on the table and took the full ashtray in her hand. "Is that good for the little one?" she asked, pointing at Nora's cigarette.

"He might as well get used to it," Nora said. Again, Nora handed me the stub as she took a new cigarette from the pack.

"She has to go to bed now!" My mother said, "Or she won't be able to get up for school tomorrow."

Sluggishly, I got up and went back to my room. I was shaking so much that my teeth were chattering and pulled the duvet all the way up to my nose. I would have to ask Nora… ask, Nora about … but my thoughts drifted away before they managed to form solid questions. From the bedroom I heard

Father say that that *goy* was nothing but a ... he said a word I didn't quite get and Mother didn't protest.

The next morning Agnete and I walked together to school.
"Well?" she said.
"Well. what?"
"The thing yesterday, how'd that go?" Her eyes beamed with anticipation.
I shook my head.
"I never want to talk about it again."
Agnete opened her mouth and closed it again.

When, later that afternoon, I put the key in the keyhole of our door I froze, gripped by an icypremonition.
"Nora!" I called. "Nora!"
It wasn't Nora, but the Gigantic Angel who came out to the hall.
"There's no need to shout like that," she said, "Nora isn't here."
In the sunroom the door leading to the garden was open, the wind grabbing hold of the curtains, alternately blowing through them and making them stretch out like sails.
It was as though all Nora's things had been blown away. The baby lift was gone and the table shone brightly with no signs of any cigarettes.
I went to the kitchen but Mother wasn't there. The Gigantic Angel was in the living room, wrapping the chord of the vacuum cleaner around her arm, for each round the knot of the scarf tied around her head bobbed up and down.

"Do you know where Nora and Mother are?" I asked.

"Your mother is helping Nora with moving," she said, smiling back, "your father found an apartment for her."

Neither Mother nor Father would say where Nora had moved. My father said that the only thing I needed to concentrate on was school, then he sat down at his writing desk and started rustling with his balance sheets.

"Nora is happy where she is now!" Mother said. She was sitting in the sun room knitting and I wasn't to start in on anything now. It had been a hard day and she was, frankly, exhausted. She just wanted to sit by herself and watch television and knit and enjoy not having to breathe Nora's constant cigarette smoke.

"Cigarettes smell better than cigars!"

She didn't answer, the knitting needles clattered.

I went down to Helle who was busy reading. She looked up from her book with a look of annoyance in her eyes and said she had no idea where Nora was.

*

Some time afterward I was to take the bus alone for the first time to Grandma's.

I closed the garden gate and looked back at Mother standing in the doorway.

"You're not scared, are you?"

I shook my head and took a few steps along the sidewalk. Turned around and waved.

"Remember to get off at Tagensvej Street! And apples,

remember to buy apples at the fruit stall! And remember to get the change back!"

"All right!"

"And don't worry, Father will come pick you up!"

"All right!"

"Are you so sure that you're not scared?"

I stomped my feet twice as hard on the pavement and was close to feeling evil when I turned at the corner without looking back again.

Snow was in the air, teeny tiny snowflakes that melted when they landed on one's clothes. I ran all the way to the bus stop. The bus gave a groan when it stopped. There were many passengers. I entered and was met by the moldy smell of wet clothes, holding out my bus card.

A man came running and stood right behind me, so close that I could feel his body pushing me. My stomach muscles contracted. What if it was *him*?

Recently, when Laila from the class had been on her way home from the frozen over lake in the park, a man had jumped out on the dark pathway by the railroad track and grabbed her. She lashed out at him with her skates and ran all the way home to me. Laila, who normally didn't get scared so easily, was gasping for air and bleeding from a scratch on her chin. Mother gave her amwad of wrung-up cotton. And when she pulled to the side the skates that hung around her neck by the laces and leaned forward toward the hall mirror, you could clearly see from the way her sweater stretched that she already had big round breasts. I asked whether we should call the police. But Father said he would drive her home!

When he came back he told me not to see Laila after school. To my mother, who stood in front of the mirror with a tweezer in her hand, he said in a tone of voice that indicated that Laila had been to blame for what happened: "She's not one for my daughter to associate with, we agree on that, right?"

She didn't answer but focused all her concentration on her reflection in the mirror.

"No...!" I began, but he whisked me away.

"There'll be no discussion!"

I turned toward my mother.

"Mother!" I said.

She didn't answer but continued to pluck the hairs from her chin.

The bus stopped short and once again I got pushed by the man's body. I couldn't breathe properly and pushed my way forward, weaving in and out between people to the end of the bus. People hissed at me but I didn't care. Luckily, he hadn't followed me and my breathing went back to normal.

I got off at the right bus stop and also found the right building. When I put my hand on the door handle I suddenly remembered the apples. Ran back to the fruit stall that almost always stood at the end of their road and asked for five Ingrid Maries.

Grandma's apron appeared in the doorway. She smiled and said, "There's my little Rhed Rhiding Hood! What have you got there for your sick grandma?"

I held out the rustling paper bag. Stepped inside and took off my coat. Heard the water running in the kitchen. Shortly after, Grandma came back carrying a bowl with the apples. We walked together into the living room and sat down at the dining room table.

She took a fruit knife in her trembling hand. Cut an apple into four quarters and started to peel away the skin in slow movements.

I looked around. A gallery of family portraits hung on the wall above the dining room table, my gaze stopped at a wedding picture of Winnie and Ben.

I, too, had been at the Synagogue. Sat between Helle and our mother and got tears in my eyes when I saw Winnie enter through the gate dressed in a long white gown. She took Uncle Jafet by the arm and in her other hand she was carrying a wedding bouquet that consisted of blue and white flowers which she held close to her body, her dress dragging behind her across the red runner.

"She's the most beautiful bride I've ever seen," I whispered to Helle.

"But you haven't seen any others!"

Aunt Pavla also cried. But it was only because she was so happy, she said afterward. And also a little bit because the wedding meant that she would have to say good-bye to Winnie.

Grandma followed my gaze and her eyes lit up.

"And Winnie is already a *mamele*, two children!"

I was reminded of the air mail envelopes with the red and blue stripes that lay on our shelf like a breath of air from the big, open but distant world. Mother always read Winnie's letters aloud to us. Housekeeping in America consisted of pushing a few buttons, they had machines for everything. The cooking was done by loading a big pile of cans in a shopping cart in the supermarket and transporting them back home. In

America there was nothing that couldn't be bought in a can! Mother got a wistful look on her face and sighed. It was hard having a husband who never touched the gas and who very rarely entered the kitchen. Then she carefully refolded the letter, the paper was so thin that just looking at it could make it fall apart. But the best thing was hearing their voices on the tape. Uncle Jafet boasted that they already spoke American English like natives. He sold men's clothes in a huge *stores*, socks and scarves in *poor wool* and that sort of thing (but it was called *pure*, Helle said). They were living with Winnie and Ben and the two little *wonders*, aunt Pavla said, they had an entire *appartment* in the American castle.

"It's fan-tastic, it's so perfect!"

I had asked Father whether we should soon go and visit them but that was completely out of the question. He also said that it was no good for parents to live with their children. Mother didn't say anything.

"Someday you'll have a wedding in the *Shynagogue*," Grandma said. "did you know that Jokke is engaged? Judith is a *fajne mejdel*."

I nodded. The Prophet was also getting married. But his fiancée wasn't Jewish so the wedding would take place at the town hall. There had been a family crisis meeting about it at Grandma and Grandpa's.

Grandpa presided at the end of the table and slammed his hands down on the table in order to penetrate the noise, everyone spoke at once. Only aunt Katja sat silently staring into space. When she finally did speak her voice was as thin as a wafer as she said, over and over, that that marriage would be doomed from the start, doomed!

Grandma, who had said what she needed to say, sat next to Grandpa crocheting, her tongue in the corner of her mouth. Her hand, that was holding the crochet needle, wriggled away with an obstinate diligence. A small, satisfied smile played on Uncle Kam's lips. Meanwhile Grandpa and Uncle Sem had shouted, a *shikse*! Had he gone completely *meshugene*?

The Prophet passed his hand across his blood-shot eyes and down across his face that was dark from his beard stubs. Pressed his hand against his mouth as though to hold back his words. Then he took his hand away and sputtered: "Hypocrites!"

Grandpa jumped from his seat.

"Hypocrite? Are you calling me a hypocrite?" he bawled, "Where would you all have been had it not been for me?" And with both his hands he straightened his combed-over hair that during the heated moment had fallen down across his face.

But the Prophet also jumped up.

"If I were to say the name "Tulle," the *shikse*, in Grandpa's shop, what would you say?" he said as he let his bloodshot glance linger on Grandpa and uncle Sem, first on one and then the other. And then back again. Then he looked at aunt Katja who had turned rather pale underneath all her rouge. She tilted her head and sent him a pleading expression.

The Prophet breathed irregularly, opening and then closing his hands. But he didn't say anything more.

Uncle Sem dried his red face with a handkerchief. Grandpa sunk back in his chair, saying, "Pfuit" like a balloon that was losing air. Uncle Kam stared into space and started tugging his beard. For a moment no one said anything.

Father had gotten up. Buttoned his jacket and nodded

to Mother, who also got up. Followed by Helle and me. We showed ourselves to the door just as the Prophet screamed, "Inge or no one!"

Mother slammed the door behind us. I cast a sidelong glance at Helle but her face was completely closed. As we drove home in the comforting shelter of the music streaming from the Captain's radio, what had happened had strangely enough never happened.

"In the *Shynagoge!*" Grandma repeated. She handed me an apple slice and saw right through me. "You shouldn't go with *di goyim* in *schkulen!*"

My cheeks turned hot. Not that long ago I had been standing in front of the bakery with some boys from the class eating "student pastry." But one of Father's Jewish business connections had recognized me and had made an informative telephone call to him. When Mother passed on the information to me there was a strange sense of delight in her voice. I had been caught! Father enforced the consequences of the revelation. From now on, that meant already from tomorrow, I was to go directly home from school! Bringing such shame to the family by hanging out in front of the bakery with *die goyim!*

"If *that's* what being Jewish means, then you can count me out!" I said, whereupon I was sent to my room with a tray. But that was only because I was so thin. I had otherwise most certainly deserved to starve!

After a little while, Mother came in, moved the pile of clothes lying on the chair to the bed where I lay with my hands beneath my head. She sat down and started talking. Not as I had expected, about shame. No, it was the student pastry! She had her "you'll get poisoned" look on her face.

"It's pure trash! They make it from the scraps they have on the floor that the bluebottles have spewed out, and the rats, not to speak of the cockroaches, do you know how many cockroaches kak at a bakery? Do you know how many have done it in that trash with which you stuff yourself? And then they cover it all up with yellow icing! That's exactly how you get the runs! That's why you always…"

I made a face. And that's when it came.

"Aren't you ashamed? In public…?"

All at once I shot up, "They're my classmates!"

"One should stick to one's own."

"You should have thought of that before. I'm now assimilated!"

"Oh, stop, Miss Impertinence! I know you better than you know yourself!"

"No, you don't! That's just something you're saying!"

But then she got up, shook her finger at me, saying "Everything I do, do you know what it is? A mother's sacrifice! And I do it with pleasure! One day you'll thank me, crying on your knees! But then it'll be too …!"

She stopped herself, picking up the tray. Then said in a persuasive voice, "Call Miranda!"

I made a face at the door she had shut behind her. Why did Mother say she knew better than I did what I meant, that is, what I in reality meant when I said something? As though I meant something completely different than what I had said? It was as though she transferred a piece of me to herself. Were mothers allowed to do that sort of thing? And why wasn't I supposed to know what I knew? Everything we never talked about!

I looked up at the poster of Cliff Richard. How he and Jens

Peter resembled one another. For the school's music day we had played guitar together. He said it didn't matter one bit to him whether I was Jewish or a gypsy, a Fourteenth Day Adventist, or whatever it was called. As long as I wasn't a Jehovah's witness!

I placed a hand on the wall. The yellow color, the same color as Agnete's, now made me nauseous. That which Mother called a mother's sacrifice just made it all the more difficult. The only thing it meant was that I would have to give up myself. But who was I?

"In the *Shynogogue!*" Grandma said with emphasis.

The apple slice fell out of my hand and onto the floor, I had to get down on all fours. Sat back down in the chair, removed a tiny speck of dust and took a bite. Waited until I had finished chewing, Then I took a deep breath.

"Grandma, could you tell me what happened back then in Russia?"

She didn't answer, but took off her glasses with the thick lenses. With her fingers she rubbed the bridge of her nose where there was a red mark and sighed, "Aj-aj-aj!" She put her glasses back on. But she didn't say anything more. In the silence, to the sound of the ticking cloock on the wall, she looked at me with eyes that didn't see me. From her eyes streamed a power that attempted to weigh down the inarticulate child which I no longer was.

At that very moment the clock struck, four chiming strokes.

Grandma looked away and placed her hands against the edge of the table. Got to her feet with great difficulty and with laborious steps walked to their bureau where their samovar stood during the winter. She pulled out the top drawer, put her hand in it searchingly and pushed it back in. Opened another drawer and took something up. Went back and placed a postcard with a photo tinged in brown on the table.

I leaned forward.

"Is that you, Grandma?"

"Da! Aj-aj-aj!"

On the photo posed an erect woman with lorgnettes. She was dressed in a dark jacket over a long pleated skirt with a low-set band around it. On her head she wore a hat which had a broad shade. On the back of the photo someone had written in Russian letters and it said "1911."

"Grandma, what happened in 1911?"

"Elias left."

"Did Grandpa go alone to Denmark?"

"Da! Da! Aj-aj-aj!" Grandma looked at me, her eyes, which the lenses made look unnaturally big, got a pleading look.

"Zing for me, that Grand-prix song, you know, the one with *die kue*?"

"You mean Klaus Jørgen, Grandma? Then you have to tell me more about that time! What happened?"

"No!" she said, this time with a firm voice. "Now, you're going to learn how to count to ten in Russian."

And even though it had been a long time since she had taught me, she started counting to ten.

The next day Agnete and I stood talking in front of the gate to her yard.

Mother called me in. Grandma had collapsed.

My heart skipped a beat.

"It's not your fault!" she said, pushing up her hair, still she asked whether anything unusual had happened the previous day.

I shook my head.

She studied me and said it would probably be best if I went with her over there so I wouldn't have to be alone after this had happened.

Grandpa let us in, Grandma was sleeping. And now that there was someone with her, he'd just quickly run down to the shop he said as he handed us some hangers.

Mother took them and gave me one. As she hung up our coats Grandpa was already putting on his coat. He wrapped a scarf around his neck and tucked both ends under. the lapel on both sides. Standing in front of the mirror, he let a comb glide through his hair, put on his hat and turned up the collar of his coat.

Mother slammed the door shut after him and sighed.

There was an acrid smell of medicine. The doctor had given Grandma an injection. Her closed face stuck out above the pile of duvets, strange and naked without the glasses. On the bedside table was a glass of water containing her false teeth.

I stared at the teeth and thought they moved. What would they say? That it was my fault? But how could you know for sure what the true cause of anything was? What if there had been no cause?

I felt an ache in my stomach. I doubled up, tiptoeing behind Mother who, with a hunted expression on her face walked back and forth between the bedroom and the living room, sighing. Put things in their proper place and checked that everything was in order in the closets and drawers. Went over to the buffet and pulled out the drawer of silverware. Reached into it and counted it. Snipped the withered leaves off the geranium in the window sill. Sighed again over the drawer with silverware. Took some underwear that lay on a chair and put it in the laundry bin in the bathroom. Sighed again. And then sighed once more over the dirty dishes. Went back once more to the bedroom. Sighed. The sighs lingered in the air and got stuck in your throat when you breathed.

"I won't ever someday come to your place to do this!" I don't know what got me to say that. I felt evil all the way to the tips of my nails.

She pursed her lips. There was no one in the family, no one but Grandma's daughter who would sacrifice herself for Grandma the way she did, she said, barely moving her lips.

"But that's how it is to be a daughter."

I tasted the word. Daughter. It almost sounded like poverty. Both words had a "t" in the middle, and an "er" sound. It was different with the word son. There was a certain swing to "son. "Son! Swing!

But daughter ... daughterty ... poverty ... and what poppa does ... again, I tiptoed in my mother's footsteps as she every now and then sighed, mumbling to herself.

She was willing to sacrifice herself, with joy even! For Grandma and for the rest of us.

In my mind it turned into: "Here you go, my girl, everything is predetermined! It's all ready and waiting for you!"

Only managed to take a few steps. Then I felt the nausea and rushed to the bathroom.

"Is everything predestined?" I asked my mother that night when she came into my room to ask how I was doing.

"You shouldn't be thinking so much about that!" she gave me a worried look and placed a hand on my forehead. "Grandma is doing much better now, Grandpa says. Go to sleep now. Good night!"

In the mornings, when Mrs. Sand opened the newspaper, she always first turned to the obituary page to see if there were any good deceased. There was nothing like crying over a good deceased, she said. The tears cleared the mind. And the sinuses. A good deceased was someone you hadn't known personally. It was a public figure, someone everyone knew.

Cousin Ralfi was the worst deceased you could imagine.

I sat next to Mrs. Sand up front on one of the wooden benches in the quiet chapel. Like in the synagogue, men and women sat in separate sections, the women wore black furs or coats, except for Mother who simply couldn't stand seeing herself dressed in black and was wearing a camel hair coat. Not the ocelot, which she put on at first, but then took off again because she thought it looked a little too festive for a funeral.

The men of the family, dressed in dark coats and hats, sat on chairs along the curved end wall close to the coffin. I looked past it and at the curved glass panes at the end wall. There were two rows of windows. The top ones were a delicate green and cast a dim light into the chapel. I counted the lit, electric candle holders that hung on the end wall, there were seven candles in each candle holder. Up front on the floor stood two tall candle holders holding thick candles.

I stared into the fluttering flames and was gripped by a strange sense of guilt. As though the fact that I was alive was a betrayal to cousin Ralfi who lay in the coffin underneath the black cloth. I thought about the last time I saw him in the hospital. He was lying on his back in the hospital bed and was as white as the bed sheets. I got tears in my eyes from seeing the twitches in his face as he tried to sit up. His apologetic smile made me sob.

For several days my thoughts had again revolved around death. Would rather not die, I had written on the slip of paper I used as a book mark. As though that could keep death away, remembering to be scared of it. In America 20 women had been murdered. They had forgotten to shut their kitchen window! Helle had read about it in the weekly journal and then described it down to every single detail. But I had to read it myself! Meanwhile they were playing "Why must I Be-ee a Teenager in Love" by Marty Wilde on the radio. The murderer had climbed through the open window. One after the other, raped and murdered. There were pictures. Blood on the walls and floor. "Why must I Be-ee." Now I would never be able to hear that song without thinking about mass murder.

You could also suddenly die. Laila's neighbor's classmate was in his freshman year of high school and collapsed in the schoolyard. He died in the middle of a break.

Now the Chief Rabbi stood at the pulpit. In a forceful voice he talked about Cousin Ralfi who had fought his illness for most of his short life. Then he said that the core of Jewish philosophy was that life and death were companions. You had to let sorrow take joy by the hand.

I had Ralfi's favorite song in my head, "Lollipop, lollipop, oh, lolli lollipop." But even though I smiled within myself, my gaze was firmly set on the green panes of glass. I was never going to see him again. Never sing or play music with him again.

It was cold being so close to death, my fingers and feet felt as though they had vanished. What happened afterward?

Mrs. Sand leaned forward and asked whether the men singing so melodically in Hebrew were called cantors. The bass voices of eternity filled the chapel and rose up toward the ceiling. Surrounded the hardness and coldness that tightened like ice in my stomach. For a brief moment a piece of eternity penetrated time and lifted the present. The chapel took a deep breath and exhaled with a deep sigh.

A rattling sound made me turn my head. The men were now lifting up the coffin. They were going to carry it through the gate of columns that faced the avenue with the beautiful trees of the cemetery. They were arbor vitaes, Mrs. Sand said. I turned my head.

The women stood in a cluster a distance away from the raised grave where the men of the family, one by one, took the small shovel from the heap of earth and cast, one, two or three shovels of earth onto the coffin.

The thuds!

The wind penetrated my jacket. I was shaking from the cold and from my tears, I felt Mother's eyes on me, her hand on my shoulder, "It's all right to show your feelings during a funeral, you're allowed to do that!" she said, "At a funeral it's perfectly OK."

The sound of a landslide when the grave diggers pushed down the heap of earth.

The Chief Rabbi said the Kaddish, the funeral prayer, and everyone turned around and faced the Vestre Prison. It had nothing to do with the prisoners, Helle said in a low voice, it was the direction of Jerusalem.

Then the sky began to cry as well, heavy, sorrowful tears. In a matter of no time the sorrow was coming down in buckets and I took shelter under the umbrella that Mrs. Sand was holding out. Yet still my shoes managed to get soaking wet. Maybe it was God's way of saying that I should have put on the rubber boots that Mother had put out for me.

Everyone shook hands with the close family members of the deceased and expressed their condolences: "I never saw anyone so sick," Uncle Sem said as he stood shifting his weight from one leg to the other.

"Now all we have left are the pictures," Aunt Katja whispered.

But life had to go on.

Already on the way out to the schoolyard I started telling Agnete about the funeral. The Chief Rabbi had said, "Earth to earth, ashes to ashes, dust to dust." We picked up our bikes but decided to wheel them all the way home. After we had walked for a little while she asked whether the Jew priest had said anything about being resurrected.

"The Chief Rabbi didn't say anything about that! Have you ever seen a dead person do that?"

Agnete parked her bike and asked me to do the same. Then she placed her hand on my shoulder and looked at me with a serious gaze, "It's the soul that does it," she said, "And you can't see it."

"What happens when you die?" I asked when I got home from school.

Mother and Mrs. Sand were sitting at the dining room table with polishing cloths in their hands. All the silverware in the house lay on newspapers that had been spread across the entire table.

Mother continued rubbing the piece of silverware she was holding and said it wasn't good for me to concern myself with such things. But then still added that nothing would happen.

But the Chief Rabbi had said the things that had once been couldn't just turn into nothing,

"How is that to be understood?"

Mrs. Sand put her polishing cloth aside and looked up. Smiling at me she said that the flesh of the deceased would get eaten by worms, "Such is life!"

And even though Mother moved her eyes and mouth in a way that could have meant anything, she did not contradict Mrs. Sand.

That night I couldn't fall asleep. As soon as I closed my eyes I thought of cousin Ralfi and started seeing worms crawling everywhere.

I turned on the light but could still feel the worms crawling around inside me.

I didn't sleep that entire night. The next morning I refused to go to school.

After three days where I slept during the day and lay awake with the worms at night, Mother called for the doctor.

He unbuttoned his coat and sat down at the edge of the bed. Took off his glasses and rubbed his closed eyes with two fingers. Then he placed his hand over mine and looked through me with penetrating eyes for a long time. Sat silently as I told him about the worms and held out my pinky so that he could see how thick the worms were. Their heads were white, a little smaller than the nail on my pinky. I bobbed my finger up and down a little to show him how they twisted and turned as they crawled around with their numerous little legs.

"Hmm!" he said as he let go of my hand and scratched his forehead.

Then he put his glasses back on his nose, fetched a prescription pad from his doctor's bag and placed it on his knees.

I was to take two kinds of pills, some that were pink and that would make me fall asleep and some that were blue that would make me ready for school.

But even though I tossed my head back, the pill remained lying on my tongue. Then I spit it back out.

And some days afterward the worms figured out for themselves how to crawl somewhere else.

Could there be a better deceased, someone who was more famous than the American President? The world held its breath. Would the Russians drop the bomb?

At school the flag was flown at half-mast. The classroom

was charged with a sense of world catastrophe when there was an assembly call in the afternoon so that we could share that which was inconceivable: John F. Kennedy, the very symbol of the free world, murdered! Shot dead in the street, in a convertible. No!

Ovesen had been home to change clothes. He stood in front of the lectern in his suit and tie and asked us to get up and observe a minute's silence.

He looked as though he were close to crying when he said afterward, "What you are witnessing is an act of evil. You young people who have witnessed this atrocity, this act of terror aimed at the very heart of our democracy, have an obligation to ensure that evil doesn't take over! We must all stand together and protect the free thought and the free word!" He concluded with a citation from the climax of Kennedy's speech in West Berlin, his declaration of solidarity with the people of West Berlin: "Ich bin ein Berliner!"

The words went straight to my stomach. I would do anything to protect the free thought and the free word. I looked around the room. Everyone's gaze lingered at Ovesen's trembling lips. Only Jens Peter stared into space, his lips pressed together.

He walked with me home from school and we walked in silence next to one another in the rugged November darkness.

At the corner of our road he tilted his head back and took a deep drag of his cigarette. Afterward he kissed me. I could feel his lips for a long time afterwards.

Grandpa saw Kennedy's murder (he said *Kenneidi*, with the emphasis on the second syllable) on the TV at our place,

Grandma was at the hospital. Grandpa, who had just come back from there, went to the kitchen wearing his coat and handed Mother a big box of chocolate. Now that Grandma was improving he wanted to pay his thanks for all the times he had been allowed to come and eat dinner with us.

She let go of what she had in her hands and went over to him.

"Oh, Dad, you shouldn't have!" she said, trying to sound strict as she accepted the chocolate and gave him a kiss on the cheek, "But of course! You're family!"

Over and over the same scenes from Dallas ran across the TV screen. The convertible with the good-looking President who had laugh lines all over his face and waved to the cheering crowd. The shots. His body collapsed and you saw Jacqueline, with a petrified look on her face and blood stains on her light Channel outfit, bent over him. The funeral. The little son of the President, who, wearing a coat, saluted his father in the coffin that was covered by the American flag.

And over and over you saw the scene where the President's murderer, Lee Harvey Oswald, who, with a twisted expression, grabbed for his stomach when Jack Ruby had pushed his way forward and shot him.

"Oswald was a gangster, Ruby was a gangster, gangsters the whole lot of them!" Grandpa said in his broken Danish, waving his big hands in the air.

"No, Father, that murder will never be solved," Father said. He offered Grandpa a cigar from the box he had brought with him and also took one for himself. "There was more than one culprit, that's as clear as day!" he said, handing Grandpa the cigar clipper.

But as the world and the Cold War had stepped in through

our door, moving into our living room and in under our skin, Helle and our mother were in the kitchen: president assassination or no president assassination, the dishes weren't going to clean themselves!

A letter came from Winnie, America was crying. Was it true what the newspapers said about Kennedy and Marilyn Monroe?

In reality there were no good deceased!

*

The time to get confirmed was getting closer. My classmates had already started to go to confirmation classes and were to be confirmed in the church across from the school. Although I had the same age as they did, fourteen, I wasn't going to be confirmed but baz-mitzvahed instead, which would to take place in the synagogue, It had all been decided beforehand.

"Not that it's anything to be ashamed of, but it's not something you need to talk about at school," Mother said.

The day my class was to start confirmation classes our last class had been in music. We sang "Now the Woods Are Turning Yellow All Over the Land." It had two melodies, one German and one Danish, and we sang the first verse using one and the rest using the other. As we were singing, I floated as though I had wings, high up in the air across the fading forest.

But all at once I returned to my body. It happened with the words Jesus Christ. My voice disappeared. I took a deep breath and tried to continue singing. But no matter how hard I tried not a sound would come out of me. I was standing between Agnete and Marianne, my classmates. Still, there was something that separated me from them, an invisible chasm. It had always been there. But now I could no longer act as though it wasn't there. My life would take on a new twist. I was going to associate with my own people. But I felt split. Who were my people? Strangers who, like Miranda, attended the Jewish school?

From the corner of my eye I saw Agnete, her lips forming the words, "faith, hope and charity." My entire body was burning like stung by nettles.

I put on my coat and wrapped my scarf around my neck a few times. Walked together with the class through the schoolyard. When the others started walking toward the gate, I turned and headed for the bicycle shed. Wheeled my bicycle out of the school yard and across to the other side of the street.

Agnete turned around and waved at me before she, too, turned down the tree lined street that led to the rectory.

When I got home I ran to the kitchen and told my mother that I had had second thoughts. Could I still be confirmed in the church together with the rest of the class, I asked.

"Jews don't do that!"

"But..." I began and didn't get any further. The paralyzing silence that followed decided everything.

Without batting an eyelid, she continued putting the cups and plates in their proper places in the cupboard. Placed two glasses on top of one another. Put them on the shelf and gave them a little push.

I only wanted one thing: to pull them all out again! Stomped through the kitchen with a half-smothered outburst stuck in my throat!

Father drove me to baz mitzvah preparation classes, the instruction took place in town, in a room in the basement of the Jewish congregation center.

Mother checked my clothes.

"Remember not to draw attention to yourself about anything!"

I opened the car door and sat down in the front seat. In my mind the contradictory thoughts buzzed like bees on their way into a beehive. None of us said anything. But when we had driven past Nørrebro's Runddel Square, Father said, "Money is everything!"

"No...!" I began but he interrupted me and repeated, "Money is everything! Wherever there is money there is love!"

The anger grew within me. He could keep his stupid saying to himself! I much preferred to read books. About real love! The anger surrounded me. Was it Mother's? No, it was mine. And it was directed at her, at the aunts and everything they always talked about with one another. You had to be careful not to turn up the heat too high. Oh yes you did! Or was it too low?

But underneath it the rejection singed. The sorrow over the fact that my opinion didn't count when I was the one who was going to get confirmed.

The first thing we learned at the baz mitzvah lessons was that God was One. That is to say, I was the only one who just learned that. All the girls knew it beforehand. They had learned it in the Jewish school.

That meant, first and foremost, that you couldn't have

any other gods than God. But everything written in the Bible had to be interpreted. So, on a more down-to earth level, this meant that whatever it was that you were doing right now was the most important thing. Being in the here and now had a value in which a part of God was present: this was the remains of the divine light. We also learned that God was both just and merciful. He didn't just punish but was also a merciful God. It was like a light that was lit inside of me.

One day Father offered the Chief Rabbi a lift. I was proud when he agreed to ride with us. I leaned back in the backseat and let the day's teachings stream through my mind.

Lots' wife had done the forbidden thing and turned around. She wanted to see Gomorra, the burning city she was leaving, one last time and turned into a pillar of salt. Even though I tried to understand the story in a bigger way than just by reading the letters on the page, it filled me with a sense of horror. But that was how we had to learn that our actions have consequences. That it was always our actions that spoke and not the thoughts behind them.

"Regardless of how noble the motive is," the Chief Rabbi said, his gaze penetrating us, "having a good intention is not enough!"

From the corner of my eye I saw Miranda and the others nodding in agreement. With a hint of shame I recalled how I had wanted to please Mother and clean up my room. But then I never got around to it. Even though I told her when she came in and demanded that I seriously do something about it, she looked around the room with a "I-told-you-so" look on her face.

"How is one to know what you've been thinking when your room looks like the destruction of Jerusalem?"

But what she had said to me didn't at all agree with what she told others: "It's always the thought that counts!"

And even though Miranda and a few of the other girls thought that buying a *triefe* hot dog at a hot dog stand if you were about to pass out due to low blood sugar could be defended, they all attended the Jewish school.

I envied all the girls who had already learned all the stories, about the Flood, the manna that rained down from the sky, and Moses that made the Red Sea separate so the Israelites could escape. And I envied Agnete and Laila and the other girls from my school. They didn't have to use their brain power to figure out what it meant to be one of the chosen people, and what did it mean to be chosen, aside from a desert of unanswered questions.

Marianne had sewed her own confirmation dress and invited me over so that I could see it. When we stepped inside her light room that had sloping walls, she, smiling, pointed at the dummy upon which the dress had been fastened with pins.

"It' *broderie anglaise*!" she said with pride.

"Wow!" I said, annoyed that I couldn't think of anything else to say. My hand quivered when I reached out for the lacy, embroidered material and the shining light-blue sash that was to be tied around the waist and…

Father's voice brought me back.

"Where would you like to be dropped off, Chief Rabbi?"

"There happens to be a synagogue in Krystalgade Street …" the Chief Rabbi said.

From the backseat I could see through the rear-view mirror

that the light in Father's face was extinguished. The face he showed the world meant otherwise so much to him that he never went in public without having shaved or put hair tonic in his hair or donned a tie or polished his shoes and would have done it even if he had to participate in a radio program.

He didn't say: How true, how true, Chief Rabbi, with that courteous, obliging voice he used with other people whom he respected. He withdrew. His lips formed a thin line.

During the drive to the synagogue very few words were exchanged, only about the freezing weather that had come early that year. I struggled to sit still and fidgeted in my seat.

Father pulled the hand brake in front of the synagogue and got out. Taking big strides, he walked around to the other side of the car, opened the door and held it open bowing stiffly.

The Chief Rabbi maneuvered with some difficulty onto the sidewalk. He thanked us for the ride and lifted his hat on parting. Then he turned around, opened the tall lattice gate and went in.

It had been the Chief Rabbi himself who had taught us that all men were equal in the eyes of God. Also a poor milkman like Tevje could speak directly to God, he said. And since everyone was equal, a Chief Rabbi was no better than a tailor. When we had turned the corner I could no longer keep my words back.

"You can speak your mind to a Chief Rabbi, he is not closer to God than anyone else…"

"Little cat, little cat, walking all alone, whose are you, whose are you, I'm goddamn my own!" The courteousness had returned in Father's voice.

But I didn't allow myself to get distracted by Piet Hein's "cat" grook.

"A Chief Rabbi is just a person," I said.

"Do me a favor."

The car stopped abruptly. He pulled the hand brake and turned around. His voice cracked. "Spare me this" he looked for words in vain and instead blurted out: "The eggs do not teach the hen!"

"But…!

"No arguments!"

The meaning of life was that you were supposed to sort out disagreements by discussing them. That's what the rabbis had been doing for almost 2000 years. There were always two sides to an issue. And often also a third. Perhaps others would perceive it in a different way, but this tickled my nose, my sense of justice and my urge to get things out on the table.

We had also learned that you had to: honor your father and your mother. But did honoring merely mean to obey? Didn't you honor much more by helping? We hadn't talked about that.

We stopped at a red light, turned away from the crowded road and drove along the frozen stream. I pressed my nose against the side window and looked out. It was foggy and the freezing fog made the air white and impenetrable. In my head there was also a fog. You had to make a serious effort yourself, we had learned. Since it was your own actions that made all the difference, things couldn't be predestined. But what I had learned at the baz mitzvah preparations did not add up with what I experienced in my real life. Between this world and the other world there was a chasm that I had to cross. And in that jump, it was as though I was being swallowed up by the empty space to later become nothing.

I had a vague sense that, for everyone else, stepping into the world was a much less complicated matter.

When you were assimilated it didn't matter one bit whether God was righteous and merciful. One or twenty-seven.

Outside the trees stretched their white-powdered branches up toward the sky.

Mother was standing in the kitchen pouring shrimps into a colander. She placed the colander between the edges of the stainless steel sink so that they could drip off.

"Are we expecting company?"

"Yes."

"Is Nora coming, too?"

"Nora is doing fine where she is," Mother said as she sighed. "Don't ask so many questions, I am actually trying to concentrate on this." She placed a lemon on the Formica bread board and sliced it up. "Could you at least help carry it in?"

"Will Mrs. Sand be coming?"

"Not today. Here, will you also take the eggs?"

"Where is Helle?"

She is studying with a friend. Mother sighed again.

Shortly afterwards the little wet click from the medicine cabinet could be heard as it was being closed. The water was running.

Father climbed up and down the cellar stairs to fetch beverages. Placed the bottles in clusters on the dining room table. Then he went out and opened the front door.

I went over there.

"Have they come?"

"No, but we need to let in some fresh air."

I stood by the open door looking out. The air was white from big falling snow flowers. A Simca came driving up our street, making black tracks in the snow. Parked at the curb. One more.

Aunt Manja and aunt Pavla shrieked and flung their arms around each other's necks. They walked together through the gate and walked arm in arm around the front yard, reaching for the white-powdered bushes and trees with their free hands upon which they wore gloves. They had to touch it all. The uncles walked directly up to the house. Took off their gloves, placed their hands on the red brick wall and patted it. Put their noses right up to it and sniffed it approvingly.

"It smells like social climbing to me!"

"No, you should invest your money in art instead!"

"Why not in liquor? It'll give you more percentages!"

"Ha ha ha! Then traveling would be better!"

"Yes, traveling, sent packing!"

"Ha ha ha!"

Mother and Father stood on the top step and took it all in with a smile.

They made a toast, let the herring and salmon swim.

"Help yourself! There's plenty more, dear Manja!" Mother held out the bowl with shrimps. Aunt Manja took it but passed it immediately on to uncle Kam who also passed it on. For a brief moment their eyes met.

Manja and Kam didn't take any shrimp today, was the expression of Mother's furrowed brow.

Shortly afterwards she got up. Collected all the fish plates and carried them to the kitchen.

The tongue was sent round. Aunt Manja took the dish.

"It is calf, right?"

"Dear Manja, I could never dream of buying anything other than calf's tongue!" Mother had gotten red blotches on her face and handed a bowl to aunt Manja. "Take this, there are also vegetables!"

"*Gott in himel!*" Aunt Katja said, "So tender that you can chew it with your…"

"Bottom cheeks!" Uncle Sem said, laughing.

"Always so witty, brother!" Uncle Kam said with his mouth full of tongue.

Aunt Katja pursed her lips and sent uncle Sem a firm glance.

"Sorry, Sis!" he said sniffling as he dapped his nose with his napkin. "It must be this cold I have!"

My father smiled as he raised the aquavit glass.

"Against illness even the gods struggle in vain. Isn't that how the saying goes?"

Mother got up and ran out to the kitchen. Returned with a big cheese plate decorated with fruit and placed it on the table. She cut the cheese in slices and handed the dish around.

"Help yourselves! There are also cheese biscuits!"

Uncle Sem sneezed a few times.

"Oh, how you long for the warm weather again," aunt Katja said, "isn't that right, Sem?"

He nodded while blowing his nose in a trumpet blast.

"What do you need bricks for when you can travel?"

For a moment aunt Katja looked like she wanted to stuff the words right back in his mouth. Then she smiled. No one else could smile and purse their lips at the same time like that.

Father, with a calm expression on his face, got up and returned carrying a lacquered cigar box in his hands. He opened the lid and with exuberance offered the cigars that lay in assorted sizes at the bottom of the cigar case which was divided into many sections.

The Ronson lighters were pulled out of the jacket pockets.

Then the three men left the dining room, leaving blue-gray wreaths of smoke from their cigars lingering in the air.

The aunts and Mother sat closer. Mother looked at me as one of her eyelids vibrated. Aloud she said,

"Don't you have any homework you have to do?"

"Yeah, at the baz mitzvah preparation we talked about…"

"More cheese, a cracker?" Mother asked across the table.

"Oh, that's right, you're getting baz mitzvahed soon," said aunt Manja as she looked at me and smiled. "What do you wish for as a present?"

"Yes, is there anything special you'd really like?" aunt Katja asked.

"Money! I'm going to America to visit…"

"Here…" Mother held out the cheese plate, "grapes aren't very filling!"

Aunt Katja took a small cluster, picked off a grape and, smiling, handed it to me.

"You're so thin that it's making me envious. Is it all that knowledge they're filling your head with?"

"Thanks!" I said and put the grape in my mouth.

"Speaking of America, when is the last time any of you have heard anything from them? It's a veeery long time since we've heard anything new." Aunt Manja put a cigarette in her cigarette holder and took out her Lady Ronson. Lit it and inhaled the smoke.

"No news is good news," Mother said, "Isn't that how the saying goes?"

"Thank you for the meal!" I took my plate and carried it to the kitchen.

In my room I sat down at my desk with a book. Helle didn't want to talk with me about what we were learning in preparation for the baz mitzvah. Once, when a friend of hers from school was visiting her and they were playing a record with Tom Lehrer, I knocked on her door. She shouted to me to leave the premises. The premises!

Instead I went upstairs where Mrs. Sand was helping Mother repair some clothes. The dining room table was covered with towels with worn-out straps.

"What does it mean to be chosen?" I asked.

"The Jews are the chosen people, that's what they say!" said Mrs. Sand as she lay her needle and thread down on the table. She gave me an encouraging look and pulled up the sleeves of her light gray cardigan.

"Yes," Mother said, "But we're not in any way orthodox..."

I interrupted her.

"If it's because God likes the Jews the most then no wonder everyone else hates us!"

"Nonsense!"

"Everybody hates the Jews, that's what Tom Lehrer sings!"

"You take everything so literally!"

"No, I don't, I just think about things!"

"You should clean your room instead!"

Mothers! The door shut behind me with a thud!

I closed my book and looked into Birdie's cage. The sand had to be changed. I opened the door to the cage. She immediately rushed out of the cage, flew a few rounds below the ceiling and landed on my shoulder. She sat there, cackling and nibbling my earlobe.

I poured the dirty sand into the garbage bin. Sprinkled some clean sand in the tray and pushed it in... then I got down on my knees in front of the cage, placed a few bird seeds on my tongue and lifted my hand in front of my mouth.

As always, she flew to the back of my hand, her beak was warm and searching, teeny tiny affectionate nubs on my tongue. Meanwhile, I moved closer and closer toward the cage. And before she knew it, she was again behind bars. I quickly closed the door to the cage.

Birdie immediately jumped over to face the mirror, moving her head up and down, lovingly rubbing her beak against her reflection in the mirror as she chatted away with hoarse sounds coming from her throat. Did she know anything about being chosen?

I went into the living room.

Mother and Father were walking back and forth between the living room and kitchen, clearing the table and carrying things out. Father collected the empty bottles and carried them down to the cellar.

"Do you know what?" Mother said when he came back up. "I could also be tempted to go someplace where it's warm. Just for a week. We could go with Manja and Kam to Israel. What do you say?"

He put the cigar case in its proper place on the smoking table in the sunroom and didn't say anything.

"Just imagine, they don't eat shrimp at all anymore since they've gone kosher. They've had to replace everything, porcelain, utensils, everything."

He still didn't say anything.

"Manja said that otherwise the young people wouldn't eat at their place. Judith comes from an "my mother tasted the word "orthodox family. But, like they say, eggs never teach the..." she spotted me and changed the tone of her voice. "Oh, there you are, do you want to come out here and help me with the dishes?"

"I'd rather go to America!"

"We're not going anywhere. What do you think, this is the Rockefeller family or something?" Father shook his head and went to turn on the TV. He pulled up his trouser legs and sat down.

I walked over to him.

"What's on?"

He gave me a tired look.

"I'm going to watch the news. Go out and help your mother with the dishes."

"But..."

"Shy! Someone's tried to escape over the Berlin wall."

*

It was the last class that Tuesday. Danielsen, our history teacher, entered the classroom and put down his briefcase. Went to stand in front of the lectern and looked across the classroom. Then he turned toward me and said loud enough for everyone to hear it, "You'd better skip the class today because we're going to be talking about the history of the Jewish people."

He didn't say that! Yes, he did! No, did he really say that?

In earlier times, I would immediately have gotten up from my chair. Would have bowed my head and dragged myself across the classroom hoping that the floor would open up and swallow me.

Now I dug my feet into the floor and moved all the way back in my chair, could feel the hard wood against my back. Then I folded my arms across my chest and gazed at the little man who looked like he had just shrunk and vanished inside his suit. And in a shrill voice that surprised me, I said, "I'm allowed to know what happened, I am after all, Jewish!"

Then I suddenly realized it: the Jew in me had jumped out of my mouth and was now standing as large as life in front of the entire class!

No one said a thing. My heart was pounding. Everyone turned around. Everyone looked. at me. Marianne, who sat in front of me, placed her hand on my arm.

Danielsen looked at me through his round horn-rimmed spectacles and continued to clear his throat over and over. You could never be sure where you had him. When we hadn't properly prepared for the lesson he would bark like a little terrier. But he was also the kind who would say, with fervor in his voice and an eagerness that would make the spit fly from his mouth in every direction, that we were never to drink hot tea without first blowing on it! Marianne's mother, who was a nurse, had let it slip that he recently had been to a rather nasty medical examination.

My blood was boiling and for the first time I wasn't the one who looked away.

Then he turned on his heels and went up to the chalkboard and pulled down the world map:

Babylon. The Roman destruction of the temple in Jerusalem. The Jewish uprising on Masada. The Crusades and the banishment of the Jews from Spain. The Pogroms in Russia and Poland, Hitler and Nazism.

Uncertainty could prick like the cactus in my windowsill. I had always carried this uncertainty in my body. A word here. A word there. Words that didn't make sense. Words that didn't have anything to do with me? Words that had everything to do with me? Uncertainty became certainty. Nightmare became reality. That had to be why it practically put my mind at ease to learn that Jews across the globe for 2000 years had been blamed for all the evilness that had happened in the word. That had to be why the knowledge that Jews everywhere had become everyone else's scapegoat gave me a feeling of near triumph.

But a second later that feeling of greatness reversed into the very opposite.

"For no other reason than that they happened to be Jews," Danielsen said.

Now he was referring to the Night of the Broken Glass. It had that name because the streets were flooded with shattered glass after the Nazis had ravaged Jewish shops and synagogues. Then Hitler and the Nazis seized power across Europe. The raids. The outbreak of the Second World War. The concentration camps.

Danielsen said that it was most likely due to coalition policies that what happened to the Jews in the rest of Europe didn't happen to the Danish Jews. "At least we know that almost all the Danish Jews managed to flee to Sweden during the autumn of 1943. And the fishermen risked their lives when they sailed the Jews across the Sound."

When the bell rang, Agnete, Marianne and several of the others formed a circle around me. Her eyes were shining, Agnete's lips moved as she tried to tell me something. But my thoughts had already left in advance and were on their way home.

Danielsen came over, too. He placed a hand on my shoulder and in a low voice asked me to follow him, I put the history book in my school bag, waved to Agnete and Marianne and trudged behind him in the hallway. Some meters further on he opened a door to the back staircase through which I also slipped before the door shut with a clicking sound. All at once the steps out there seemed never-ending. I dragged myself up the stairs, leaned out from the bannister and looked up into a landscape of glass, steel and concrete. Surfaces and edges, window panes and bars spread out, criss-crossing one another as in an abstract piece of art.

I winced and when I turned my head and looked down into the abyss of the staircase my head began to swim. Still, I continued, placing one foot in front of the other, going up and up following in the heels of Danielsen.

He stopped at a landing and opened an orange door which led to a passageway with more doors. They were blue. He selected one and I followed him across the threshold. Were there more levels of hallways and rooms outside of one another? The interior of the school, the assembly hall, from the ground floor all the way up to the glass roof with balconeys surrounding it on every floor and doors leading to the classrooms, was like the stomach of a gigantic whale. This was where we would meet for the morning song. By and by we would separate between the ribs of the whale until the last bell of the afternoon would make us ride its wave and wash us back to the world. I was now in a small office. Danielsen pointed to the armchair by the window and asked me to take a seat while he went out to get something.

I looked around. There was a bright-colored poster hanging on the wall above the bookshelf. Chagall, it said in black letters. I recognized the motif. A couple floating as one body in the air across the roofs of the city's houses, away from Vitebsk?

Danielsen returned with two steaming cups of tea. He handed me one of the cups and asked me to be sure to…but I already knew that.

Then he sat at his writing desk and cleared his throat. He was sorry about the unpleasantries he had had to confront me with that day, he really had assumed that I already knew all about it. He blew on his tea and took a sip. But then he had seen by the look on my face that it must have been the first time I had ever heard about it. He was sorry about that. And if there was anything he could do for me while he was still there at the school, he was waiting to get admitted, yes, he was soon to be hospitalized.

He had been talking into space. Now he opened a drawer and took a notebook in his hand. Turned around and handed it to me.

I got on my feet and took the notebook.

He was still looking at me.

"If you could write a little bit down, in fact, that's what I usually do myself," he said, giving me small smile, "just some scattered impressions, that which you heard today must have…"

He interrupted himself and remained silent for a little bit. Meanwhile I sat gripping the mug to warm up my freezing fingers.

Then he spoke again. As a history teacher he couldn't imagine parents, not to say anything bad about mine, they had no doubt had their reasons, he couldn't imagine parents who would allow their child to grow up outside of history, so to speak.

"Historyless." He turned the word in his mouth showing clear signs of unpleasantness, cleared his throat and continued, "To be historyless! That is like a vessel without a compass. History itself has taught us that! And if there's anything you ever want to talk with me about, just let me know!"

The last words were said with the same fervor as when he spoke about tea.

I took a different route home. Everything was covered in frosty snow. The sunlight sparkled in the trees, through the hedges and on the rooftops, the snow had transformed the residential neighborhood to a dazzling white fairy tale landscape. When we said good-bye, Danielsen had said he would inform my mother about what had happened today. He even had the feeling that my parents were merely waiting for the right moment to broach the topic. And he said he hoped, giving my hand a warm squeeze, that his effort would prove useful and beneficial for the conversation that undoubtedly lay ahead between me and my parents.

Pogroms and gas chambers. The Jews' escape to Sweden. As I tried to transform the bustle of thoughts that filled my skull into questions I could ask, I had crossed the park and was now standing in front of the stream.

Something was lying on the lumpy ice and I had to squat to see what it was. It was a dead bird, a sparrow. It lay on its side a little distance from the bank. I reached out for the dead body of the bird. It had frozen into the ice. Only its head and one of its wings was sticking up.

That evening Father sat at the dining table looking at some of his old photographs. I walked over to him. Looked at the furrows on the skin of his face and sought traces of the things I had heard about at school that day. Right now it was all distant and unreal. In front of him lay a pile of photographs which he spread across the table.

"Look!" he said as he pointed to a picture of some racing cyclists, "there I am, and can you see who the others are?"

"Isn't it Kay Werner and Evan Klamer?" I asked.

"Yes!" he nodded, smiling up to both ears. "And who is he? The one standing next to me and smiling?"

"It resembles Gunnar Nu Hansen."

"It is Gunnar Nu! Ah yes, that was a great period!"

Mother entered the dining room.

"Are you sitting there again looking at those old pictures?"

I turned around and looked at her. But there were no signs of history to be seen in her face, either.

Night after night I waited for Mother and Father to call for me and say that there was something important they wanted to talk with me about. I would secretly study their faces for signs, for a crack in our everyday life. And Helle's. She had to know? My hope died for each day that passed. Monday night Mother and Helle went to the hospital to visit Grandma. I realized that what I was waiting for would never happen.

But then Father called for me. I was to immediately come into the living room and, with my heart pounding all the way up in my throat, I ran in there.

He was standing in front of the TV, pointing at the screen and saying that something would be coming on which I *must* see: sex education.

Then he left the living room. A little later his footsteps could be heard going down the cellar staircase.

I trodded back to my room and sat down at my writing desk. Danielsen's notebook lay in front of me and on the first page I wrote in capital letters NORA!

The following day it wasn't Danielsen who entered the classroom but a young substitute teacher wearing blue jeans and a sweater. With belligerent movements of her hands, which were in direct contrast to her slender appearance and bashful glance, she banged the chalkboard with a piece of chalk and wrote her name: Lone Krog. She turned around and said, "I will be substituting for your history teacher while he's in the hospital."

She walked to the front of the lectern, constantly running both hands through her short hair and looked across the classroom. Letting her eyes rest on me she said, "Danielsen has informed me how far you got last time on the history of the Jews."

She turned around and took out a book from her bag. She skimmed through it and placed it on the lectern. Then she went to the chalkboard and pulled down the world map.

"I would like to talk with you about the foundation of the State of Israel. And I might as well say it like it is: in my opinion, the West played a little too much Robin Hood when it gave the land to the Jews."

She continued talking, moving her pointer back and forth across the map.

"And this area here in the Middle East contains the biggest mistake of history. But we'll save that talk for next time."

Theodor Herzl and Zionism. The Balfour declaration. The British White Papers, the Second World War, the UN's Partition Plan for Palestine, the vote on Nov 29, 1947, the suggestion to divide Palestine into an independent Arab state, an independent Jewish state and an international command over Jerusalem was adopted 33 to 13, 10 did not vote.

"What was a triumph for one was a catastrophe for another. The Arabs said no, no, no!"

The bell rang. Krog's voice cut through the usual noise of chairs banging against each other.

"Listen! Go home and talk about it with your parents!"

Agnete and I walked together to our bicycles. Hung our school bags on our luggage racks and unlocked our bikes.

"I think it was absolutely right that the Jews got Israel!" she said in a voice that shimmered like crushed velvet.

"The Middle East!" A shadow crossed Father's face as he with slow movements ran his finger back and forth around the front of his throat inside the collar of his shirt.

Then he shook his head and made a sweeping gesture, "There's nothing to discuss, there'll never be peace down there!"

*

Tikøbgade Street, number 8, first floor to the left, Tove had said. That was where Nora lived with Mikkel, as the boy was called. It was in Nørrebro, according to the map. And I was now on my way there.

For weeks I had biked into Vesterbro. Always during the afternoon when people had returned from work. I always made sure to be back home before my parents returned from the shop. The streets looked like one another, narrow, dark and worn streets where the houses loomed and where it teemed with dogs and cats and small shops and all different kinds of people.

I wheeled my bike through the crowd, down one street and up another, dizzy from all the exhaust coming from the cars and all the noise. The clamor as from a thousand voices echoed in my head. I had a vague memory of where the street was but had of course forgotten the name of it. The only thing I had to go on was a mere mailbox. A mailbox where the "B" was missing.

Tikøbgade was a dead end street. Number 8 was at the very bottom, by the elevated tracks which passed close to the house at the top. I parked my bike against an iron grille that surrounded a small garden for the apartment on the ground floor. Inside the grille a baby carriage stood on the grass.

I went into the hallway, took a deep breath and rang the doorbell.

Nora's face lit up when she saw that it was me. But as she stood there in her tight brown dress, her arms hanging down along her sides, she practically became one with the battered, brown-colored door frames.

"Well, I'll say!" she said with a dry snap in her voice, "Sure you're not too refined to come out here?" she leaned a little forward, pointing toward the baby carriage in the yard. "In your circles that sort of thing is gotten rid of!"

"Nora, if you only knew... they know nothing about me coming here, Tove was the one who gave me your address."

Then she pulled me inside and hugged me.

"Sit down in the living room! I can hear Mikkel's awake, I'll just get him."

The living room faced the street and was airy. There wasn't that much furniture. Through the window pane I saw Nora pick up Mikkel from the baby carriage. On a shelf next to the window there were a number of photographs. Next to a photo of Lasse there was one of Helle and me.

Mikkel had been given something to eat and was sitting on the floor playing, Nora and I sat down on the couch. I could no longer withhold the words.

"Did my mother and father also go to Sweden?"

Nora nodded.

"They were lucky. Not everyone managed to get across." She lit a cigarette, blew out some smoke and said, "Shortly after the government was dissolved, the country was in a state of emergency. That was in 1943, at the start of September. At the start of October, the Germans let it leak out that they were planning a campaign against the Jews. There were raids and a number of Jews were caught and sent to Theresienstadt. Your family doctor hid many Jewish families in his office at night. Including yours. And along the entire east coast of Zealand the fishermen organized major relief work by sailing Jews to Sweden, several thousands." Nora took in another whiff of smoke. "Then you could once again be proud to be a Dane."

"But how ...?"

"Your mother and father were told to drive to a harbor someplace up north. A boat would be waiting for them there. But when they got up there they got quite a shock. The fishermen weren't willing to let your sister go with them. You must understand that it could have jeopardized the lives of everyone on the boat. If they had gotten caught, that is. But your mother refused to leave Helle behind, she was only six months old. So they gave her an injection. But there were many who weren't allowed to take their babies with them. Your cousin Ralfi had to live with a Danish family who hid him."

"Cousin Ralfi had to be hidden? Do you know he died?"

Nora breathed in as she said yes.

For a moment none of us said anything. Then she continued, "It was all very dramatic. As they were crossing, the engine suddenly died and Helle woke up and started screaming. The Germans were in the vicinity, you see, and your mother feared she might get thrown overboard." Nora crushed the cigarette in the ashtray. She lit another cigarette and drew the smoke into her lungs.

"Yes, your eyes are so big, but they managed to get across and later got to Stockholm. Then, after the war, it all came out what had happened to the Jews all across Europe."

"Where do you know all that from?"

"Your mother had been so strong and brave through the whole ordeal. But when the worst of it was over she broke down. The doctor sent her to a sanatorium, a place in Jutland. Meanwhile I moved in with your father and sister. She was about two years old. I got close to your father back then." She paused before continuing. "He hadn't had an easy life with his father, your grandfather."

"I never knew him."

"Did you know your father had an Orthodox upbringing?"

"My father?"

Nora coughed a few times and nodded.

"When your mother returned from the sanatorium they agreed to put it all behind them. The future was all that mattered. Your father built up a new business and your mother helped him. But she was still very fragile and I stayed with them for a while. Mrs. Sand also came over to help get their day-to-day routine to hang together. Then you came, the new little hope of the family."

Nora sent me a little, crooked smile.

"But you weren't like your sister. And if anyone's having a hard time of it, then it's her. You couldn't help it, of course, but Helle felt that you took all the attention away from her and your mother protected her from you. You were pretty and extroverted and she was shy and toothless. She has been jealous of you, always.

"Helle!"

"Yes, you were a rebel no one could get to shut up. You asked questions and demanded answers, no, they couldn't get you to shut up."

"But how ...?"

Nora took a last whiff of the cigarette bud and crushed it in the ashtray with an impatient movement of her hand, "What could you possibly know, no one ever told you anything." She took another cigarette from the package, held it in her hand as she sat looking at it. Then she lifted her gaze, "But that which had once been dangerous was no longer dangerous. Still the fear remained in them. The fear that your mother fed your sister at an early age. In your mother's eyes Helle would always be a vulnerable little baby whom she would have to protect with her very life. She has never properly let go of that."

I nodded. My whole body felt like it was aflame.

"I know that. Helle is my mother's right hand. And do you know what? Marianne from my class is going to sew my baz mitzvah dress, last week I tried it on with the pins still in it. Mother and Helle came into my room and lavishly praised Marianne. But when I had left the room with her and came back I saw Helle bent over my writing desk. She turned around and said that Marianne had written my essay. Of course, I said that that wasn't true but she kept saying that it wasn't my handwriting, I wrote in script writing. I said that I was practicing writing like Marianne, her "j"s and "g"s had loops and you don't use that in script writing! And do you know what, Nora? She wouldn't believe me! I was so angry that I stamped my feet on the floor. But *I'm* the one who's helping Marianne with spelling and commas. Her grades in written Danish have gone up from 7 to a 9 +! And the worst of it is," my voice cracked, "my mother…immediately took Helle's side. She didn't even ask me!"

Nora had sat patiently listening holding her cigarette in her hand. When I paused she let out a sigh of frustration and lit the cigarette. Then she said, "That's nothing to make your teeth clatter. The most important thing is to have a clear conscience, that you can look yourself in the eye. Because if you can do that, then you can look the whole world in the eye. Remember that!"

Mikkel came over and whimpered. Nora put down the smoking cigarette on the edge of the ashtray and lifted him up on her knee. Cradling him in her arms.

"Incomprehensible, isn't it?" she said. "Here you are, this beautiful baby, and your father doesn't know you at all."

"Who is he, Nora? Mikkel's father?" I said and couldn't make out the glance she gave me.

"I might tell you some day. But for now, all I'll say is that when Mikkel grows up one day he'll have to make a choice. If he wants to amount to anything then he should choose his father's surname. But if he'd rather live it up it would probably be wisest to take an ordinary name like Jensen. There are advantages to everything!" Nora said and laughed. Then she grew serious again. "That story has done more damage to the soul than your parents would care to admit. I've always said to them that they have an obligation to tell you kids your family history. But they believed it was safest for you not to know."

When I got home I went to the bathroom. I turned the key in the lock that I was only allowed to lock if I *wasn't* going to take a bath. Safest for us not to know! My knees were shaking and I sank down on the bath mat. Could I trust Nora? Had my mother pushed Nora away because she had talked about the war? Or were there other reasons? When I asked Nora what was going on between her and Mother she said, "It's not the first time we've been on bad terms. I've always been frank with her ... But your mother's always come around again. And I'm sure she will this time, too, if your father lets her. I grabbed hold of her when you were going to the Jewish school. They shouldn't take you out of that school again! Nothing would be gained from that other than that you'd get confused. But your father insisted on it. You and your sister were to be nothing but Danish."

"But that's not how it is at all."

"But you have to understand that they felt they had to keep a low profile after what they went through! All they wanted was to forget about it. They partied, Good grief how they partied! Your mother was really out showing off her ocelot! But the fear was in their bodies and that wouldn't go away on its own."

Nora fell silent and shifted in the couch.

I said, "Whenever I come home too late, Mother always looks like I've risen from the dead. And once when they didn't come home at the time they normally do, I ran all the way down to the big intersection to look for them. What if they never came back home? When I saw the Captain turn at the corner I started to cry. 'How foolish! A big girl like you!' my mother said. Then I was ashamed of myself. They could drive off again, as far as I was concerned! And do you know what, Nora? When it's dark, Helle doesn't dare walk alone from the bus stop by herself. Then I bike down to the bus stop to get her!"

"Yes, that's exactly what I'm saying, you're going to manage just fine!" Nora said, lit another cigarette and sat for a long time staring at the smoke. Then she got up and walked out of the living room.

Shortly afterwards she came back with a bottle in her hand. Poured a little into her glass and emptied it.

"'I guess we can talk about it,' I said to your mother. But she wouldn't speak up. She heard what you and I were talking about that night. But she's sure to come around again!" Nora said as though to convince herself. Put out the cigarette in the ashtray and poured herself another glass of schnapps.

"You know your father's principles, he won't budge an

inch. But one thing's for sure, he's got the right connections! The next day he called your mother to say that there was a two-and a half bedroom apartment ready for me. And then she quickly got me installed in there. She washed the entire apartment, polished all the windows. Filled my refrigerator with food. Do you have any idea what it means for someone like me to be able to say, "My refrigerator?" Nora looked at me with starry, shining eyes. "Your parents have always helped me. I've always paid every dime back. But ever since I've moved in I haven't heard a word from your angel of a mother! But she'll come around again." Nora's voice had grown grainy.

I was to visit Nora again. Or come by her new job, she was working at the bureau of the Danish National Archives now. Then she'd help look for information about the family, it would be good for me to know more, she thought.

But how was I to see Nora without Mother discovering it? My angel of a mother who, as she said in the telephone, had an eye on every finger. It made me think of "The Angel of Light" which was one of the songs we sung at morning assembly. Didn't she know that? Didn't she know that her Jewish, non-orthodox hands had been returned to favor by the Angel of Light? And that the diamond ring that always sat on her finger had an otherworldly shine to it? "Shining color from above"? It surrounded her hands and everything they touched. In my mother's presence I would get sucked in, in my mother's presence I was trapped in a teeny tiny idiotic and ignorant present, now. How could I not see Nora?

Without thinking about it I had begun to undress. Got to my feet and took off my pants, socks and underwear. Left them on the bath mat and climbed into the bathtub. Turned up the faucets, didn't put the stopper in. I lifted the shower head from its cradle and leaned my head back against the cool enamel of the bathtub and passed the jets of water across my body. The lukewarm jets felt gentle on the skin, like the brush of an angel's wing that made me forget everything and little by little made me float.

I closed my eyes, letting the Water Angel take me upon its wings, all the way up to "The Angel of Light."

Helle studied psychology and for several days she had been looking at me in a strange way. So one evening when we sat down for dinner I decided that I might just as well make a clean break of it.

"I've found out where…"

But Helle broke in, "Mother says that you've started talking in your sleep, about angels, water angels. Have you started drinking holy water instead of water from the tap?"

"Mind your own business, you fat…!"

"Now, now, girls!" Mother entered with a bowl of cucumber salad and sat down at the dinner table.

Helle began helping herself to the food, but continued in that teasing tone, "And I guess you don't think anyone knows about your little secret?" She made a telling pause. "But it starts with a 'J'," she made a telling pause, "and then comes 'P'…" My hand squeezed the fork so hard that my knuckles turned white.

I was lying in my room. Trying to settle down and read.

The sickle moon came into view above the apple tree. I stared up at the star-filled darkness and thought about Nora. While we had talked it had all made sense in my mind. Now it was strangely unreal, as though it had absolutely nothing to do with me. Was Helle really jealous of me?

I let my fingers slide across the wall where I had fastened a postcard from Lasse with some thumbnails. A square with plane trees. A landscape of lavender fields. He had been confirmed. In France it was called a "communion." He had sent a picture of himself where he was standing in front of the church with his broad shoulders and looking handsome in his navy colored suit. He was staying at a place for the treatment and rehabilitation of polio. His father was teaching at a school close by. Lasse wanted to study literature, he said.

The last time I had taken the bus to his house was shortly before I turned 14. The farewell made me choke. I fixed my gaze on his shirt pocket as we tried to talk as though he wasn't moving to France. He was looking forward to it. After all.

"I'm going to see the house where Marcel Proust lived. It's a museum now. Blue. The house is in Illiers Combray." he pronounced the name in French. "Illeeyers-Combray." And with an awkward movement he placed his hand over mine. "You should come down and visit us."

But that would be inconceivable, Father said.

Nora's words returned. In my mind's eye I saw a boat that sailed from a harbor. A wake of foaming whirlpools. A sense of drowsiness settled over me, a warm wave that rolled through me. And as the warmth spread through my body, I felt something take shape in my skull, something I was to do. But just before I grasped what it was, I had fallen asleep.

Tormented, I opened my eyes. The sun was stinging. I got up and got dressed. Took a mouthful of tea and walked with Agnete to school, but I didn't wake up until later in the day.

*

It was Saturday afternoon. I parked my bike in the carport and locked it. When I went inside the house, Mother came out to the hallway. "Where have you been?" she asked overly nonchalant as she looked at her reflection in the mirror and straightened her hair with both hands.

"Just out biking."

"You're lying!" She had turned around and looked at me with a strange sort of delight shining in her eyes. "You were at Nora's. We saw you and followed you with the car. It's not the first time, is it? Is it?"

I looked at her without blinking. I had been in to visit Nora four times and I intended to continue doing so.

"But today was the last day you're ever visiting her, just so you know!"

I ran to the bathroom! Slammed the door behind me and turned the key.

SMASH!

The mirror would be an appropriate start! But when I peered into it I sneered at myself. I was just about to cry.

"Idiot!" a voice was screaming within me.

Instead, I turned on the faucets in the sink at full blast. It splashed everywhere. Also in the bathtub. I stomped back and forth between the bathtub and sink, the sink and the bathtub. Idiot!

I stuck my hand in my pocket. My fingers felt something, a crumpled cigarette package. One left! I straightened it and lit it with the matches that always lay in the ashtray. They were burnt to drown out the worst stench of our Jewish shit. I puffed away in front of the mirror. It had almost gotten completely steamy. Just like my glasses. Ladies and gentlemen, I puffed, before you now is the smoke from a Blue Northstate. I got dizzy.

I winced. Someone was turning the door handle. Rattling it. Mother's voice cut through the noise,

"Are you in there? I can hear the water running and you know you're not allowed to lock the door when you take a bath!"

My "Yeah" didn't reach to the other side of the door.

"Are you there?" She rattled the door knob again.

"Yes!"

"Open up!"

Silence.

"What's taking you so long?" Again, she rattled the door knob up and down.

"What are you doing?"

"Practicing hymns!" In a loud voice I started singing, "The Angel of Light" as I quickly threw the cigarette stub in the toilet, flushed and grabbed hold of the faucets to turn them off. They were stuck. I pulled and tore at them. They wouldn't budge. Niagara Falls had come to stay. Once we had to get a hold of the plumber. The toilet was clogged. Mother said, "Who else but you would throw all that into the...?"

Well, that didn't matter now! Come on, you damn faucets! Then I realized something and tried turning them in the opposite direction.

Afterward I looked around, if you could call it looking. I took off my glasses. Put them in my pocket. The steam billowed. The water was trickling down the walls. There were pools of water on the floor. I slid when I reached for a towel. It remained hanging and the strap made a sound. I pulled the towel again. Another little rip. And one more time. The strap gave way a little bit more. Another tug. Now it was practically torn off. Now I just needed the three other ones. And the guest towel. I mopped up here and there.

"Open up already!" Now Helle was out there rattling the doorknob. "Mom has taken diuretics, open up now!"

At the very same moment that I turned the key in the door knob the door swung open. Helle tumbled in with Mother right at her heels. "I hope I make it, I hope I make it!"

"Hymns!" Helle tapped me.

I wriggled out past her. I hadn't gotten a chance to open the window.

A while later I dialed Marianne's number.

At that very moment Mother entered the sunroom, sat down and took a hold of her crochet work.

"One moment," I said to Marianne, removed the receiver from my ear and cupped my hand over the mouthpiece. "Would you mind? I'm talking!"

"No, I'm going to sit right here!" She sat down and took a hold of the crochet hook.

Once again, I said "One moment" to Marianne and added that I would continue talking from the bedroom, bent down and pulled out the plug. Not only the plug but the entire outlet came loose! Light gray dust sprinkled out from the wall.

That night I refused to go with my parents to a family visit. Told them I had to write an essay. I *wanted* to stay home!

"I want to decide over my own life! Helle does, too!"

"She's a grown-up," Mother said, straightening the sleeve of my sweater.

"I will be, too, soon!"

But just as my parents were about to go out the door the telephone rang, aunt Katja had come down with something. So my parents weren't to go there after all.

Shortly afterward someone rang the doorbell. I ran out to open it.

On the staircase stood Marianne, Jens Peter and Hans.

Recently the class had been at Hans'. The parents had sat with their ski socks up on the sofa and discussed things with us as we sat on pillows on the floor. Words and concepts flew through the air. With a sinking feeling in the stomach I listened to Hans' father who explained to us about the Cold War, and the Truman-doctrine that led to the Berlin wall.

Now Hans looked at me, smiling. "We saw that there was lights on at your place and wanted to ask whether you'd invite us in for tea?"

Would they be allowed to come inside? I stood before the front door which was open, in the line of fire between the two fronts of the Cold War at home: my suppressive, principled Russia and the free America of my classmates and turned my head hesitantly from side to side.

With her eyes, Mother sent a "I-can't-take-responsibility-for-saying-no" gaze to my father who immediately returned it. This continued an indefinite amount of times.

I grew breathless at the sight of Jens Peter's figure dressed in black standing in the glow of the garden lamp. I longed to be able to open up my arms and say, "Come on in! My room's this way!"

The glances that Jens Peter and Hans gave each other made me feel uncomfortable. Due to a reason that never even occurred to them, they were not welcome in my home.

Marianne smiled. The wind played with her hair. She moved her lips without making any sound. What did she want to say? I could feel tears were on their way, I blinked.

Mother won. She made a resigned movement with her shoulders and sent a friendly nod to America. And then she voiced her demand to me: "You have an essay to write, so you'll have to tell them to leave!"

I tried to catch Jens Peter's gaze. But he avoided my eyes. My stomach ached. It burned like a licorice lozenge on a blistered tongue.

The world was unfair. Unfair and evil. Every cell of my body stung when I lay down on the bed and opened a book. A little while later I lifted my head. Birdie's sounds when she cracked corn with her beak. She stopped eating, settled herself properly on her perch and started cleaning the feathers on her wings. Without anyone ever showing her how she had discovered on her own how to clean the wing feathers. She herself didn't know where she had that knowledge from. That was the difference between animals and people: the awareness of the self, and with that came pain and fear. The animals weren't afraid of dying. Only if they felt threatened would they defend their lives.

Now Birdie spread her wing, grabbed ahold of a new feather with her beak, aligning it from the inside of the body and out again in one long flowing movement. Let go of the feather and grabbed a hold of a new one.

At the very moment she saw me put my book aside, she puffed out, turning into a ball-shaped shuttlecock with a beak and claws. Then she shook herself, returned to her normal bird-shape and began jumping from perch to perch with anticipation. Basked and cackled. Teeny tiny downs lay strewn through the entire cage, falling like snowflakes.

She flew out the very moment I opened the latch.

I waited until everything was completely quiet on the opposite side of the door to my parents' bedroom. Then I got up and tip-toed out of the other door that led to the living room. On the desk flap lay a pile of written invitations to my baz mitzvah. Inside a shelf in the bookcase I found some leftover invitation cards. I sat down and wrote another invitation. Put a stamp on the envelope and placed it in the pile of invitations.

*

The synagogue's gold below the chandeliers cast a golden glow down on the festively dressed relatives seated on the rows of benches, women to the left and men to the right, and not like at ordinary services where the women were always seated in the gallery.

All faces were turned towards us, who were about to be baz mitzvahed. We were sitting on the dais up front in the synagogue's center on rows of chairs facing each other.

I looked around. Up in the gallery a woman leaned across the railing and waved. Nora?

Everything that had happened in the weeks leading up to the baz mitzvah ran through my mind:

"By the way, Nora called today to say thank you for the invitation and that she was looking forward to it!" Mother smiled in a way that could mean a lot of things. I felt my cheeks flush. That night harsh words about Nora could be heard again coming from the bedroom. It seemed they were arguing about Mikkel's father. But Mother said in no uncertain terms that no matter what had taken place in the past you had to keep a straight face during a baz mitzvah. And on the telephone she said that everything was in a frenzy of excitement. The house cleaning, the seating arrangement, Grandma in and out of the hospital and again no news from America. This time she was really…!

We had just sat down after saying the Statement of Faith out loud in unison. Just across from me, on the outermost chair, Miranda sat looking at me. But her myopic, kohl eyes looked without seeing. Her bangs, that normally reached all the way over her eyebrows, had been brushed back and the rest of her hair had been pulled up. Without her glasses and bangs she looked serious. Vulnerable.

At the pulpit in front of the Torah arch the Chief Rabbi stood dressed in his long black pulpit robe and hat. Now he was making the sign. I had a sinking feeling in my stomach and I followed the white-dressed girls with my eyes as they, one at a time, with measured steps, walked to the right along the red carpeted steps to receive the blessing. And back down on the left side.

Now the Chief Rabbi was placing his hand on Miranda's head. Leaned forward and moved his lips. In a moment I would have to stand up. The fear of doing something wrong had haunted me. My mother's gaze would be monitoring every single one of my movements. Lot's wife didn't get a chance to say anything in her own defense. The punishment just fell. With one stroke! Then she was turned into a pillar of salt. A shiver trembled through my body. Miranda had started to go down. I got to my feet.

Then I stood there myself. The Chief Rabbi's mouth was close to my ear, I felt the whiff from his pungent cigar breath. Even though he spoke in a low voice, I was almost certain that I heard the word "chosen."

The rest of the ceremony faded through me. I was there but I didn't sense it.

The party was held at home. There were flowers, candlelight, songs and speeches. Helle, in a new pigeon blue dress with a balloon skirt which aunt Manja (whispering, but not low enough) found very unstrategic, said in her speech that she admired me and sat back down, her cheeks glowing red. Nora, who sat next to me, whispered that fortunately we weren't all shaped like penguins, broad at the top and narrow at the bottom. I leaned a little forward, looked at aunt Manja, her black dress with the distended white insert, and couldn't help smiling. She smiled back and lifted her glass.

Then Nora got up. With festive arm movements and fluttering sleeves, she pointed at the flower decorations that ran through the middle of the party table and let it slip out that she, in honor of the day's rare occasion, had managed to bust her budget by investing in a silk blouse.

"Bravo, bravo!" shouted uncle Sem, who clapped his hands as the first to be joined by other scattered claps of applause around the room.

And she not only thanked me but also the four of us and Grandpa for not going to America. Because otherwise she would never have met us!

"Akkuratnik!" Grandpa bawled and jumped out of his chair. Then he lifted his glass and got everyone around the table to give a toast to Nora and the rest of us.

With laughter in his eyes and a cigar stub in his mouth, uncle Sem got to his feet and grabbed his harmonica from the buffet. While there were shouts and cheers he stuck his arms inside the straps and gave a flourish with a curled-up tail that glided into a medley of Jewish and Russian melodies. The whole table sang along and clapped in time and Father once again passed around the house silver tray with tobacco in the vibrating air with the fluttering flames of the candles below the chandelier.

Nora had given me an envelope. Besides a bank note, there were copies of Grandma and Grandpa's entry papers from the years 1911 and 1912. Grandpa had gotten Danish citizenship in 1946. On a different piece of paper it said that Grandma and Grandpa had been among the approximately 3000 Jewish refugees from Russia and Poland who came to Denmark at the start of the 20th century. The remaining 700,000 went to America, Canada, New Zealand and Australia.

"You can see it all in print, now!" she said, laughing. "That way you always know where you belong should you be in doubt."

Mrs. Sand, who helped serve wearing a black dress with a white ruffled apron came over and gave me a telegram that had been delivered at the door.

"Agnete sends her greetings and says congratulations!" she said and smiled.

The whole class had signed it.

A little while later the Giant Angel emerged in the doorway. She was also dressed in black with a white apron. Father whispered that there probably weren't ruffles in her size, smiled up to both ears and said, "Wait'll you see this!"

Upon the lifted, rear-facing palm of the Giant Angel balanced an oblong steel dish containing an ice cream gateau in which there had been placed a sizzling bouquet. The chandelier was turned off, the whole table applauded and the photographer, who had been contracted to memorialize the day, snapped and snapped.

At that very moment could be heard noise, voices and howls of laughter from the hall.

The lights were turned back on and a moment later uncle Jafet and aunt Pavla stepped into the room followed by Winnie who held a child in each hand.

"Hi family!" uncle Jafet shouted, looked around and added, "Congratulations!"

"*Gott in himel!*"

The aunts shrieked, everyone spoke all at once. And everyone, with the exception of Grandma, who was unable to get up on her own, jumped from their chairs to go over and embrace the returned emigrants, as uncle Sem laughingly called them.

Aunt Pavla came over and lifted out my dress. Inhaled audibly as she turned her gaze to the ceiling. Then she kissed me on both cheeks and congratulated me.

Winnie also came over and opened her arms.

"But I was supposed to come over and visit you in America!" I blurted out.

Then she called over her children so that they also could congratulate me. The curly, fair girl was called Anna and would soon turn four, the boy, Albert was one and a half.

Winnie's voice cracked and, crying, she embraced Mother. "I'm sorry that we just barged in on your party like this!"

"But, of course, you're family!"

Father had also gotten to his feet. He put his hand on the knot of his tie and smiled all the way to the back of his neck. "This calls for a story. Herschkel met his friend Merschkel on the street. 'Oy,' lamented Herschkel, 'I'm completely *ojseinander*. I just came with the train and have been riding in reverse the whole way home.' 'But Herschkel,' said Merschkel, 'Couldn't you have asked someone across from you if they could trade seats with you?' 'No,' Herschkel said, 'because there was no one sitting there!'"

The uncles tilted back their heads.

Uncle Jafet came over, could my father lend him some money for the taxi, he asked.

"We only have dollars, sorry," he snorted.

Uncle Sem and Uncle Kam took uncle Jafet under the arms and went out with him to help with the luggage.

Grandpa squatted down in front of the boy who still hadn't said a word as he stood in the middle of the floor and sucked on his finger.

"*Nuh*, little Al, do you speak English?"

The following day the newly baz mitzvahed met at the home of the Chief Rabbi who served us fruit juice.

I sat down on a chair by the window and looked around the group of newly bar mitzvahed dressed in their day-after outfits. Several had put on lipstick in a red color à la the aunts. In most of our cases, our grandparents had fled from Poland and Russia. In all our cases, our families had had to flee for their lives. I wondered whether they ever talked about it at home.

The very first day when we heard about the Creation, I had poked my neighbor, "I also think all this religion is difficult," I whispered.

"But it's *Bereshit*," she said.

My cheeks started to burn.

She smiled apologetically, adding, "That means in the beginning,"

Now she was wearing a white flower in the collar of her light blue outfit. She took sips from her yellow juice and smiled, looking as though she felt very much at ease.

When Father picked me up he was smiling up from ear to ear and asked me if I wasn't happy with being baz mitzvahed after all.

I nodded.

He talked about the party and the gifts. Everything had gone so well. And it was all already over with. And to top it all off, the emigrants had come home to stay. They were all to stay with us until they found their own place to live.

"Imagine, baz mitzvahed!" He looked at me and said that he would put all the money I had received as presents into my bank account.

But wasn't there more to a baz mitzvah than that? I took a deep breath and asked the question that had been burning on my tongue, "What about the commandments? Everything it says in the Bible?"

A shadow crossed my father's face. He started a sentence but then stopped himself. A muscle in his cheek began to quiver.

"Let me tell you one thing! I learned all of that, too, once. You see, my father was a devil! He forced religion upon us. But then I discovered that it was all fabrications and was more than happy to wash the floors on Saturdays rather than go with him to the synagogue! Religion," he said, the corners of his mouth turning down, "is nothing for you. Do you want to know what religious men do? Every morning they thank God that they weren't born a woman! But there is no God!"

"Why did I get a Jewish baz mitzvah, then?"

"Because it is best to be with like-minded people."

"Like-minded?"

"Yes," he said and then he smiled again. "It's so very simple. It's the same God that isn't there!"

"But why did you take me out of the Jewish school, then?"

"Now, now, not so much discussion!"

"I closed my eyes, moved my lips silently. Dear God, if it turns out that You do exist, could You please let a miracle happen?

*

"Green is the hedge of Spring" we sang in school at the morning assembly. The chestnut trees along the stream had big buds ready to burst. The birds chirped and there were rustling, swishing and scratching sounds in the light green hedges. Blue and yellow flower pillows spread across the flagstones on the sidewalk. the air was filled with pollen and anticipation.

But you sweet world outside! You, world of inaccessible longing! Why had I not been born in Agnete's home? Or Marianne's? Laila's? Anyone at all. Was language not created to transport content from one person to another? Wasn't that the normal way things worked? And wasn't that known as having a conversation with one another? That was what we did at school. That was how it worked at my friends' home. Or was that just wishful thinking?

In my world language had become a military weapon. The words were bullets that flew through the air. Or a shield between two fighters. Bullets that penetrated through the shields were the same as poison that had a prolonged effect.

It was all because of the second day's parties.

"You're not attending the second day's parties with di goyim!" Father said, waving his index finger in the air.

"Of course I am!" I said without ducking. "Since that's the school I'm going to!"

"No!" the answer rang out like a shot "And there'll be no more discussion about it!"

It didn't help that we were now nine people sitting at the dinner table in the evenings and that Mother was always on the verge of exploding into a fit every time Winnie used a clean dish cloth to wipe the children's mouths.

Once Uncle Jafet tried to intervene. "Let her go, it's just her friends from school…"

But he received a glance from Father that spoke its own clear language. In what was then the current housing situation the wisest thing to do was to surrender and shut up.

It wasn't God who came to my rescue. It was Marianne ... Or...? I held my breath, wasn't that precisely the way in which God came to people's rescue? Through a messenger who came to offer their help?

Right there, in my own room, on my own bed, where Marianne was sitting next to me, a miracle happened! The world opened up to me. Thank you! Thank you! I sang within myself. The greatness of that moment made me feel as though I were being lifted.

"My mother!" Marianne said smiling as she placed her hand on my arm.

She had a dimple in one cheek.

When, with equal amounts of joy and deceit in my heart, I went to get Marianne, whom I was allowed to visit, we continued on to the home of someone else in the class. Then her mother would call if it became necessary.

"And remember, I trust you!" she said, smiling as she looked up from the 3000 piece jig saw puzzle displayed on their hexagonal table in their library room where she was sitting with Marianne's sisters. It was from her mother Marianne had her dimple.

Marianne's father was a tall, friendly man. The fact that he was a judge gave Mother a sense of security. Also, the fact that their three-storied house was close by. For Marianne's second day party the tall judge had personally planted torches in the ground along the lawn. The gleam from the torches soon transformed the yard into a magical space outside of time. The fairy tale also included the Gangway, a densely grown path on the other side of the yard. A dilapidated gate led out to it.

The Gangway was at our free disposal. You were only young once, the judge said.

Despite the fact that I was in constant fear of being discovered, a stolen sense of freedom tasted better than none at all. In the morning I woke all the way up to the very roots of my hair. The blackbird was singing. There were still several hours before I had to be at school. I floated in and out of my newfound ecstasy: Jens Peter.

I hated lying. Even more than I hated being different and not included in the class fellowship. One day I summoned up my courage! When all the others were allowed to I should be, too! It was only a matter of time until I would manage to impose the necessary reforms. This first one was crucial. I wanted to impose some normality!

One Saturday I said, "Today there's a second-day's party at Jens Peter's!"

Helle wasn't at home and was therefore in neutral territory. How I envied her! Winnie and aunt Pavla were busy bathing Anna and Albert. From the bathroom could be heard shouts, screams and splashes.

The battle ended with a ban.

With uncle Jafet's sympathetic eyes at my back, I staggered into my room and fell onto my bed. In my mind's eye I saw Jens Peter put his arm around Laila when I wasn't there. Lead her to his room. Saw them closely entwined, sink down on the sheepskin carpet. Heard his hoarse voice mumble sweet words in her hair.

But I wanted to not care about the world! I cursed my own honesty.

"The naked truth" they said. Just like the legend we had learned about at the baz mitzvah preparation lessons, lies were dressed and never appeared without their clothes. Which they had stolen from the truth. "Truth and Lie bathed in the ocean at the same beach. While Truth cooled off its body in the waves, Lie snuck up from out of the water, dressed in Truth's clothes and disappeared from sight.

"I am the one who is Truth," Lie claimed. Through a simple theft Lie had managed to creep into Truth's clothes and make Truth stand naked with the shame. The shame that belonged to the Lie.

I had gotten it all ready so that I wouldn't have to turn on the light. The guests of the house were fortunately sleeping in the cellar. And when it grew quiet on the other side of the door of my parents' bedroom, I got up and got dressed. Opened the door to the living room and sneaked out on my tippy toes through the sleeping house. In the hall I let my hands glide across the wall, found the button for the burglar alarm and turned it off. Snuck back to my room.

I put on a windbreaker jacket and put my keys in my pocket. Grabbed the school bag in which I had packed a few clothes. Then I lifted the latches from the window and swung one leg over the window sill. Shortly thereafter I was standing on the terrace and pushing the window shut. The cool wind felt pleasant against my burning cheeks. The full moon shone down with an insistent, ethereal gleam that divided the yard into fields of light and shadow and made the illuminated grass and trees glisten silvery. I walked around the house and found my bike, turned on my bike light.

As I biked my thoughts were in a turmoil. I was more confused than ever. Confused and furious! The confirmation and baz mitzvah were the ticket to the big world. For the others it was no cliché, everyone in the class talked about it. Laila had gotten a ticket to Gaza where her father was stationed as a UN soldier. Agnete was going to England to attend a language school for the summer. Marianne wanted to be a clothes designer and was going to Paris. I would never have been allowed to visit Winnie in America.

Even though there were hardly any cars in the street, I stopped at a red light. Late on the night of the baz mitzvah, Winnie had taken me by the hand and led me down to the cellar where her children lay sleeping in our old pull-out couch. She went over to her luggage, opened it and took out one of her American dresses. Held the dress, which was made of red mohair, up for me to see. I was to have it! Then she told me she was getting divorced. Never going back to America. They had left the country illegally. She pointed at Anna and Albert that lay with their heads toward one another and breathed deeply and said, "Aren't they wonderful? They can't help the fact that their father is such a damned--" she stopped herself and continued with a breaking voice, "Do you know what the strange thing is? My mother and father are completely crazy about the kids. But they could neglect me for a whole weekend. They were just conked out on the couch, they were always out partying the whole night. Had I not had your mother and father back then I don't know what I would have done. You have no idea how lucky you are!"

When I asked Winnie whether they had ever talked about the history she said that for her John was dead!

"But..." I said but never got a chance to continue. For at

that very moment aunt Pavla and uncle Jafet joined us. He had gotten a migraine attack and had to go to bed. The trip back home had been too much for him, he lamented, clutching his head and apologizing for all the fuss. Aunt Pavla scolded him, saying he shouldn't have drunk those last three shots. And while the best quality whisky of the house left uncle Jafet's stomach before he had reached all the way back up the stairs, they called the on-call doctor who came and gave him an injection. Helle said he was a drug addict.

In a matter of almost no time I had reached Lygten Sreet and made a right turn. There were no people on the street. All at once I remembered a night when Helle hadn't come home. With death in her eyes, Mother sat chained to the telephone, calling everyone in the world. Meanwhile Father paced restlessly back and forth, going down to the cellar and back up again. Helle didn't come home til the next day. She never told me where she had been. For the first time I experienced for a second that we were connected, But I also remembered that shortly before my baz mitzvah I had gone down to her room. Said I wanted to talk to her and told her what I had been talking with Nora about. The only thing I left out was what Nora had told me about Helle and me. She listened. Afterward she looked at me overbearingly.

"What happened happened. Leave the past alone." And she added that she might as well tell it like was. She was going to quit her study of psychology. She didn't believe in it anymore.

"Things are the way they are. There's nothing you can do to change them!"

"But do you think everything is predestined? Doesn't

it matter at all what you yourself do? I mean, what if the fishermen hadn't sailed you to Sweden?"

"They got money for it!" Helle checked herself and added in the same breath, "But I don't think it was only for the money. I know that they put their lives at risk."

"But that's not the point! Can't you see what that piece of family history has done to us? Continues to do to us?"

Helle got an exasperated look on her face.

"Don't you think I know? But I don't have the energy to go into that history, I want to move away from home! Get out of here! I'm going abroad this coming autumn!"

I turned down the dark, dead-end road and leaned my bike against the iron grille. Locked it. With my heart pounding all the way up to my throat, I entered the hall and rang the doorbell. Waited. Pressed the doorbell one more time. No one answered. My heart sank. I let myself collapse on the mat, leaned against the door between Nora's scratched doorframes. My eyes closed.

I was awakened by the sound of voices and because the door at that very same moment opened and disappeared behind my back. I tumbled in backward and the light in the hallway was switched on.

"What the deuce?" said a tall, stocky man who at that same moment was making his way out of the apartment and very nearly managed to step on me in the process. He ran his fingers through his dark, curly hair and pointed at me, giving Nora a quizzical glance. She nodded.

"See you!" he said and went out into the street.

I slowly got to my feet, uncertain as to what I should say. So I didn't say anything.

Nora was wearing a robe and had a lit cigarette in her hand. She opened the door wide.

"Well, well, looks like someone's run away from home," she said, sending me a crooked little smile. "Come on in, you can sleep here tonight. But tomorrow we'll call your mother and father! There's no need to make matters worse than they are, right?"

"I don't want to go back home!"

"Now, now!" Nora lay down next to me. Lying in Nora's bed with her arms around me, I told her everything. But what had I expected? Even though she felt for me, she couldn't invalidate the laws of my home, she said. Instead, she tried to cheer me up.

"Do you remember when you were little and lay in your bed, you'd call for me, 'Nora!' you shouted, 'Come here and turn on the light, I can't see to sleep!'"

That made us laugh. We lay there talking until there were no more words.

The next day Father came to get me. He looked at me but didn't say anything. Greeted Nora properly but reservedly and thanked her for the help.

On the street Father took hold of my bike to place it in the trunk but I held onto it, I was determined to bike home.

"But it's pouring down!" he said.

"So?!" I said and got on the bike.

Then he shrugged his shoulders and sat down behind the wheel, driving behind me all the way home.

I ignored the Captain. Because Nora and I had a proper plan now!

If you wanted to do well in life you had to be able to do

what was necessary, Nora had said. The plan was devised so brilliantly that it would pull the rug under our domestic cold war! The floor included!

The rain drenched down and my feet squished in my shoes, but I didn't care.

Part III
Who knows?

The sand was burning under the soles of my feet as I started making my way from the sand dunes toward the water. The beach was packed, I zig-zagged between the beach chairs, sunbathers, towels and beach baskets and was close to stepping on a forest of thermos bottles that had been planted in the sand Got hot dog and ice cream paper stuck between my toes as I dodged a cluster of mothers with their small children. Squinted because of the sunlight that made the air flicker. Flicker.

I stopped close to the water's edge. Stood still inhaling the scent of the sea. I longed to run along the water's edge. Overcome the initial resistance to finally reach the flying sensation of my legs running automatically on their own accord. But death was something no one could run away from.

First Mr. Sand died. Else had come home for the funeral and when she returned to Sydney she took Mrs. Sand with her. She was going to stay there for a whole year.

Then Grandma died. She had died in her sleep during the night at the hospital Mother said one morning during my spring break when I came out to the kitchen to eat breakfast. She sat on a chair with her hands in her lap and looked sad. Father stood next to her with his hand on her shoulder. I went over to her. Her hands were like ice.

After the funeral there was to be a family gathering at our house. Nora was also invited. You only have one life, Mother said on the telephone.

The Chief Rabbi had spoken beautifully of Grandma and about life and death: Grandma had had to flee for her life twice. He stressed that something could not turn into nothing. The implication was that as long as the family continued talking about Grandma she would continue to live in our memories.

The coffee and cold cuts had been placed on the table and, with feeling, aunt Manja said that the tradition of sitting down together to reminisce about the deceased was a *richtigeh* tradition indeed.

"And in Grandma's spirit, too, with cold cuts from the Jewish butcher!" uncle Kam said with his mouth full of food.

"And the beer!" uncle Sem said.

Aunt Katja, who was busy freshening up her lipstick, gave a start and she looked up from her makeup mirror.

But Father had already gotten up.

"That's no problem, there's beer in the cellar. Anyone else?" he asked as he looked around the table.

Uncle Jafet raised his hand, then Grandpa and others.

"Sorry, Sis," uncle Sem said.

"But of course! You're family!"

"The last time I called Grandma to wish her a happy birthday," Winnie said as she dried her eyes and a little mascara from her cheeks with the napkin, "She said to me, 'He hasn't *kushed* me on my *burshday*, so I won't *kush* him either on his *burshday*!' 'What do you say to that? Heee!"

Everyone laughed, including Grandpa. A little while later he put his hands to his face and cried.

Aunt Pavla and uncle Jafet had in the meantime moved and gotten their own place to live where Winnie, Anna and Albert also lived in a three-room apartment in Valby. When they moved, Helle let out a howl of joy that lingered in the air like a struck guitar chord and could be heard all the way to Valby. Uncle Jafet never locked the door when going to the bathroom. Even though there was nothing to see while he was sitting down, judging by the look on her face, the outrage of having to be exposed to that sort of thing was on the scale of the Fall of Man. She even claimed that it took away her appetite for several days afterward.

But in the telephone Mother said that Helle's compulsive eating had escalated and that it didn't help her that the excuse he managed to come up with when someone came barging in like that while he was out there, always came from the heart.

When they left after the funeral aunt Pavla and uncle Jafet gave my mother a hug and said she ought to try to get away for a bit. They were all going to the beach town and had rented a house in the old fishing neighborhood close to the church. It would be exactly like in the old days. Grandpa would manage, he was a survivor. And life had to go on.

Mother nodded, she had been thinking about it herself. Then she turned toward me and said, "How about getting a room up there a couple of weeks during the summer vacation? Just the two of us? Helle can help Father in the shop and drive up with him on the weekends."

I looked across the Sound. The waves rolled in toward the beach, rising and breaking into white, flattened and licked the edge of the beach, forceful and foaming, pulled back again, leaving the sand dark and glistening.

When the Germans stopped turning a blind eye to them, the crossings had to take place at night, Nora said. There hadn't been enough fishing boats to take everyone. Some had attempted to row, others to swim across the Sound. Not everyone had made it across alive. I had been visiting Nora again and it had been nice not to have to lie about it. We were going to meet after the summer vacation and continue working on our secret plan. I got breathless thinking about the plan. Pushed it all away and looked across the beach.

In the drowsy summer wind a flag wound affectionately around the flag pole by the lifeguard tower and swished its tail every so often. From the wisps of lyme grass on the dunes to the borders of seaweed at the water's edge where flocks of sand-hoppers made the air come alive in dancing dots, the beach stretched itself before my eyes like a painting in motion. I wondered whether Katrinn was here. I looked for her but she was nowhere to be seen.

But there, in front of the tower, the figure by the post! He was holding binoculars in front of his eyes and was looking out across the sea. I stood completely still and dug my toes in the sand. Let my glance wander across his body: the curve of his head, the straight bridge of his nose, his powerful neck and shoulders. White Bermuda shorts fluttered about his tanned thighs when he shifted his weight from one leg to the other.

I ran the last few meters over there, "You!" I said.

The sun's rays fell on his cheek when he removed the binoculars from his eyes and looked at me. His face lit up in a smile.

"It *is* you, isn't it?"

The next second he turned his head, again looking across the water.

"I'm afraid I'm going to have to..." he said in an apologizing voice.

That very moment an ice cream man passed close by us, his arms around the white ice-box that hung from a strap around his neck.

Without turning his gaze from the surface of the water, he asked for two ice-cream cones, stuck his hand in his pocket, and took out a bank note which was exchanged for two dewy ice cream cones wrapped in tinfoil which were placed in his hand.

Still without taking his eyes off the surface of the water he handed one of the cones to me.

"Thanks!" The cold ice cream cone wrapped in tinfoil that I was holding in my hand was like a breeze from the past. A fragment of a fleeting narration. A boy with black, curly hair running after a girl with black curly hair in a schoolyard, pushes her from behind or tugs at her hair. But who constantly bustles about her. Every time she turns around she sees the same round boy's face that lights up in mischievous smile. *His*.

He hadn't grown all that tall. He had the face of a grown man now. But it was *him*! It was Boj!

And as I pulled off the tinfoil, it was like tearing into time. I unwrapped the past and took a bite.

"Do you live up here?" Boj asked between mouthfuls of ice cream. His gaze still panned much further across the green surface of the water that was cleaved by a throng of heads and bodies, floating mattresses and beach toys in constant motion. Further out than even the most daring swimmers would ever venture to go, a couple of speed boats were rocking, their engines turned off, on the deep blue water, white and luminous.

I nodded.

"Where?"

I said the address and he wrote it down in his mind. Invisible sparks flew through the air between us as he seemingly unaffected continued to look across the water. A slight quivering of his upper lip was the only sign of his emotional state.

The summer vacation opened up like a swarm of fireflies that with a burst spread out everywhere.

I pushed open the backdoor of the house and stepped out into the light evening. Looked up at a snatch of eternity and started walking toward the driveway. Mother had said I should just go down to the harbor ahead of her as she got herself ready.

When I turned at the corner I started. There he was, leaning against the fence, wearing blue jeans and a black t-shirt. With his finger he was holding the strap of his leather jacket which he had flung over his shoulder. You knew as much, didn't you? His eyes said. I held out my hand. He took it and pulled me toward him. Afterwards I could barely stand on my feet.

Boj studied me.

"Can you walk?"

I could fly! But I nodded and we went out to the street. I looked up at the open window to our room where Mother stood smiling.

I signaled with my hands: am going for a walk with Boj, okay?

She nodded and lifted her hand in greeting.

People on the street were heading for the harbor. Boj said he didn't feel like going to the pier.

"Wouldn't you rather go somewhere where we can talk *peacefully*?"

I nodded. We turned right at the path to the woods and walked in the direction of the plantation. It was mostly Boj who talked. Strange that we hadn't run into each other before, wasn't it? He had continued in the Jewish school until 7th grade. Now he was attending gymnasium. He shared the job as a life saver with one of his friends, Danny. Recently he had saved a drunk Swede who had fallen asleep on a floating air mattress. But it had been *no big deal*.

But I wanted to know more about him. Who was he underneath all his fancy English expressions? He asked whether I had anything against them. No, I said, I had just noticed it.

He said he wanted to be a journalist. His parents had a summerhouse close to the plantation, not far from the place from which they had fled to Sweden during the Second World War.

We had passed the beach hotel and could once again see the Sound that sparkled golden out there between the big houses and trees with gnarled, black trunks.

"Where did your parents cross?"

I told him and he nodded. Then he said it was the million dollar question of our generation. Where did your parents cross? Damage due to the environment.

"Damage due to the environment? Some months ago I wouldn't have been able to answer," I said.

"Really?"

"My parents have never spoken about it. Nora was the one who told me."

"Who's Nora?"

"It's a long story."

It was late before he walked me home. My heart was pounding all the way to my throat when I stepped into the room. But Mother calmly looked up from the magazine she was reading.

"Well, well, I must say! The life guard!" And her eyes said something along the lines of: The two of us have certainly done well, haven't we?

Later I lay in the dark next to her in the twin bed. She was already breathing deeply. But when I closed my eyes I saw Boj before me, standing with his binoculars before his eyes. His smile when he recognized me. When we said good-bye he had kissed me. It was like having rediscovered a part of myself that I had forgotten, that I had lost. But what if his parents hadn't survived the crossing. If he had never been born? My heart skipped a beat. I breathed deeply and tried to hold the fear that something might happen to him at arm's length. While he was saving drunken Swedes, he himself might drown. I saw him lying lifeless at the water's edge. Turned around on the other side.

*

Every day Mother and I walked together down to the beach. She would settle herself on a blanket next to the aunts and gave me the freedom to see Boj as I pleased. Around lunch time we would go together to the butcher and buy open faced sandwiches which we'd eat together in the room. We relaxed in one another's company and didn't talk about anything other than what we wanted to eat and the nice weather. Then we would go back to the beach.

And every day I would meet Boj down there. He introduced me to his friends. One of them had a boat and took us on a sailing trip along the beach. At night he would come and get me. Then we'd wander about the town, dance at the beach hotel or go for a walk in the plantation.

One night, when his parents had to go out, we drank tea together with his little brother at their summerhouse. Gaj also played the guitar and taught me some Israeli songs.

On Saturday Father and Helle came for the weekend. Father looked happy and kissed Mother. We were going out to eat at a restaurant.

She said something to Father, almost without moving her lips. He nodded. Then she asked whether I would like to invite Boj to join us.

I told Helle about him when we walked together to the beach. She wanted to go down there to get a little color, her boyfriend was coming the next day.

Before we left home Mother checked my dress. Then she looked at me and said, "Now remember not to say the first thing that enters you head."

I made a sound with my tongue.

We were to meet at 7 pm at the graveled square in front of the restaurant. He was already standing there filling the whole square with light!

Helle nudged me with her elbow and whispered something. But I only saw Boj. He must have borrowed his father's blazer and beige pants. The trouser legs were wide and had sharp creases and were slightly too short. But he still looked extremely handsome! A tie. Beneath the blazer the white collar of his shirt fit snugly on the tanned skin of his neck. I swallowed, how soft that skin had felt against my lips.

He smelled like after-shave and told me that he had had to shave twice a day already from when he was 12 years old. Once he let his beard grow but his father and little brother had teased him, saying that he looked like something from the previous century. He himself was able to see it as well and shaved it off again.

"Boj!" He held out his hand and bowed.

Mother smiled and shook hands with him. Afterward Helle did as well. I held my breath. But Father also held out his hand. It was the first time he had shaken hands with one of my friends. His smile reached all the way from ear to ear. Like when I was little and we walked hand in hand to the candy store. I was allowed to choose for myself what I wanted.

"Whatever I want?" His smile, when he nodded.

Inside me, heaven and earth took one another by the hand.

Boj took me by the elbow and let me walk in front. I walked into the door frame.

"Klutz!" Helle said in a teasing voice from behind.

The restaurant was filled with guests. A waiter pointed to a window table. Boj pulled out a chair for me. I could feel Mother's and Helle's eyes on me as I took my seat across from them. Boj sat down next to me.

Father sat at the head of the table. Put his hand up to the knot of his tie and read aloud from the list of open face sandwiches.

"Herring, salmon, fish fillet, smoked herring, eggs and tomatoes, potatoes. Cheese. Any of these things of interest to your Excellencies?

For a moment Helle and my eyes met in silent agreement. Today we were not going to have roast pork. Ham with Italian salad or roast beef which my mother always ate if it wasn't too red. No, what we were going to eat today were all things that you could put in your mouth without having to reveal your Jewish observation. It was a convenient little show. Only Jews could act it out. And only in the company of one another.

As we waited for the food the topic of conversation was everything and nothing. Father did the talking, all smiles and forthcoming. Who was Boj's father, and what had been his mother's maiden name? His father was a professor. They had an unexpected address which became apparent through a small wrinkle of surprise on my mother's brow as she drank from the mineral water which the waiter had poured in her glass.

The family was active in the Jewish congregation with regard to providing information and raising money for Israel, but belonged to the older Danish-Jewish lineages. They were to be regarded as a kind of aristocracy that stood above our low-status position of belonging to the group of Eastern European immigrants. Since they didn't live in a house it had to be a big apartment, Mother's brow indicated. They also had a summerhouse.

As Boj talked about himself, well-articulated and self-confident - only that tiny quivering on his upper lip showed me that something was going on within him which he didn't say out loud- I assumed my new role in clammy silence. Paralyzed, I sat by his side. I was painfully aware of it myself but was unable to cut through and listen to my own thoughts. It felt as though the inside of my skull was smeared in prejudices, in a sticky mass of honey in which my own thoughts were stuck. I was embarrassed and ashamed for having gone along with the outing. Cast a sidelong glance at Helle who, her nose somewhat red from sunburn, sat looking down into her plate. Her boyfriend did not belong to the lineage of older Danish-Jewish stock.

When we left home, she had teasingly said that she had heard that going to the Jewish school made you pious. But aside from his hair color, Boj had absolutely no resemblance to the so-called pious who, wearing their yarmulkes, would frequent the sand dunes in their rather not so pious swimming trunks, spoke in loud voices and acted as though they owned the whole beach and the whole of Denmark.

All at once I remembered Helle's laughter the time she told about the cross examination she had been through when her boyfriend had introduced her to his family. Who is your father? What was your mother's maiden name?

The dishes were brought in and placed on stilts. All the open-faced sandwiches were garnished with lettuce leaves. There were capers on the herring. The salty taste of herring gave a pleasant sensation on your tongue when you had been outside all day sweating in the sun. I maneuvered the fish filet onto my plate. Squeezed some lemon juice on the remoulade. Salt and pepper.

Then I felt his lips next to my ear. "Have you repressed yourself or what? Why are you just sitting there? Say something, *come on!*"

*

The next day Boj was not on the beach. His friend, Danny, was there, long-limbed and fair-skinned, standing in front of the life guard tower, holding his binoculars in front of his eyes. He didn't look in my direction when, throughout the day, I trudged back and forth between the water's edge and the sand dunes looking for Boj. When I for the umpteenth time returned to our sand dune and toppled onto my beach towel and Mother once again, with ill-concealed concern in her voice, asked about Boj, I didn't answer. I just closed my eyes and surrendered to the uncertainty that was tearing within me.

That night I pushed open the backdoor and went outside. Held my breath and looked over toward the corner by the tool shed under the ash tree where Boj usually stood smoking. He was there!

I breathed a sigh of relief and rushed over to greet him. He was wearing his own clothes again, jeans and a t-shirt. His jacket hung loose over his shoulder upon which he also was carrying a gray linen bag. He looked at me and smiled, "Thanks for the evening yesterday!" He threw away the cigarette stub and stepped on it.

"I thought you never wanted to see me again," I said.

"Hey," Boj placed his hand on my shoulder and squeezed it. "I had to drive my mother to Copenhagen for an errand. Yesterday was o.k. That's how it is when you belong in the duck pond. *Take it or leave it.*" He fixed his gaze on me, "What now?"

"It's up to you!"

I happily walked with him in the opposite direction of the harbor, along the practically deserted beach. A narrow path led to the plantation. He flicked a branch to the side, held it there and let me pass through before he let go of it.

That which he had whispered in my ear in the restaurant about repressing myself. I couldn't get it out of my head. What had he meant by it?

He put his hand on the back of his neck and asked, "Does anything come to mind if I say... Freud?"

"Freud?"

"Papa Freud. Psychoanalysis. Freud discovered that people get sick from repressing things. His theories are used today. People like us born after the War ... our parents, that is, people who have war traumas in their baggage. My folks have worked with it." He gave me a small smile.

"How worked?" A shiver ran down my spine.

"Talked it out. The escape, the fear of getting caught. The guilt of having survived when so many others didn't, a feeling of having betrayed the dead. But most of all learned to live with it. With the fear that it might happen again. To live life to the fullest despite it. They belonged to a group. They still do. That group has stayed together ever since. That sort of thing never goes entirely away."

I wanted to say something but no words escaped my mouth. Then he said that his parents associated with Miranda's parents. Mine did, too, I said, when I went to the Jewish school. But when I stopped going there they also stopped seeing them.

His ran his finegrs through his hair.

"We are several that drank it in with our mother's milk."

I inhaled from the very bottom of my stomach, "Do you know the feeling of being vulnerable, threatened..." I struggled to say the words, "of being scared of disappearing. Dying?"

"But that's the price you pay for being alive!" he said without batting an eyelid, "And Jews have always lived dangerously!"

I didn't answer. Didn't he sound like a book? Or like he was just repeating something he had heard before. But his words had opened a door ajar within me. I pretended that I had gotten something stuck in my shoe. I sat down on a tree stump and took off one of my sneakers. Shook it. Took a long time tying my shoelace. He offered a hand and helped me get up. We walked on in silence.

Then he said, "The rescue of the Danish Jews is unique

when you think about what happened in the rest of Europe. It was a success. But below the surface the fear and guilt, everything in connection with the escape left traces in the psyche. Just because something isn't visible doesn't mean it isn't there."

A loud outburst came from me.

"No, you're not the only one. But there are many variations of that story. Did you know that there were Jewish children that were in hiding with Danish families when their parents fled?"

I nodded. "One of my cousins was hidden with a family. He's dead now."

"Some have grown up with their parents talking about it all the time. Danny's told me that no matter what happened to him, whether he hurt his knee or his bike got stolen, whatever, it was considered to be nothing, nothing at all! His parents met each other in Theresienstadt."

"How do you know all that?" I asked.

"Me and Danny, he wants to be a journalist too. and a couple of others are working on a pioneer project where we examine those of us who were born after the Second World War. The second generation after the victims and survivors of the War. We talk with people. They tell us their stories and we record it on tape."

"Who are the people you talk with?"

"First and foremost the ones who have gone to the Jewish school. But also others. There are many of our generation who have existential issues and problems with identity. We have discovered that it may have to do with our parents' escape from Denmark. Everything that hasn't been talked about or that has filled the whole landscape has been passed on to the next generation. We're just beginning, but one day we want to write something about how that history has left its marks on the second generation." He slapped a mosquito on his arm. "Come to a meeting when summer vacation is over, you could contribute with your story. Would you do that?"

He sounded like a book! Still, I said, "Why haven't we met until now?"

Boj smiled, took my hand and led me to a fallen tree trunk. He sat down, hung his bag on a branch and gestured with his hand. I was to sit next to him. He put his arm around me and I rested my cheek against his shoulder. After a little while I got up. Looked at him directly and said, "I have always had the feeling that I was standing in front of a glass pane looking out into the rain and had to make do with getting tears in my eyes."

Boj got up as well. In the tenderness that streamed from his eyes, there was a mixture of something that went against the current, a glimpse of irony or a certain distancing? Then he said it was common for Jews to cling to the role of the victim. But doing that was almost just as traumatic as that which had made Jews victims.

"You need to break free of your inherited glass cage!"

He took hold of my shoulders and shook me. "Have you heard of Proust, the French author Marcel Proust? He wrote about the same things as Freud, just in a different way."

I opened my mouth to say something but Boj was faster. " Did you know that Proust was among the first to collect protest signatures during the Dreyfus affair?"

I shook my head. "Dreyfus became the *point of no return*, a *stinking* expression for classic anti-Semitism. In any event it got the world to stop believing that Jews could be assimilated in Europe. And that was just a prelude. To the Second World War, that is!" Again he paused for a brief moment before continuing in a somber voice, "Things like that are why we are condemned to have to deal with our history!"

"I'm breaking out of it, though, Nora and I ..."

He didn't listen but took my hand. Held it up high in the air, "Well, tonight at least we got further than just scratching the polish." And he let his thumb glide across my fingernails as though he wanted to scratch off the nail polish. "Why do you put up with that circus of parental monitoring?" Now there was irritation in his voice,

I shrugged my shoulders. "If they mean well?"

"It's right out of the book!"

"What?"

"That you now start to defend them. Last night you sat at that table and died. I saw it with my own eyes!"

"Why didn't you say all of this yesterday, then? To them?"

Boj placed a hand on my mouth.

"You should have stayed at the Jewish school!"

"But I wasn't the one who ..." my words drowned in the palm of his hand. I tried to bite.

"*Roots!* You have a choice!"

I tore his hand away and spurted out, "You're so harsh!"

He didn't answer. Looked about in search of something. He said he wanted to take a series of pictures of me. Then he took his camera out of his bag.

"You confuse me," I said. "Everything you've been saying is all that I have longed for someone to say. Always. But you make me feel wrong. As though it's my fault that we had to keep it a secret. Your parents did something about it."

"*True!*"

There was a pressure growing within me, below my skin feelings were boxing with one another, pulling me in each their direction. When I was new at the school, Morten from my class had run after me on my way back from school even though he lived in the opposite direction.

"Are you an Indian or something like that, a gypsy? Your hair is pitch black."

I started shaking all over.

"And that's not allowed?"

"Yes, it looks nice! But there are no other kids in the class who have black hair, so I was just wondering..." Morten said.

Now it was clear as day to me what I should have said.

"Jew!" I should have said, "I'm a Jew! Are you satisfied now?" But I didn't do it. I dragged myself home while a repulsive feeling swept through me...the shame that I hadn't admitted to what I was.

Boj took the cap off the lens and held the camera up to his eyes. I did what he asked me to do: unzipped my jacket, Squatted and tried to keep my balance on a thick-stemmed tree. He snapped one picture after another. Went down on his knees. Straightened up again, moved about and took pictures of me and the tree from all angles. I looked at him and smiled. But he said I was to look serious, turn my cheek towards the tree trunk. It scratched. The dream! I had dreamed it again that night.

In a landscape were two separate iron staircases that merged to become one way up high. The staircase went further up, so high that the very top step was covered in clouds. I was to meet Boj up there. He was way ahead of me, was already standing at the top step. I was still standing on the ground. I didn't understand why I always remained standing on the ground in that dream, why didn't I just go up? Then I saw it! My ladder was missing all the bottom steps!

The muscles in my calves quivered. Boj held out his hand. I accepted it and got to my feet. Shook both my feet .

We slowly continued on our way. A blackbird was singing. Another one responded further away. The forest floor was a carpet of red-brown needles that gave way under our feet. Muffled our steps. Below us a space opened up, the endless abyss. The earth, roots, crawling worms. It was as though all of it was inside of me. At the center a core that was glowing, bleeding.

We left the plantation and started to head toward the town. The sun had set but it was still light. We turned at the big road.

"There's Katrinn!" I said. In a purple mini-skirt and high-heeled wooden sandals she strutted past the grill on the other side of the road.

Boj had also caught sight of her and once again draped his arm around my shoulder. I wanted to shout "hi" but he closed my mouth with a kiss. Afterward he said, "What about a little appreciation?"

"I do appreciate you!"

"For making it so clear to her that I'm with you!"

I followed Katrinn's swaying hips with my eyes. Remembered last summer when she and I had walked the pier together.

We had met at the harbor kiosk and merged into the river of pedestrians. Of voices and laughter. The gossip that was paraded out in combination with the dogs being taken for a walk. Who had gotten married? Who was expecting? Who was expecting and not married? Katrinn was the oldest and knew everything about everybody. I took it all in.

We went out to the furthest edge of the pier and sat on the big rocks in front of it. The stones were as smooth as silk against the palm of your hands and gave off heat like small ovens through your dress. We sat right up close to each other, our bodies trembling and ready to burst. Wrapped our arms around our knees as we listened to water striking against the rocks and pulling back with a slurping sound. Followed with our eyes the glowing ball sinking toward the horizon. Out there where the sea gleamed against the sky, out where Lolita, Atilol, or rather Lilato-like golden violet tones merged into a kiss of death We remained sitting that way until somebody called for us. On lucky nights until nature's drama had settled down in drowsy colorlessness. Like closed eyes right before sleep.

We saw Lolita in each other's eyes. We *were* Lolita. But that name was on everybody's lips that summer. And the Russian sounding name, Nabokov. We watched the movie at the cinema in the beach town. Wallowed in Lolita's mother who gawked at Humbert Humbert who gawked at Lolita-Dolores.

Like her father, Katrinn had brown eyes. She had her hair color from her mother who was Swedish. Her hair was cut in a Lolita style hairdo that daringly framed her broad cheekbones.

"Do you want to hear my little secret?" she said as she took hold of the Star of David on the thin gold chain that hung around her neck, "I can't become a member of the Judiska youth club. In their eyes I'm not a Jew because my mother isn't Jewish. My father got so damned angry and said I should just go there even though they demanded that I first get converted. There was a bitterness in her voice when she added, "You don't know how lucky you are, both your parents are ... you're full-blooded!"

"But..." I started.

She didn't listen.

"All that talk about being conversion was too much 'Jewishness' for my mother. Then my father got enraged at her, too. And then my grandma got enraged at my father. It was the same story all over, she said, and she had said so from the beginning!" She continued in a lower tone of voice, "I went to a party in the youth club. And I met a smashing boy there. He's Danish. He took me to a Jewish youth club in Copenhagen. But then he also talked about how I should get converted. And now..."

Katrinn hadn't said smashing boy but smashing Boj! My eyes were swimming.

"Hey, where are you?" Boj waved his hand up and down in front of my eyes.

I pushed his hand aside.

"I asked if you wanted to come with me? We can just make it!"

I looked around. Like someone asleep I had followed him through the town's streets. Across the main road where cars with shining headlights moved at a snail's pace in both directions. We were now standing in front of the cinema. The sign was bathed in the gleam of the projector:

"Summer cavalcade" it said in capital letters, "Tonight, Lolita."

*

I by turns rode a wave and got my head covered by the water that washed over me. Swallowed water and spit it out.

"Is that what you call swimming?" Boj placed his arm under my body and ordered me to relax and float. He was a supporter of *learning by doing,* he said. And without my realizing it, he had pulled his arm back. The water was carrying me. I turned on my back and tilted my head back. Looked straight up into the sky. It slurped and bubbled in my ears and made the shouts from the other bathers echo. Again, I turned on my stomach. Tilted my head to the side on the surface of the water. Blinked. A bosom swelling over a low-cut black bathing suit was heading directly my way. I quickly placed my feet on the sandy bottom. The light of the sun blinded me and it took a little while before I realized that it was Winnie who was standing before me.

"Come and hug your cousin" she said as she, as always, placed all her effort in pronouncing each syllable with all her heart. She pulled up the straps of her bathing suit.

I leaned forward and our cheeks brushed against each other. Then she put her hands on her lips that were painted with blood-red lipstick.

"Sorry if my lipstick is smudgy, that's no excuse for not introducing us," she nodded toward Boj and laughed.

"This is Winnie," I said. "My cousin, and this is..."

"Boj" Boj said as he held out his hand and bowed.

Winnie took his hand and shook it in the wave that came rolling in on us at that very moment.

"One isn't exactly a Lolita any longer," she put one of her arms in front of her chest, bent over and lost her balance. Got on her feet and laughed again.

People around us saw it and started laughing. That was the way Winnie was. She could get a full-house audience in no time.

"Come visit us one day! And now you must excuse me, I have some weight I have to lose," She leaned forward again. Then she took a few strokes and disappeared out of sight.

"That's what I call a ... real cousin," Boj said with a crooked smile. "Do you have more of those?"

We swam together along the beach a good distance from the shore. At the second sand bank we stopped to catch our breath.

Suddenly Boj tore off my glasses and let them fall into the water!

I was in shock. Was standing in water up to my armpits. Shouted that I couldn't make do without them!

"Then get them!"

I hurled myself into the water. But had to come up again to gasp for more breath. I dived in once more, swimming back and forth under the water. Found the glasses down at the bottom and came back up to the surface, coughing and sputtering! Removed a little seaweed hanging over one of the glasses and put them back on. And without waiting for Boj I hurled myself into the water and swam toward the shore with long steady pulls.

"*Learning by d*oing!" he shouted at me, laughing.

When I waded into the shallow water close to the beach I started shaking.

But it was right out of the book, he had said. Grabbed me from behind and knocked me down at the water's edge.

I had swum my anger away. So I surrendered and played along. Made my arms as limp as a baby's when he positioned me. People stopped and stared. They could go home and tell they had seen someone drowning and getting mouth to mouth resuscitation for all I cared!

At that very moment a scream penetrated the noise of the beach and slashed the air. Boj let go of me and ran after the noise. I looked in the direction he was running. Flying.

A woman in a black bathing suit staggered up to the beach. In her arms she was holding a small child whose arms and legs were hanging much too limply at its sides.

Completely beside myself, I started running. Boj was already over there and shortly after came Danny.

When I got over there and managed to squeeze my way in through the crowd the two life guards were on their knees in the sand working on the little boy who, without moving, lay between them. For a moment everything in my mind stood completely still. Then I saw that the boy had red hair, that he wasn't Winnie's Albert.

A gurgling sound rose up from the little boy's throat and he started regurgitating water.

Sometime later, when the ambulance that had been sent for drove off again with the mother and child my mother suddenly stood before us. She complimented Boj on his efforts and sent greetings from the aunts. She asked if he would care to join them in the sand dune for a cup of coffee.

We looked at one another.

"This is Boj!" Mother's theatrical glance went back and forth between us and the aunts' buzzing noses.

Boj held out his hand and presented his broadest smile.

Aunt Manja took a hold of the straps on her black and white bathing suit that, liberated from their dead weight, hung idly down her upper arms, lifted them up over her fleshy round shoulders and with a few vigorous tugs managed to maneuver it all into place. Then she held out her hand and looked at Boj with the usual expression of surprise on her face.

"And you've taken your life guard with you!" Aunt Katja pulled down the skirt of her shocking pink bikini a little and sent us both a carrot-colored smile.

"Winnie's mother," I whispered when he shook hands with aunt Pavla who hastily rearranged her beach towel so that it covered her bosom.

It hit me like needles behind my eyeballs: It wasn't at all Boj who was the focus of attention here. Mother held her head high and was basking, not in what she clearly thought was the case, the approving eyes of the aunts, they had turned towards each other, but rather, in her own perception of greatness: that the success of the daughter reflects on the mother, she is her very raison d'être, it said in clear letters across her brow as she passed the box of cookies round.

"Well, I'll have to be heading back to the tower now," Boj said when she, once again, asked for the details regarding the rescue mission. And with a bow he handed the empty coffee cup to her.

"Thank you for excellent coffee!" he said. Then he put his

arm around me, pulled me along pushing me with his hip for every step we took.

"He is in *gymnasium!*" she said to our backs, "working as a life guard is just a temporary summer job. His father is a professor!"

When we reached the life guard tower I borrowed Boj's binoculars and saw Mother sitting with her hand on her forehead and observing us from her spot in the sand dune. Her mouth didn't stop moving for one second. I couldn't hear what she was saying, of course, but I didn't need to. I had heard it all enough times already. Already in the morning she had begun to share her future plans for me with the aunts: "I think we'll end up with a little Lilly bridal gown!"

"It's much healthier to let the young people decide for themselves!" Aunt Pavla said. But was she really one to speak? She, who had crossed the Atlantic Ocean to follow in her daughter's footsteps? Aunt Katja and Aunt Manja agreed with my mother. It couldn't hurt to give luck a hand along the way.

I handed the binoculars back to Boj. He took them, put them up to his eyes and looked across the ocean.

I sank down on my beach towel that lay at his feet. Tried to read in the book I had bought on the way to the beach, *Katten der fik feber (The Cat that Caught a Fever)*, I felt as though I myself had a fever.

"Part of a Mother's joy is taking pride in her daughter's success!" she said, pinching me on the cheek when I changed clothes at night before meeting with Boj. And when I stood in front of the mirror to fix my hair it was her face that I saw. She always came over and positioned herself right in back of me and started fixing her hair. But I was the one she was looking at! And she didn't just look! Her gaze was like a sponge, a hairy mother sponge that sucked everything out of me. All that vigor that made my body smooth and supple. In a flash I saw myself as a 90-year-old, with wrinkly and flabby skin. And the mother sponge swelled, sucked and swelled. And sucked.

With my last energy I turned around to push her from my range of vision! I hesitated. Wasn't I being ungrateful in wanting it all for myself? My own life. Could one even talk about having the right to one's own life? What about her, the one who had given me life, made it possible? The one who had carried me and given birth to me. Had filled my stomach with her lukewarm liquid of life. What about all the pain she had to endure because of me? The seven stitches. The hemorrhage. Everything I had done wrong! What about Grandma's illness? And death. Didn't she, the motherless one, have a right to be allowed into my paradise? Now that she so desperately wanted to? As a poor band-aid on all the wounds that life and I had inflicted on her. The wounds from the Second World War.

I had gotten my vigor back! I was fit to be wrung from sweating profusely. But the snake had gotten into the garden as well! Underneath my new feelings of greatness at finding myself on the stage basking in the light of the mother projector, a feeling of shame cavorted. The shame of allowing her will to be done, since it and my own unexpectedly had become best friends. Boj had been the cause of my getting sucked right back into my raison d'être: the mother sponge.

I gave up reading. Put the book aside and turned on my back. Closed my eyes and tried in vain to turn off my racing thoughts. Helle felt somewhat pushed aside. Perhaps it had something to do with the lineage. She didn't say it aloud. But what she needed to get out slipped out anyway, as that sort of thing always did. While lying in our beds in the room that we shared in the weekend, she had said that I shouldn't take it too hard, that is, the thing with the hemorrhages. She herself had to live with the fact that she had caused Mother a breast infection in both breasts.

It eased things a bit that Helle, in her own way, tried to lift my feelings of guilt a little from my shoulders. But just before she sat down next to Father in the Captain to drive back to the city she let it slip out: Boj and me would never last!

That night I lay again in the twin bed next to my raison d'être, listened to it breathing in its sleep. Turned my back to its half-open lips. Its innocent snoring sounds. In the morning I woke with the birds, lay still as death with my eyes closed until I heard my raison d'être swing her legs over the edge of the bed and get up. In order to escape that which had become her most beloved greeting in the morning:

"So, there you see. Like attracts like, right?"

Towards evening my raison d'être took advantage of the rare moments that Boj wasn't present. And she helped me with my zipper in the back of my dress, brushed some dandruff I hadn't noticed I had off the collar of my dress, straightened my belt, my glasses, my hair. Finally she gave my arm a confidential squeeze.

"You know you can always come to me if there's anything, right?"

I nodded. But I had always done the wrong thing. I had always been disapproved of. Like the truth. Unwanted because it was dangerous. Dangerous because it was naked and didn't know anything about the world. In a way, just as innocent as Yvonne.

We had once taken Yvonne with us to the beach. But no one had taught her that Adam had covered his nudity with a fig leaf when he discovered the truth of his nakedness! She couldn't help that. So she just took off all her clothes at the beach. And people turned around and stared at her naked body that already had round breasts and fox-red hair.

I felt as though I were being roasted over open flames. With a start I sat up. The world was spinning round and round. Boj, who was leaning over me, was spinning as well. Why was he hitting me on the head? But he was holding both my hands in his. The pain, an incessant throbbing in my temples, must be coming from the inside.

*

I pushed the door open, saw Boj throw away the cigarette stub and stomp on it. I stepped outside and went over to him with a feeling of being chosen while at the same time infinitely vulnerable!

"Does your little head feel better today?" He placed his hand on my head. Gently.

I nodded. Boj had escorted me up to the sand dunes up to the aunts. Contrary to what was normally the case, they were in complete agreement: I had had a sunstroke and had to go home and go to bed. Mother took me under the arm, supporting me all the way home. I threw up on the way. I slept for the rest of the day and the night as well. The whole day I had remained lying in the ocher colored glow from the roller blinds that had been pulled halfway down. And even though I floated in and out of delirium and could barely distinguish between dream and reality I felt clear in my mind. The headache had worn off.

We had reached the plantation, walking closely together. The forest dimmed the light, letting my eyes rest. I looked far into the dream-like, hazy air among the pine trees when I heard Boj say that he had seen me get baz mitzvahed. He had even taken special notice of me. I turned around and smiled.

"But that was only because your hairdo was the ugliest I have ever seen." Again, he put his hand on my head and ran his fingers through my hair.

"*Never again* a back-comb, ok?"

Gaj had been bar-mitzvahed the previous year, Boj said. He had given him a Bob Dylan record. Did I know that he was Jewish? In reality his name was Robert Allen Zimmerman. But that wouldn't sound so good for an artist's name, would it? The whole family had been to Israel afterward. In a synagogue in Jerusalem there had been a pregnant rabbi. That was too reformed for his father. In Krystalgade Street at least you knew what you got!

"Do you often go to the synagogue?" I asked.

"I like going there. My family goes there. Many of my friends do, too. It's ok."

"You don't seem to be ... I mean ..." I got stuck.

"I'm not sure whether I'm religious, if that's what you mean," he said, giving me a small, crooked smile. "What does it mean to be religious? In reality, being Jewish isn't so much about being or not being. It's about doing! Traditions. Rituals. And going in there for me is like entering a social and cultural community. The synagogue is a meeting house. You should try going there!"

"I've been there after my baz mitzvah. But I don't think it's for me. Is it necessary for one to go there? I mean, isn't one first and foremost a human being?'"

"Not with our history! And 'one'! Say 'I' instead! *You* are who it's all about. You! You sound like someone who hasn't taken a stand. Break out of your glass cage! I'm not saying you have to do anything specific. The only thing I'm asking is that you break free of the shit you inherited. figure out what you yourself want. If Wizo isn't for you, then find something else!" His burning eyes looked straight through me.

"I ..." I began and squirmed, "is it written anywhere that men and women aren't equal?"

"Orthodox Judaism isn't something you can just change." Boj wrinkled his brow and looked thoughtful. "The philosopher Hannah Arendt is interesting to us, she deals with the psychological effects of the Second World War: the problem of maintaining a positive Jewish identity after the Holocaust. This affects Jews in the diaspora, everyone who has a double identity. And also those of us born after the War. If we don't use the Jewish sides of ourselves in our identity, we get cut off from our roots. Then the Jewish identity risks rotting away and infecting the rest, causing us to be without a surrounding world, is what she implies. And if you can't find it in the religion, then seek it in the culture, literature, philosophy, history, music, Hebrew." Boj looked at me and got a teasing expression in his eyes. "But there's plenty of material in you to follow in your mama's footsteps!"

I lunged at him and got a hold of the sleeve of his black t-shirt.

"Oh, so you want to fight? Well, come on, then!"

He flexed his muscles and came toward me with all of his weight ... I had to let go of his sleeve. Suddenly remembered that I had some liquorice Pirate Coins. I stuck my hand in my pocket and pulled out the bag, offered one to Boj and took one for myself.

"By the way, my mother's started to ask about you, how you look and that sort of thing. She says we could use an active girl in the family."

I felt my cheeks starting to burn. "What did you say?"

"I said you're OK!"

"And what is she like, then?"

"Who?"

"Who do you think? Your mother, of course!"

"Oh, her! She's OK"

"Oh, she's also OK?"

"She is! She's found her own way. She's a member of a Wizo group."

"My mother is, too!"

"But aside from work at the congregation, she makes ceramics. They are really nice!" With his hands he formed the image of a bowl in the air.

"What about your farther"

"He's a professor in the history of religion. Also OK. Aside from that, the professor can be a little kinky sometimes when it pleases him."

"Kinky?"

"Once I borrowed the professor's jacket, without permission. I couldn't really ask him when he wasn't at home, could I? But I'm telling you, he went berserk over it, it was the Fall of Man! Do you know what was in the pocket of the jacket?"

I shook my head.

"A pack of condoms!"

"What was he going to use those for? I *know* what he was going to use them for, but..."

"Gaj and I talked about it afterward, too." Boj shrugged. "Other than that, he's ok. And we have a baby, a real cutey!"

Boj stopped.

"Hey, I just got an idea. The Fall of Man!"

"The Fall of Man?"

"Yes. And Don't look so nervous. You can just treat it as an experience. So, was Eve created from Adam's rib? Or were they created at the same time? Or, put in a different way... Are men and women equal?"

"Why do religious men thank God that they weren't created as women?"

"My, you know a lot!"

Again, I lunged at him. He caught my arm. Held it firmly.

"Listen to this: Is Eve more guilty than Adam? Imagine that Adam had been standing next to Eve the whole time. He could actually just as well have done that. You can look it up! The first Book of Moses, chapter 3, verse 1-6."

"Oh, I suppose you know the whole Bible by heart?" I asked as I pulled back my arm.

"My religion instructor got pissed because I knew the whole thing beforehand. He said I was sabotaging the instruction. So I was excused from that class." Boj kicked a stone. "But I could ask it this way. What would you rather be, yourself, or one of my ribs?"

"You're so dumb!"

"You know what?" Boj looked directly at me, "I also think it was cheap to let the world's first woman take all the blame when it was really the snake!"

"The snake?"

"Listen. The snake asked: Did God really say you're not allowed to eat the fruit in the garden?" and Eve answered that it was only the fruit in the middle of the garden. Because otherwise they'd die." Boj looked at me, "Do you see?"

I nodded.

"And the snake was a real snake. It said that they wouldn't die. God would just prevent them from eating the fruit. Because then they were able to distinguish between good and bad. In a God-like way.

That was how the snake beat Eve with its winning argument. That the fruit was in reality the source of wisdom."

I walked into a branch. Put my hand up to my cheek.

"Would you say that again?"

Boj repeated it and explained it. And once more. And again. He seemed to be enjoying his role!

"It doesn't say anywhere that Eve called to Adam. Neither does it say that he needed to be convinced! So it can't be Eve's fault alone! Still, it is far from many who see it that way. But the brilliant thing about is that you can be on it yourself!"

"On it?"

"Find your own way of understanding it! The core of the problem of evil: where does evil come from?" Boj had warmed to his subject. "You have to take responsibility for your actions, right?"

I nodded.

"But God couldn't ask the snake to do that. That was why

He got angry. But in reality He was angry at Himself. The snake had to be, in some way or other, His ally, since it knew what lay behind the prohibition. But when it betrayed God, He sent Adam and Eve out of the garden into exile! Punishment! And the snake, too! Conclusion: good and evil come from the same place!"

"Where did you learn all of that? From your father?"

"We have our verbal fights. Also Gaj. My mother doesn't hold back either. But that's just one way of looking at it. A construction. A little modern Jewish way of understanding the world. The beginning of the end of paradise, man's story of exile. And on its slimy stomach, the snake crept into the story with the tips of its tongue hanging out of its mouth, dripping with poison!" he stuck his tongue out so that it almost reached his chin.

"Your tongue is all black!"

"I wouldn't mind another Pirate Coin, by the way."

I found the bag, took two, put one in his mouth and took the other one for myself.

"Pirate Coins!" I said.

He snatched at my fingers.

"No! One Pirate Coin. Two Pirate Coins!" He took my hand, swinging it back and forth. I allowed myself to be led.

Barely paid attention to where I put my feet as I withdrew into myself and saw Boj climb the steps that went all the way to heaven. I had dreamed the stairway dream again. I was still on the ground. And when I saw him move further and further away from me it felt as though I myself was starting to disappear!

Boj broke the silence:

"Do you know what I think? I think you're more Jewish than you yourself think. Miranda says so, too."

"What have you two been talking about?" It sounded sharper than I had intended.

"Nothing special! Hey!" Boj pointed up in the air. "Look! A squirrel!"

I turned my head in the direction of his hand and saw a red-brown tail disappear in a treetop.

*

We took the boat to Helsingborg the day he had off from work. To do something else together besides going to the plantation. My mother gave me permission. Just like with everything else during the vacation. When it came to going out with Boj! When we were about to leave she folded a few bills and put them in my hand, then closed my hand with hers.

"Buy some fancy underwear for yourself," she whispered.

I bought underwear at EPA. Afterward we walked along the city streets, had a sausage with mashed potatoes. We sat down on a bench at the square. I couldn't finish the whole thing. So he also finished mine.

"I didn't think you ate that sort of thing."

"I'm only kosher at home. When I go out I eat everything."

"Is that just you?"

"Yes. And Gaj a little, too. My folks would be pissed if they knew"

"Why do you do it, then?"

"We all have to find our own way. I might stop doing it at some point, *who knows*?"

We took the boat back. Stood close together by the rail of the stern and looked across the water. Followed the foamy eddies of the wake with our eyes.

"My parents got to Stockholm back then."

"Are you always thinking about it?"

I turned around and said, "Let's go to the front of the ship!"

"OK." He put his arm around my shoulder.

In front of us lay the towers of Kronborg enveloped in a haze of heat. On the sides the sky and sea merged into one silent, silent blue.

We followed the crowd of passengers and went ashore. Took the regional train back.

When we stepped onto the platform at the beach town the sun was still high in the sky.

We turned off the road and walked among the trees. I asked, "What are you going to do after high school?"

"Travel. Go to the US. Maybe Israel for a year."

"What's it like in Israel?"

"If I were to describe it in a single word it would be: *electricity*. The same impatient electricity reigns everywhere, an omnipresent vibration which gives you a sense of an intensity of life which I haven't experienced anywhere else. On the other hand, there is no other country in the world whose neighbors on all sides threaten to throw the entire population into the sea: a sense of life spiced up with the fear of being annihilated. If you are able to stand it, then..." he spread out his arms, "But when they hung Eichmann there was one idiot less in the world."

"I want to go to Israel, too."

Boj didn't answer.

The light lay like a deafening veil in the air among the trees. In the meantime it had grown cloudy, at least the glints of sun on the forest floor had disappeared. When I said that my legs needed a rest he took off his jacket. Spread it on the forest floor.

We sat close together, our backs against a pine trunk, took turns drinking soda which he had bought on the boat. I put the EPA bag aside. The white light of the sea could be seen between the trees.

"Aren't you going to try this on?" He took the EPA bag, put his hand in it and pulled out a bra. Pulled up my shirt.

"Someone could come!"

"They won't see anything other than what God has created!"

"But I don't want to! Not here!"

"Why do you always have to be so boring? Come on!"

"No!" I pushed his hand away.

Then he jumped up and ran toward the sea. A feeling of unreality gripped me. I got to my feet and picked up Boj's jacket. Followed him with dragging feet. Stepped out from the canopy of trees and squinted when my eyes encountered the light. Walked the last few meters toward him. He stood on the narrow part of the beach close to the water's edge.

"Here!" I said, "your jacket." I let it go and it fell to his feet.

"Mmm" he grunted barely audibly without turning his head.

There was thunder in the air now, not a breeze. There wasn't a single ripple on the glossy surface of the sea. There was an invisible wall of silence in the air between us. He bent down, picked up a skipping stone and threw it into the water, looked at it wistfully.

I squatted, took a few stones and rolled them between my hands. Straightened my legs, let my arms hang loose at my sides. A sadness like the cover of the low hanging thunder clouds settled around my forehead.

He bent down again, found a yellow skipping stone, threw

it outward and got it to skip, four, five, six, seven times. I felt I was the one he had thrown into the water. That it was my head that had gone under water all seven times. That it was me that now was lying way out there, sunken to the bottom of the sea below the rings that spread in soft circles. They grew bigger and bigger. Until they disappeared and merged with the mirror of the water's surface. Soon the summer would be over.

All at once the sound of screeching seagulls penetrated the air. I turned my head towards the sound. A flock of seagulls circled above the water, took a dive and flew back up. Toward the beach. Then outwards again. The enormous power in their wings. The screeches became longer and longer, as though they were being pulled out across the sea, remained lingering in the air!

At that very moment I felt Boj grab my arms, shake me.

"What's happening? We'll continue seeing each other! You're coming to our meetings. We also have to develop the pictures I took of you! Come on!

I shook my head, nodded, and couldn't stop at all. Had to sprint along the beach. Back again.

He caught me in his arms, turned us. Round and round!

*

I ran down the staircase, two steps at a time. And like every evening during this summer vacation, my heart throbbed all the way to my throat. At the bottom of the staircase in the semi-dark hall I remained standing and tried to get my breathing back to normal. I put my hand on the door handle to the back door and took a deep breath. Sucked the air all the way down. Let it go again from my stomach. I did that twice. But it didn't help. I pressed the door handle down and pushed open the door.

Sunlight fell on the birch trees and made the foliage shine like gold. There, below the low-hanging branches, stood Boj smoking. He held the unfiltered Camel cigarette between his two fingers and took a last whiff. Threw the stub into the grass and looked up. He caught sight of me and smiled.

My feet barely hit the ground when I skipped over to him. And glided into his outstretched arms and heard a small snap.

"You're *electric*!" Boj said as he held me out before him. "But you should always wear white!"

As always before sunset the street was full of people. We walked against the crowd down toward the beach. Left the road and climbed up a concrete ramp that led to the beach area. A little further in the distance the ramp made a sharp right toward the beach restaurant. We stopped there and took off our sandals. In our bare feet we jumped down from the ramp and sank into the soft, warm sand that reached our ankles.

Neither one of us said anything as we moved along the top of the dune. The glances we gave one another said all that was necessary. We were here now. Boj put his hand around my shoulder and I leaned my head against his armpit. Inhaled the smell of his body that filled me with a dizzyingly great feeling. Almost everything about Boj had that effect on me. And to that which didn't I closed my eyes. Soon the vacation would be over. I pushed the thought aside.

I heard voices shouting and looked down on the beach across from the beach hotel. With a touch of unpleasantness, I thought back on it.

One night we had gone in there. When we met, Boj had seemed restless, barely looked at me. I followed him into the dimly lit restaurant where an orchestra was playing. There were many people but we found a free table. I sat down. He said he would get us something to drink and left. A waiter came with a coca cola and poured it into my glass. Boj didn't come back. I sipped the cola and began getting restless. Looked around the room. My stomach turned to ice. He was on the dance floor with Katrinn.

I shook off the sense of unpleasantness. Below at the hotel a group of evening bathers were on their way into the water. They were holding one another's hands, ran out and hurled themselves in the waves. We continued walking further and soon all that could be heard was the sound of our breathing and the breaking waves against the beach. The sun hung low in the sky and enveloped the entire beach in a dream-like glow of fire.

All at once Boj let go of my hand and began walking toward the sand dune.

"Where are you going?" I called to his back.

He didn't answer but walked about searchingly in the thicket on the backside of the dunes. A good distance ahead he turned and made a gesture with his arm.

I started walking down the slope but had to keep an eye on where I placed my feet. There was no path here and no matter where I stepped it prickled my feet. When I looked up again he was gone. I turned my head from one side to the other but all I could see were dense clusters of rosehip bushes. They spread all the way to the beach lot where the trees shaded the houses. I continued anyway.

I stopped at the place where I thought he had been standing

when he signaled for me to come and again I looked across the dune landscape. I sniffed the air. The scent of rosehip tickled my nose. But there was no sign of Boj. For a moment everything stood still in my mind. And a feeling of loss and of having been abandoned made the muscles in my stomach contract. He was gone. I would never see him again. I was close to turning around and going back when I saw a hand protruding from a thicket and walked over there.

He was kneeling in a sand-filled hollow surrounded by rosehip bushes. I stepped across the bushes. Fell down on my knees across from him and threw my sandals in the sand. With his knees in the sand he moved closer. A tickling sensation ran though my body, a tingling sensation that made the tiny hairs on my skin rise. The light evening sky arched above us. There wasn't a cloud as far as the eye could see. The air hugged my body with the remains of the heat of the day. On the sides the hollow was shielded by the thicket-like brushwood of the fragrant rosehips. And if that which I saw in his eyes shining toward me and reflected in every grain of sand and which made every cell in my body dance wasn't love, what was it then?

It practically threw off sparks when our hands met. Clutched and intertwined. He pulled me to him and pushed me down onto the lair of the beach. A butterfly fluttered past us and landed in the rosehip close to my hair. I turned my head toward its white wings and at that very moment felt his lips on my neck. His mouth glided further up across my cheek, closed around mine. His skin tasted of salt, of trickling drops from sun sweat, of all the berries and fruits of the summer. The button on my jeans was opened. His hands and mouth.

The sea. I felt warm waves rise in my body. Rise and rise. I closed my eyes and let the waves lead me, suck me toward them.

Slowly I returned, tried to move. One of my legs was asleep. Boj still lay heavily on top of me. Had he fallen asleep?

When I said his name, he didn't answer at first. The third time I said it he lifted his head and gave me a tired smile. Slowly sat up. Got on his feet and stood swaying for a moment.

"Come on, let's go for a swim," he said.

"Is there anything wrong? You sound strange, almost as though you're drunk."

"I have a headache, I probably just need to cool off a little."

My hands trembled slightly as I collected all our clothes. Had to go back to get our sandals and ran after Boj who had gone ahead of me. I caught up with him at the beach and took his hand.

We stood in water that reached above our knees when Boj's hand slid out of mine and he hurled himself into a wave.

But when he remained lying where he had fallen I turned him around and lifted his face from the water. He looked practically surprised and when I said his name he didn't answer. Just remained lying there, his head resting in my arms.

I refused to believe anything other than that he was testing me, and so I continued talking to him.

"Come on, this isn't funny anymore!"

When he still didn't respond, I grabbed him under the arms from behind and started pulling him ashore. My knees were shaking as I alternately pulled and pushed his lifeless body free of the tongues of waves that licked across the beach.

Then I got on my knees and forced myself to give him mouth to mouth resuscitation, closed my mouth about his cold nose and exhaled. Waited. Did it again. And again.

After a while I realized that it was of no use. He wasn't breathing, his heart wasn't beating. He lay lifeless and motionless at the water's edge with the same almost surprised look on his face. At first, I died. But then something happened which I never thought possible for me: I was gripped by a great and deep sense of calmness.

I quickly got dressed and spread some clothes across his naked body.

That was where he lay when the ambulance crew came to get him.

Gaj was the one who told me about Boj's aneurysm. Said there wasn't anything I could have done better than what I did. No one could have prevented it from happening. No one had known it would happen. A brief hug.

I closed the door to the room and heard Gaj's footsteps as he went down the stairs.

The local doctor that Mother took me to see explained that an aneurysm was a small bulge in a blood vessel that could burst. That was all there was to it.

He said I had had a shock and wrote out a prescription for some sedatives.

I had just finished a long letter to Nora. I told her everything. From my first meeting with Boj to the night *it* happened.

How I mechanically ran for help up in one of the houses. Rang the ambulance and the police.

Went back and sat quietly next to Boj's covered body and waited. A white moon came into view in the sky and cast an umbilical cord of light across the water, white and flickering.

It ran through my mind again and again: I didn't know him at all. He had once filled my body with his hunger. Still I didn't know who he was behind all his ... big words. Behind his ... pioneer project ... as he called it, which he said was just the beginning.

"We never got done finishing the beginning," I said to the motionless figure that was covered up.

After I had told the two police officers what I could tell they drove me home.

It wasn't until I saw Mother that I broke down sobbing.

Putting it all into words had been a relief to me. It was like having to reinvent the words. Or as though the words that were so familiar had been given a new meaning. Words like "really" and "death." The word "shock." Mother did everything she could to comfort me. But what could comfort someone who wasn't done grasping what had just happened?

I said I wanted to go home. But she wanted us to stay those last few days in the countryside since we had paid for them anyway. Father was to join us that weekend and going home wasn't going to make me feel any better, she said. And, for God's sake, I had to remember to take my pills!

It was Saturday, the last weekend of the vacation. From the window above I saw the Captain pull into the courtyard and went down to greet Father. He stepped out of the car, got a very serious look on his face as he studied me. Then he nodded and placed his hand on my shoulder, but didn't say anything

It was raining so we weren't going to be going down to the pier. Mother had talked me into going over to aunt Pavla, uncle Jafet and Winnie in the fisherman's cottage they had rented.

"It's not good for you to be alone!" she said.

In silence we walked together side by side through the semi-deserted streets in the dark smell of soil dampened by the summer rain. When we had passed the harbor we turned away from the big road and entered the fishermen's neighborhood.

We stepped into a yard in which red and yellow roses meandered along the fence. The scent from a fragrant jasmine bush went right to my stomach.

Uncle Jafet came to meet us, briefly greeted my mother and father and then went over to me. Put his arm around my shoulder and led me into the house.

"My poor little friend!" he said over and over.

Winnie came over and gave me a hug.

"How are you getting along?" she asked.

I told it like it was, that I no longer felt I had any reason to get up in the mornings.

"Listen to her!" Winnie said in the living room as she

turned her palms to the ceiling, "only fourteen and a half and she says she has nothing to wake up to!"

"She hasn't eaten anything for three days! Nothing!" Mother said in a voice that was a mix of both concern and pride, "and she talks to herself at night," she lowered her voice, "about fate and God and who knows what. I'm at a loss as to what to do with her. But she's been prescribed medication and then there is not much more one can do."

The aunts came over, showering her with consolation and sympathy. Then they took turns kissing me on both cheeks and felt my waist.

"Skin and bones, *Gott in...* "Aunt Katja sighed and grew silent.

Aunt Manja and Aunt Pavla nodded, exchanging telling glances.

I sat poking at a chicken wing and when Anna and Albert were given permission to leave the table I got up, too. When I walked past Uncle Kam, he reached out for me, "Come and sit down on your uncle's knee, you're not too old for that!" he said in his greasy uncle-voice as he clicked his tongue.

I wriggled myself free of his grip and sat down on the floor in the opposite end of the living room where there was a rag rug of indefinable colors. A little while later Anna came and placed a book on my lap. Asked if I would read to her.

I nodded.

She looked at me with large, expressive eyes and said, "You're the one who has a dead boyfriend, right?"

Again, I nodded.

"Oh my God," she said and put her little warm hand on top of mine, "but aren't you going to get a new boyfriend, then?"

The uncles guffawed. Winnie and the aunts in turns let out a series of shrill shrieks of laughter.

Little Albert ran back and forth getting toys that he wanted to show me. "Bus, bus," he said, lisping in American and placing a little yellow double-decker on top of the open book.

Aunt Pavla called to me, "Come here and have a cup of coffee!"

"Oh my God, Grandma!" Anna said, "Can't you see she's reading to me?"

"She's fan-tastic!"

"*Gott in himel!*" And everyone around the table laughed again.

I lifted my gaze from the book and looked over there.

Aunt Manja sat restlessly on her chair, tapping her feet in the high-heeled wooden sandals she always wore in the summer. Followed uncle Kam with her eyes who, together with my father and the other uncles, had gotten up. The Ronson lighters were pulled from the pockets of their jackets and, enveloped in a cloud of cigar smoke, they went into the next room to play cards.

Aunt Pavla removed the dishes and returned carrying a thermos jug. Praised aunt Manja's new white dress, it matched her bronze colored tan smashingly well. The coffee was passed around.

"Yes, you can say a lot about Kam, but one thing he's always been is generous," aunt Manja said as she nodded, making her heavy earrings dance about her cheeks as her ear lobes grew longer and longer.

I had looked into her wardrobe once. I almost lost my breath at the sight of all her dresses, light, dark, flowery, shiny. And I remembered the sight of Mother standing in front of Father, the diamond ring sparkling on her outstretched beggar's hand as she asked him for money. Money that the men earned. Money that made beggars out of women. Beggars that were dependent on their husbands. And if you were dependent, you were at their mercy.

Aunt Katja extended her arm to take the thermos jug. Her purple shirt slid up, revealing some bare skin above the waistband of her skirt. The image became another: I once lay on their couch in their living room and watched her walk around in her long nightgown that fluttered about her legs all the way down to her polished toenails. With a shudder, I faintly saw through the thin white material of her nightgown something dark where her thighs ended. Uncle Sem called out whether she expected him to wait for her all night. She came over to me anyway and sat down next to me and caressed my cheek. I fell asleep in her fragrance.

Now aunt Katja was pouring coffee into her cup. Then she took a sugar cube, dipped it in the coffee and started sucking on it. Looked at aunt Manja who was busy putting a cigarette into her cigarette holder saying between mouthfuls of sugar. "But I think you can still be satisfied when they come back home at night. What you don't know won't hurt you!"

"No, really..." Winnie began, but Mother interrupted her:

"Now, sweet Winnie, what you don't know won't hurt you!"

"Yes, it will!"

"No, it won't!"

"Yes!"

I turned my head and looked at Anna. The concentration that was in her gaze revealed that she, despite her four years, was attentively following the grown-ups' conversation as their words became imprinted in her mind.

"Do you know what?" she lowered her voice in confidence, "I think you can borrow one of my mother's boyfriends, she has many and they don't even know that she has me and Albert. She says that I'll get a boyfriend too someday. But you can only choose Jews, they've been circumcised, or you might get cancer!"

I looked at her and wished only for one thing: to be four years old again.

*

I lifted the latches off, pushed open the window and leaned out. It was no longer summer, not even late summer. The leaves of the apple tree had started to turn yellow, there was a rawness in the air. I shuddered slightly and shut the window.

I pulled myself together and painted my room again. Blue walls. Cliff Richard was thrown in the garbage. The guitar placed in the corner. I hadn't told anyone at school about Boj, not even Agnete or Marianne. During classes I sensed Jens Peter's glances. I looked past him. Then he started going out with Laila. Well!

I applied myself assiduously at school. Struggled with math. Read till late in the night. High school lay before me, a twinkling sea of longing for nourishment that could fill up the empty space after Boj. Father's appreciative nod when he came in to wake me in the mornings.

One late afternoon someone knocked on my door. I was busy pulling down the shades which were giving me a hard time and had become crooked. Before I had a chance to answer, Helle stepped inside. She smiled. A serious small smile. She just wanted to say something, she said, as she sat down at the edge of my bed.

"Your shirt looks nice, is it new?" I asked.

"Oh, that," she said, looking right through me.

Tears filled my eyes. The four words she said: "Remember, life goes on."

I decided that now was the time and told her about Nora's and my plan.

Helle made a defensive gesture with her arms.

"You can't ask me to do that!" she said.

"But that's what I'm doing!" I said, putting my hands on my hips.

"But, I'm leaving!" she said.

"Not until afterward!" I said, "Think about it, please?"

She promised she would.

Once again, I pulled myself together and said yes when Miranda asked me if I wanted to come to her place and see her new cat.

"I'm happy you came!" was the first thing she said as she took my coat. I nodded and followed her into her room.

"Do you notice them?" Miranda had turned around, staring at me with her wide open kohl eyes.

"Who?" I shook my head.

"The contacts! Can't you see I'm wearing contact lenses?" she nudged me with her elbow. "You seem totally depressed!"

"It's..." I started and then got stuck.

She placed her hand on my arm.

"It's such a pity for you!" she said, "I remember he was

always running after you in first grade. But he was a little bit of a nerd. Like the other ones in that student club gang. Holocaust on the brain."

She tapped her temple with her finger.

"I think they're onto something. I always thought I was the only one ... I mean there weren't any others ..." Again, I got stuck. Together with Boj my thoughts had had wings. Now they crumpled up.

She didn't answer but pulled the knitted sweater that reached her bottom down a little. Straightened her leather belt resting on her hips. I waited for a moment, maybe she wanted to say something. But she didn't. so, I asked, "Were you one of the people Boj interviewed for his project?"

"I'm not interested in all that Jewish navel-gazing, I'd rather go to Israel, then. That's what I told him. I only want to look toward the future. And you should, too!"

"But..." I started but didn't get further. My skull was like a garbage bin filled with crumpled thoughts.

"Think of his parents, of Gaj! They have lost something irreplaceable, a son, a brother. You can just go out and get another boyfriend." She gave me a nudge so that I lost my balance and fell onto the couch. Then she turned around and put the Beatles on the record player. Said that I could snuggle with Randy, which was the name of the cat, while she got us some tea.

I pulled off my boots and leaned back against the wall. Randy sprang up to me and curled up against my thigh. I warmed my hand in her soft speckled fur. Looked around. Miranda's walls were plastered all over with Beatles posters.

A little while later she returned with a tray of tea and bread. She placed it on the edge of her writing desk. Settled down in a sack chair and poured the tea. Handed me a mug.

"You must taste my mother's rosehip marmalade, I'm telling you, it's super!" she said, then she blinked quickly a few times right after the other. Got down on all fours and started sweeping the floor with her hand across the floor boards.

"What is it?" I asked.

"My contact lens! I've lost one of my contacts! Go away!" She gave Randy who had jumped down from the couch a shove which made her skid on her nails across the floor.

"Yeah!" Miranda sat up and put the lens in her mouth. Turned it a few times. Then she took it out and placed it on the tip of her index finger. Held her finger away from her body.

I leaned forward. "I thought they were bigger."

Then she leaned over a small mirror. Opened her eye wide open and put the lens in. Blinked.

"Doesn't it hurt?"

"Not anymore. It's just so damn irritating when they fall out."

As we smeared butter and marmalade on the bread she said I should go with her to a party.

"Are they all from your school?"

"Who?"

"Who do you think? The ones at the party."

"We'll find another little Jewish boy for you!"

"Mira..."

"No one there bites. Come on, say yes!"

We met as agreed in front of number 20 in a quiet street in Østerbro. Miranda pressed the button on the paging system and made eyes at me.

"Be careful of your contacts!"

Then came the sound of the dial tone and we went into the hall. When we reached the right floor Miranda, in a way that seemed very familiar to her, tried the door that stood ajar and was the first to step across the threshold to what proved to be a very big apartment. I followed her into a hall which was at least 100 meters long. We hung our coats on top of the others that were hanging in several layers on the coat rack on the brown-colored walls.

"See, they have two floors," she pointed at a spiral staircase at the end of an entrance hall.

"I took my friend with me, she needs a little cheering up," she said to a short-legged guy who had come over to us, and adding in a whisper loud enough for me to hear it, "Boj's last flame." Then she threw her arms around him.

"Mira!"

He let her go and took my hand. Kissed the back of it. He had a dimple on his chin.

"Then you've come to the right place!" he said, turned around and started walking. We followed him.

The party was in full swing in the other rooms. No one noticed us. After a little while Miranda disappeared. I let my hand glide across the red dress I had gotten from Winnie and looked at the group of dancing couples. Most of the girls were wearing black. Or was the lighting dim?

I stood in the corner of a room that was the size of a ballroom and smoked. Looked for something to use as an ashtray when he came over and held out a saucer. It was the short-legged guy with the dimple on his chin.

"Thanks!" I said and crushed the stub.

He put his arm around me and pulled me to him. His breath was sweet. He didn't say anything as we danced. So I didn't either. He scratched me lightly on the back with his two fingers and then let his hands glide up front. Beatles. Rolling Stones. Herman's Hermits. Millie. I was taller than him, I didn't care. When he led me up the spiral staircase I didn't resist.

Up in his room I kept my dress on. Afterward he said that I was cute. I said that I wasn't interested in anything steady, I was starting high school. He preferred making a buck, he said.

Then he kissed me and walked with me down back to the living room. Said that we could take one more dance. I didn't care.

Someone had thrown up in the bathtub. I held my nose and peed. Went back out in a hurry. In the ballroom I sank into an arm chair. Watched the dancing couples in the dark as they merged with the furniture.

Then the midnight snack was served. Miranda and I shared a taxi.

The next morning, I had what felt like shards in my throat. Throughout the day I felt Mother's gaze on me, searching and suffocating. I had to keep myself from throwing something heavy at her!

Helle got back to me. She had thought about it and could see that I had a point. As Nora had said, she was probably the only one who could talk my mother into it. But I could hear by the sound of her voice that it was no longer just for my sake that she was willing to go along with the plan.

Nora would take care of the rest. She even considered going to my father in the shop and taking the bull by its horns, as she said. The only thing left to do was to wait.

*

Ever since the summer vacation the thought of it had been scratching against the inside of my skull. During the first weeks of September I was 100% convinced. I went into the living room. Mother was sitting on the couch and crocheting. Then I said it, "I intend to fast for Yom Kippur!"

She winced! The crochet hook flew from her fingers and fell down on the ground with a long jingling sound.

"You're not turning *religious*, are you?" she said, making it sound like an invective.

She got down on her knees, stuck her arm under the couch and looked up at me with every indication of discomfort.

"I'm just trying to find my own way!"

She found the crochet hook and took it in her hand. Got on her feet and stood for a moment, turning her head back and forth between me and the empty space next to me. Then she sent a series of nods in the direction of Father's shop.

I was convinced that at that very moment he would be overtaken by a sudden emerging passion. It would make him rush over and tear open the door to the shop and stand in the doorway in his bare sleeves.

That same night she said to Father that it was the silliest thing she had ever heard, that I, who had become so thin that my ribs stuck through my clothes, was going to start fasting.

"Do something!" her voice was shrill.

But he didn't say a word!

I had also armored myself. The artillery lay ready. While other Jews in the world were fasting for Yom Kippur! You had to do something yourself!

I sat all day on the bench furthest back in the women's gallery of the synagogue and tried to repent. That was what you were supposed to do. To start with I was proud of myself, Helle had never done it. But the hunger in my stomach started to gnaw at me and I got a headache from the poor air quality in the women's section which was right under the roof. You may have been physically closer to God up there but you were a considerable distance from the men's ritual gesticulations on the floor. The whole day through I showed my solidarity and thought only of the suffering of the Jews.

Well, maybe not only. I don't want to make myself sound better than I was. As I repented for having lied when I said I had gone over to Marianne's, my thoughts revolved around food. I repented for the scrumping with Agnete, the yellow sweater. For biting into a crispy, juicy apple. I repented for the broken telephone socket and felt the waters in my mouth rise at the thought of crunching a doubly forbidden bacon rind. The straps of a towel, to sink my teeth into a student pastry. Cigarettes I had stolen from the cigarette holder, a miserable piece of matzoh. *That thing,* yes that too I repented. Everything that possibly came to my mind of sins I had committed or thought about committing, anything

But I wanted to be willful, show solidarity. I didn't stoop so low as to checking whether I had a leftover piece of candy in my purse. I did everything to commemorate the struggles of the Jews while, in my imagination, seeing manna fall from the sky. I tried to identify with the pain and suffering that the Jews had endured. Persecution. Escape, Horror. All the ones who just thought they were going for a shower! Forced my thoughts to focus on the ones who were starving, who were surrounding me, the women who wore hats who, with their prayer books open, followed what was going on way down below in the building.

Miranda wasn't there. But while the lamenting tones of the cantos went straight to my stomach, I recognized some of the other girls I had been baz mitzvahed with. I gazed down and didn't want to be recognized. I incorporated that into my repenting as well, being the miserable and sinful person that I was. Within me there were no other greater feelings than hunger. And could you call hunger a feeling?

Although the woman sitting next to me kindly handed me her prayer book several times and pointed to the place we had reached I shook my head. Tried to bring forth a smile. Silently I let myself sink inward, to the very bottom of myself where hunger must have fallen asleep by then.

The women around me closed their prayer books. Got up and greeted one another in Hebrew. The service was over and I got up, too. I was a little dizzy when I went to the cloakroom to get my coat. Walked with the women wearing hats down the stairs. It felt as though I had been in the distant past and was now on my way back to the present.

On the bottom floor I stepped into the gateway where men and women are allowed to be close to one another. The couples who had been separated found one another and we greeted one another with heartfelt but faded expressions.

When I walked toward the exit someone poked my shoulder.

I turned around and looked into Danny's eyes. Or rather up into, he was tall and had a stoop and was wearing a brown woolen coat.

"Here," he said, smiling as he handed me an apple. "I always have a few in my pocket for the way home. Oddly enough, when you can manage to fast for a full day, if you ask me. But the trip back home is unbearable without having something to put in your mouth."

I thanked him. We followed the stream of people wearing yarmulkes and hats through the wrought-iron gate and walked along the sidewalk toward Daells Varehus. I took a bite. The apple was crisp and crunchy.

Danny also took a bite of his apple. Chewed and smiled again. Then he said he was happy to see me there and asked me what I had thought of it.

"I didn't think that you liked me?"

"I didn't think so either. To be frank, I thought of you as a silly goose. But you'll get a second chance. Meet me on Saturday, should we say Nørreport station, at the corner of Nørregade Street, at 8 pm?

When I got home the table was set for dinner consisting of soup and chicken. Of all of us, only I and Grandma, my father's mother, had fasted. Grandpa had never done it, not in Russia either. He wasn't born for suffering or want he said in broken Danish and laughed so that his eyes disappeared in a net of wrinkles. But he was grateful to the ones who took it upon themselves to fast. They ensured that there was a little bit of balance in the world.

He had never spoken like that before.

"*Herein, herojs*! The one who sins is full and content!" he added with a glow of laughter in his voice as he rubbed his big hands together.

Father repressed a laugh.

"My father is a billy goat," my mother said on the phone. But she didn't meddle in that! As long as there were the right number of silver spoons in the drawer.

At the same moment that the steaming and pleasantly smelling plate was set on the table I devoured the soup. Out of the corner of my eye I saw Mother who, with a spoon in her hand, and a mix of disapproval and pride in her gaze watched my somewhat miraculous appetite emerge.

Father glanced at me in a way that could have meant many things. And from Helle's eyes there streamed something that could have been interpreted as admiration. No one said anything and after a while all that could be heard were the spoons that clattered against the porcelain.

Then Grandma asked in a somewhat prosecutorial tone: "Didn't you drink a little *beet* of water when you brushed your teeth, just a teeny tiny drop?"

I stopped shoveling soup into my mouth. Mother used to say on the telephone that Father's mother always looked so well-groomed, but...! And without being able to decipher what lay in that "but" I now looked over at the old woman, who, well-coiffed and with a white shawl over her blue flowery dress had put her spoon aside as she waited for my answer. I forced myself to smile when I in all honesty said that I had not!

"Then you're more *from* than I am!" the white haired lady said with an emphasis on "I."

I didn't answer.

I had been close to canceling. Went down to Helle and told her about Danny. Remembered what Boj had said, that Danny's manner was like a silver paper wrapping around a piece of soft nougat.

When I got off the trolley he was already waiting there wearing his brown coat that reached below his ankles. In the wind and rain we trotted through the city streets. There wasn't much soft nougat in that. It was mostly Danny who spoke. Just as Boj had said, he was studying for his degree in journalism.

"Pipe cleaner!" someone shouted at him as we crossed the pedestrian street, Strøget. He just kept talking.

We walked into the Tokanten café and found a free table. He asked me what I wanted to drink and I said a Coca-Cola.

It was still mostly him who did the talking. Meanwhile he sat and looked at me with a glow in his eyes and puffed at his pipe. The loss of Boj had by no means meant that he or others had lost their spark. Meanwhile Gaj had entered the project and more or less taken over Boj's role. One day the world would discover that the Holocaust had left its marks, The marks were passed on from generation to generation. Even though there was a difference between whether the parents had been in Theresienstadt or Sweden their lives had been threatened. And how they lived their lives afterward was important. He pointed at me with his pipe and said, "I'll give you this much: that those of you who have grown up in a family that has suppressed or repressed what happened have holes in your family history. (with his hands he formed a parenthesis around the word 'family') and are worse off than those of us who had it stuffed down our throats day and night."

A waiter placed our beverages on the table. Poured. When he left, Danny continued where he had left off.

"When the Holocaust experience (again, he formed a parenthesis around the word 'Holocaust') has been out of one's reach, then you have neither an awareness nor a language that you can use. Then you have become cut off from your Jewish roots and the problem becomes invisible. A sense of social security cannot replace the existential insecurity that is the result of the double identity (yet still another parenthesis around the word 'double') that has not been anchored. It corresponds to getting a nip here and a tuck there, to lacking all the lower steps of the ladder of realization."

I almost choked on my cola and coughed.

He gave me an ingratiating smile. I had clearly nodded in the right places and hoped that he at least would learn to write in a way so that it could be understood. More so than Boj, Danny spoke like a book or rather like a foreign alphabet. Yet still his words resounded in me. Double identity? No, neither one nor the other.

He puffed at his pipe a couple of times.

"As I see it, the goal itself with the project must be Judaism." he said. "Judaism has existed for over four thousand years. The Holocaust should not be allowed to upset the apple cart of a positive Jewish identity." Puff....puff. "An identity, mind you, that is both historically aware and thinks in terms of the future."

His words to me at the synagogue came back to me, he had perceived me as a goose! As a Jew I felt like a newly hatched duckling: ugly.

We went back to Nørreport Station. His ego was as big as the Round Tower in Copenhagen, I thought, when we passed the brick wall damp from rain. But when we said good-bye we agreed that I should visit him at his place. Then he would interview me for the project. He was convinced that a day would come when there would be a demand for exactly this form of perception. In reality it wasn't just about us, but about all families that had been through traumatic experiences, as for example, children of resistance fighters or children of Nazis. There could be others. Who knows what the future might produce of that sort! And he had nothing against leading the way!

Luckily, he didn't try anything.

*

It was the day before Nora's and my plan was to take place. As Helle had suggested, I went to Nora's and slept over at her place. As we ate dinner we talked the whole thing through. There was nothing more we could do now, she said. And when we had eaten dessert, Mikkel had to be put to bed. Meanwhile I could watch TV or read. At any rate, she was tired here at the end of the week and wanted to go to bed early so that she would be rested for the next day where our plan would be put to its final test.

"It can only go one way," she said, turning her thumb upward.

"Do you think so? But what if...?"

Nora broke in, "We could also just call the whole thing off, just to be on the safe side," she said teasingly

"Give up in advance? Over my dead body!"

"I wouldn't have expected that of you, either," Nora said, banging her fist on the table

The pancakes were her idea. That way I had something to do that would take my mind off of things a little. I held the frying pan in front of me and flipped the last pancake in the air. It splashed over the edge and a little burnt crumbling fell on the white enamel between the burner and the grate.

Nora laughed and turned off the gas, and I placed the pancake on top of the stack on the plate. Then I put the pan in the sink and turned on the warm water. It sizzled and sputtered and the steam made my glasses mist up.

Again, we sat down at the folding table in her kitchen that faced the courtyard. Mikkel, who had dark eyes and curly hair, sat on his knees in his chair, beating his fork on the tabletop.

"Mikkel have, too!"

"Yes, yes, you'll get some. Look, it's on its way!" Nora said as she cut a pancake into small squares, placed the plate in front of Mikkel who immediately threw his fork on the floor and started stuffing his mouth using both hands.

Nora bent down and picked up the fork. Handed it to him.

"Here, you can use the fork yourself."

He knocked the fork out of her hand.

"More, more!" he shouted.

"I don't have the energy to get angry now," Nora put another piece into his mouth. Then she lifted him from the chair and placed him down on the floor. He started screaming, but went over and opened one of the cabinets anyway. Sat down on the floor in front of the cabinet and started pulling things out. Turned around and looked at his mother.

She nodded.

"Yes, you can play with whatever is in that cabinet."

"From whom does Mikkel have his brown eyes?" I asked, trying to sound as casual as possible.

"Oh no, not today, I'm too tired for that!" Nora stretched her arms above her head and yawned.

I poked my fork into a pancake. Placed it on the plate and topped it with sugar and marmalade. Took a bite and saw Boj before me ... he had made Danish apple cakes. Wearing a striped chef's apron, he had moved about in the kitchen in their summerhouse as though he had been doing nothing else his whole life. He had cracked the eggs in a glass one at a time before pouring it into the dough. One egg was thrown in the garbage can.

"Why did you throw that one out?" I had asked.

"The egg was fertilized. That means there's blood in it and we're not allowed to eat that!"

Two thousand years of collective Jewish history was connected to that act. His identity would crack if he didn't do it, he had said.

I told Nora about it as we ate while Mikkel went back and forth, playing. I also told her about Danny and that whole project. That Gaj had joined it.

"What does his little brother look like, then?"

"He has black hair. Brown eyes. But Gaj is a little taller than Boj ... was."

Nora leaned back and stretched again: "Do you realize that you're smiling from to ear to ear when you talk about Gaj?"

"No, I'm not!"

"Oh yes you are!"

The next day we got off the train at around 2 pm. I wrapped my scarf a few times around my neck. The strong wind blew through our hair. Nora lifted her nose in the air and sniffed, "The air is good in these northern regions. You can almost smell the whiskey."

"Aren't you cold?" I asked.

She shook her head. Leaned forward and tilted the back rest of the baby carriage down. Covered Mikkel, who had fallen asleep on the train. with a blanket, tucked in the edges of his blanket well below his feet. Then she took a small bottle from her purse. Unscrewed the cap and put it to her mouth.

"Ah! This gives you an inner warmth!" she held the bottle forth, "You look like you could use a sip yourself."

I shook my head. "It's just because when I don't sleep well at night, I always feel so cold the next day."

"Take it easy! See how easy I'm taking it!" she said and laughed. Took a sip from the bottle and put it back in her purse. Then she fastened a few buttons on her coat and grabbed a hold of the handle on the baby carriage.

We walked over to the other side of the station building and reached a paved parking lot. Continued along the exit that led to a bigger road.

"Come on, we have to go over there!" Nora said, pointing toward the forest on the other side of the busy street.

Shortly afterwards we were walking among the trees. I looked up and was sucked into a world of dense yellow foliage. From both sides of the forest path the branches of the trees reached in toward one another high above our heads.

"Listen to the wind rushing through the treetops. These old oak trees have a lot of stories to tell, if they could speak. It was into this forest that the Jewish refugees ran to hide. Like hunted animals."

I trembled and asked, "Right here?"

"Yes, and further into the forest."

"How do you know that?"

"I looked into the archives of the area and found some reports. They were made public shortly after the War. I thought you might want to know more. That is, what happened here around the time that your parents fled. Can I get you to push the baby carriage. I need a cigarette!"

I nodded and took the handle. Nora lit her cigarette. Blew out some smoke and said, "The air was thick with rumors. Some had claimed that they had seen the Gestapo go into a house. Others thought they had seen informers. But no one knew anything for certain. And those poor people had taken the train here. What else could they do but go into the forest? Apparently the weather was the worst you could imagine: extremely cold and pouring rain so the forest floor was a swamp. It wasn't exactly fun to be there!" she pointed at the thick tree trunks.

Again, I trembled and said, "But there's something I don't understand. Why weren't they just sailed across?"

"Because on the night of October 4th the overt transportations were stopped. Gestapo was suddenly standing down at the harbor. Some unsuspecting fishermen were on their way into the harbor after a transportation and were taken. The Gestapo also took one of the houses up on the slope. It had big panoramic windows facing the harbor. So, no one dared take any more chances sailing during daylight. But fisher families in the whole area took care of the refugees as much as they could. Helped trying to find hiding places for them, in the attic, in the cellar or in an out-of-the way barn. The local doctor also participated. The police. But that's how it also was along the coast further down south and up north. Everywhere along the east coast of Zealand."

"And my mother and father had crossed to Sweden at that point?"

Nora nodded.

"Yes, they had been seen to! But your aunt Pavla and uncle Jafet, and also your cousin Winnie, that was another story, things didn't go so smoothly for them!"

"Winnie!"

"Yes, they had been hiding in the loft of a church further north together with many other Jews. Someone had given them away. But because your aunt was Swedish they avoided having to go to Theresienstadt."

We walked for a little while in silence as I tried to get Nora's words to make sense in my mind. The words that had nothing to do with me, the words that had everything to do with me. Then I asked, "Do you think everything is predestined?"

"No, you are every bit as much in charge of making things happen. All the people who did things during the War! The community, the solidarity, the omnipresent responsibility for the Jews that the Danes felt in this country, I believe in that! And yet still there is something greater than us little humans. That great thing is also within is, if we dare to feel it!"

"Is that great thing... God? Or...? It's all so confusing, my father says there is no God. But at the baz mitzvah preparation classes we learned that..."

Nora broke in, "You know, this talk is actually getting a little too large for little me!" Again, she took the bottle and put it to her mouth. "Let's see if we can get back down to earth again."

I nodded. A little while later we stopped walking.

"Nora!"

She stopped, too. Turned around and looked at me quizzically.

"The man I saw coming out of our apartment that night I ran away from home, Is he our non-existing uncle? And is he Mikkel's father? I mean, is that why you're doing all this?"

"Well, well, it all slipped out, didn't it?" she said, "I sensed that you were mulling on that. But I'm going to tell you something. You're old enough to know now!" With a swift movement of her hand she brushed a lock of hair from her forehead. "I was once married, at the start of the War. But he was on the wrong side! Shortly after, we got divorced and he died. And I discovered that I was pregnant. It was a little girl. I gave her away!" She sniffled and said in a different tone of voice, "But I couldn't forgive myself for that ...your mother was the one who found me!"

I put my hand on her arm.

"Yes, well, I live with it now. While your mother was at the sanatorium and I was taking care of Helle..." she took a deep breath and exhaled, "not one day went by when I wasn't thinking of my own little girl. And again, when you came. And I still do. It will never go away. But shouldn't we take one thing at a time? Let's first make sure that Helle cuts the umbilical cord and gets out into...!"

"So, it's for Helle that you're doing this?"

Once again, Nora had taken the bottle out, her hands were shaking.

My cheeks grew red hot.

"I'm sorry, Nora! I'll never be able to thank you enough!"

"Don't mention it, Miss," she said dryly.

We had walked through the forest. Stood for a moment looking around. Then we crossed a parking lot and went out to Strandvejen Street. On the other side of the street a big lawn sloped toward the beach.

"Is it here?"

"No, not right here. From here the refugees were sailed out in rowboats during the night, from those jetties." She pointed. "Can you see them?"

I nodded.

"Come, we have to walk a little further, past the houses," she said, "And imagine, in almost every house they hid people until there was an opportunity for them to sail over. It was highly dangerous. But they also demanded a lot of money to sail them. 1000 DKK a person. That was a lot of money back then. And some had to pay even more than that!"

"What about the ones who didn't have money?"

"They got over anyway. That was the kind of thing that made you proud to be a Dane!"

Now we were able to see a harbor but Nora said we were to go further around the bend. We had plenty of time and Mikkel lay with his head to one side and was still far away.

I asked, "What did you yourself do during the War?"

"I did a little bit of everything. But it's nothing to speak of.

Not compared to what other people did. That's what I want to show you."

Outside of some modern hotel buildings Nora stopped and pointed, "This was once an inn. The owner of the inn was a former captain. He is known to have once said that there wasn't much difference between running an inn and sailing a ship. It was a matter of keeping a steady course and that's what he did! Even when it was too dangerous to let Jews stay at the hotel, that didn't hold him back!" Nora pointed toward a window in the main building of the hotel. "He sat in there and cheated the Gestapo. Right in there! And he wasn't the only one, it abounded with stories of people putting their lives at risk! But someone gave him away and he was sent to a concentration camp. Neuengamme. He died in 1944."

For a moment neither of us said anything. Then she looked at her watch again.

"But we'd better be heading back."

When we were again able to see the harbor, a ripple ran through my body.

"What are you shaking for?" Nora looked at me and laughed. But her laughter didn't sound like its usual self.

She took a hold of the baby stroller and we crossed the street and entered the harbor area. A mixture of seaweed and tar burned my nose. I said I had to pee.

She pointed at a red-painted wooden building.

"They must have a toilet in the clubhouse!"

"That took you awhile," Nora said, shuffling her feet.

"My stomach suddenly went haywire, sorry!"

I held on to the baby stroller and looked around. There

weren't that many people at the harbor. People looked normal, walked, chattering, or in silence as they looked at boats and did ordinary, common things.

After Nora had used the toilet we went over to look at the fishing vessels that lay in rows in the basin of the harbor.

"Well," she said after a little while, "Look who's coming there!"

I turned around and my heart skipped a beat.

The yellow Captain could be seen pulling into the parking lot on the opposite side of Strandvejen street..

Mother and Father got out. Helle, who had been driving, locked the car. Handed the keys to Father who put them in his coat pocket. Then they all three crossed the street. Came toward us.

My knees were shaking.

Once after Boj's death all four of us had had an argument. It was about Helle's trip. I sat in my room listening to how they both were trying to talk her out if it. Then Helle, completely beside herself, shouted that she should have left years ago and that no one was to prevent her from going!

I had gotten up and tore open the door of my room. Father stood in the middle of the room gesticulating his arms. Then he said in a voice cracking from emotion, "If you leave you'll kill Mother! Is that what you want?"

She sat in the sofa hiding her face in her hands.

I shouted, "This isn't normal! It's because you've never talked openly about the War!"

"Nonsense!" Mother had taken her hands away from her face. "We're not talking about that!"

Father said she should ignore me. But I didn't let anyone stop me, saying over and over, "This isn't normal! This isn't normal!"

"I don't want to hear anymore!" she whispered. Got on her feet and staggered to the bathroom. Father followed her.

Helle went with me into my room. We were both shaking so that our teeth were clattering. The words came pouring out of Helle, pent-up anger, "And if you knew how I have loathed myself because I wasn't like you...envied you because you dared to do the things I didn't dare to..."

"At least you didn't get deported!" I said.

"And now I'm deporting myself" Helle said, "I'm not staying in this...house....and NO ONE is going to prevent me from leaving! Not this time!" She was breathing heavily. "The worst of it is that I feel so cheated" she said and looked at me with big, somber eyes "I don't know what I would have done without Nora...and you of course," she added.

I met her gaze and saw a little, awkward toothless girl whom I had not seen before.

Now there was nothing showing in their faces.

Nora and I looked at each other and took a few steps toward them.

My gaze sought out my father. Wasn't there a hesitation in his movements, the way he put one leg in front of the other, as though he were considering a final way out and might turn around and leave? I held my breath. But he walked all the way over to us. Looked at Nora. Whatever he was thinking, he was hiding it well. He didn't say, who does she think she is dragging me all the way up here, Nora, a goy!

Then he looked at me. He didn't say that eggs don't teach the hen. On the contrary, he put on a guarded expression. Then he lifted his hat and pressed it down on his head again and again, and out his hand, smiling at both of us.

"Don't I know you ladies?"

I looked at Mother and my breathing grew irregular. What had I expected? I hadn't given it much thought. But there was no hesitation in her movements. With her hand she held the collar of her ocelot fur together, went directly over to the baby stroller and looked down at Mikkel. She lit up in a smile and said, "How big he's gotten, Nora! that certainly happened fast!"

I looked at Nora. She also stood looking down into the baby stroller A small, proud smile played about her lips.

Then Mother placed her hand on my head but didn't say anything. Helle didn't say anything either. She put her hands in her big coat pockets. I got them up here, now the rest is up to you, her eyes were saying.

Father stood for a moment, his shoulders drooping, looking out across the harbor basin. A muscle quivered in his chin. Then he puffed himself up. The man of the world had returned and he looked as though he was about to tell us one of his stories when he said, "Do your Excellencies know what day it is today?"

Nora looked at me. There, you see? her eyes said.

He continued: "It's the third of October. It was 21 years ago today precisely!" He swept his hand across his face and took a deep breath. Exhaled and opened his mouth to say more.

But Mother was fast.

"We took a taxi up along Strandvejen Street. At Bellevue Hotel we changed cars. There were soldiers everywhere. But they didn't bother us. We stopped over there," she turned around and pointed. "Then a man came rushing toward us, one of Grandpa's contacts, he an Grandma had gotten away a few days earlier. He said we should immediately run out on the jetty. It was here, right here, where we're standing.

I shook my head. A humongous sense of bewilderment swept through me, she sounded happy! Then she turned toward Helle:

"Father carried you in his arms. In the rush he dropped his hat and shouted for me to continue. But I ran back and got the hat." A small laughter came from her lips, "It was such a good hat."

I looked at Father whose cheeks had turned white. He put his hand up to his hat and once again pulled the brim down over his head. Mother smiling looking at us, from one to the other. For all those years, the War had been no man's land, a place nowhere, and here she was talking about it in a tone of voice as had she been telling about a Sunday family trip!"

Helle and I looked at each other. I could tell by her eyes that we were thinking the same thing, my mother!

I looked for Father's gaze but he turned his head away. I felt ill at ease, empty, abandoned.

Mother took Helle by the arm and started walking toward the jetty. The rest of us followed. Nora walked behind us with the baby stroller.

In a loud voice Mother said, "Do you remember the trolley in Stockholm? When the conductor rang the bell you thought it was the telephone and you said 'Hello, papa!' Do you remember that?" She gesticulated and turned her head from side to side as she spoke to Helle, as though she were two years old.

I caught up and was walking next to Helle. She didn't answer but her face expressed that she might crack at any moment.

At the very end of the tip of the jetty we stopped and looked down in the black gray foamy water. The waves struck the wharf on the narrow piece of open water between the northern and southern jetty, between the basin of the harbor and the Sound. No one said anything.

Then Mother began speaking again.

"We crossed with the last boat," she pointed. "It was called Håbet (Hope). It was over there."

Again, Father brushed his hand down across his face. For a moment his eyes were hidden. When he removed his hand his face seemed relaxed. He smiled and said, "Listen to this! In Sweden once I was out fishing and caught a salmon! I quickly threw it back in the water." He laughed. "Do you think a poor tailor could afford salmon during the War?"

Mother giggled. Helle's face was closed. I turned around and looked for Nora as a feeling that approached desperation grew within me. It made me think of the time I had lost track of time and Jens Peter drove me home on his bike. Father had gone out to look for me and was standing by the stream in front of the iron gate that led into the park. And then he saw it with his own eyes. His daughter sitting on the bar of a bike ridden by a goy!

I immediately jumped off the bike. Told Jens Peter to turn around and walked the last meters to my father. But Jens Peter wanted to go over there and say hi.

"Jens Peter" he said, putting out his hand and bowing deeply.

Father didn't accept my classmate's hand. And he didn't speak to me for a whole week afterward.

But my whole life he had neglected to tell me about the history of my family and people! Had taken me out of the Jewish school and, on the pretext that I was to be assimilated, let me loose into a world he himself didn't want me to be a part of, to later force me back in, back inside the Jewish walls. And here he was cracking a joke to me and Helle! But what had I expected?

The next moment it was crystal clear to me: Both Father and Mother were doing everything they could to meet Helle and me halfway! Everything they were capable of! But between us there was a chasm that couldn't be bridged.

I looked across the Sound. The clouds hung low, layer upon layer of thick gray ringlets. Boj had been right. You can't assimilate your way out of a history like ours. When I turned my head and looked at Helle her face had come to life! My hope returned.

"But why didn't you ever say anything? She asked.

"We wanted to protect you!" Mother said.

"Protect us?" Helle and I exclaimed all at once, our voices shrill.

For a moment she looked surprised.

"Mistakes have been made!" Father said in a serious voice. "But from now on ..." he turned toward Helle and hesitated.

Nora gave me an encouraging nod. Then I asked my question.

"But weren't you scared?"

"No," Mother said as she smiled, baring both her gold

crowned teeth, "Downright scared is something I don't think one was back then, you just did what you were told to do, here and now, right?" She looked quizzically at my father.

I held my breath. She didn't say that. Yes, she did. Whatever it was she had felt back then was now inaccessible to her! Repressed, as Boj had said, and once again it struck me how right he had been. Whatever I chose to do in my future life, I would have to find my own way. And the only thing I knew for sure was that I didn't want to live in a deepening twilight, separated from my feelings. I wanted to be whole! Alive! I met Helle's eyes in which my own determination was reflected!

A seagull landed on the wharf and flew up again with a screech! At that very moment it struck me: back then, 21 years ago, Mother would have been in her early twenties, exactly the same age as Helle was now! And if they hadn't all three been sailed over to Sweden then we four wouldn't be standing here today! None of us, that is to say, I wouldn't either! The thought made me dizzy.

Father stood looking across the Sound. Shortly afterward he turned around looking from one to the other. He cleared his throat but didn't say anything. He looked as though he had shrunk into his coat. Mother stood by his side fiddling with her fur collar over and over. All at once I saw their vulnerability. Was filled with tenderness and a need to protect them.

Nora went over to my mother and stretched out her hands, "Let's not waste any more precious time," she said, "you and I need to have a talk!" then Nora put her arms around her and cradled her as had she been rocking a child.

At that very moment Mikkel woke up and started crying, loud and piercing.

*

Nora had managed to convince both my father and mother. They had to let go of Helle and let her live her own life.

Nora didn't want to tell me how she had done the impossible, just sat on my bed smiling secretly. I said to her that I had my suspicions. She didn't care about that, she said, as long as I kept them to myself. So I did.

Helle had left and I was on my way to Danny's. I was going to meet the others from the pioneer project. At Nørreport Station I got off the trolley and as I slipped into the crowded streets and walked up toward Købmagergade Street I thought about the farewell to Helle. She had asked me to go with her to the train. Together with a friend from high school she was now on her way to Southern France. First they would attend a language school. Later they would travel around the country. She would write.

All the silly things we had said to each other. But they hadn't been silly. She had put her boyfriend on hold, they'd have to see when she came back home, she said.

"So you finally cut the umbilical cord!" I said.

"Yes, I feel quite guilty!" she said, "And one day it will be your turn!"

I nodded and we hugged one another. The scent of hair shampoo surrounded her head like an invisible cloud and put our mother's "You hair smells sour!" to shame. I looked at her. She had gotten her ponytail chopped off, and her dark, pageboy hair fell freely about her cheeks. She turned around and lifted her luggage. Turned her head back around and looked at me smiling. I noticed a beauty mark right above the corner of her mouth that I didn't remember seeing before. And as she stood there in her traveling outfit carrying her luggage and with her foot on the very bottom step of the train carriage, it was for real: she was on her way to her new life.

I lifted my hand to wish her farewell.

Her last words to me were: "It's strange. Now that I'm leaving it feels as though you and I are closer than ever before. And that that feeling of closeness won't ever disappear."

Yes, it was strange. Helle had to be hundreds of kilometers away yet still she was right here. Within me.

At Kulturtorvet Square a young man stood playing a guitar and singing. A shiver went down my spine: he looked so much like Cousin Ralfi! His eyes. His hair about his head like a bird's nest of red-brown curls. On the square, in front of his feet, were a flock of pigeons pecking the asphalt.

I stopped and listened to his song: "Bye bye love. Bye bye happiness. Hello loneliness."

I went over to him and put a coin on the sidewalk, his face lit up in a sorrowful smile.

Then I hurried off toward Hauser Plads Square where Danny lived. For each step I took, my heart beat a little faster. He had said that Gaj would also be coming.

Behind me I heard the clattering sound of a flock of pigeons taking off. I turned and looked up and saw the pigeons ascend and spread across the sky.

NINA SOKOL is a poet and translator in the midst of translating novels, short stories, plays and poems by Danish writers. She was a grant poet-in-residence at The Vermont Studio Center in 2011. She has received several grants from the Danish Arts Council to translate plays, including a play written by the fairy tale writer H.C. Andersen which was published by the journal InTranslation. She has also translated an excerpt from one of the winning novels of last year's EU Prize for Literature (Danish, 2016) as well as translated such authors Niviaq Korneliussen and Bjørn Rasmussen. Her own poems have appeared in American journals, including Miller's Pond and the Hiram Poetry Review, and a collection was published by Lapwing Publications in Belfast, Ireland (2015).

BIRTE KONT is the former chief editor of the Danish Jewish Community's monthly magazine, as well as a writer and woman of letters. Using her Master's thesis on Franz Kafka as her point of departure, she wrote *Kafka's Guilt Identity: a Modern Jewish Skeptic Wrestles with the Law*, which was published in 2002, and she received a work grant in 2000 and in 2003 from the Danish Arts Council for cultural essay writing. She has participated in, among other things, the Kafka's Matliary Festival in 2008 in Slovakia, where she gave lectures, as well as in the Kafka Marathon in LiteraturHaus in Copenhagen in 2009. She debuted as a fiction writer in 2011 with the novel *En by i Rusland (A Place Nowhere)*, and in 2012 received a work grant from the Danish Arts Council for fiction writing. The novel was re-published in 2015 as an e-book. She is a member of the board for Fiction Writers in the Danish Writers Guild.

www.ingramcontent.com/pod-product-compliance
Lightning Source LLC
LaVergne TN
LVHW032004070526
838202LV00058B/6289